PROTECT HERO

Cartel vs Navy Seal

Gil Ortega

Protect Hero Book Reviews

In Ortega's debut thriller, a U.S. Navy SEAL commander finds his personal life shattered by a kidnapping. Ortega infuses the action scenes with realism and adds a dark element to the final outcome that elevates it beyond the action genre. A worthwhile thriller primarily for fans of military action. -KIRKUS REVIEW

His novel presents a roller coaster ride of compelling story lines one after the next filled with very believable characters---the surprises keep coming and will have every reader wondering what will come next. Excellent use of characters, writing, storyline and use of technical data. -BRETT L., AMAZON REVIEW

The action grabbed me from the first chapter and I found myself reading until 2am just to find out what happens next! I look forward to the next books in the series. -KEVIN J., AMAZON REVIEW

Action, excitement and suspense keep you on the edge from beginning to end as you follow the life of a Navy SEAL. Although this story is fictional it is all to relative to today's international chaos. I picked it up and couldn't put it down until finished. -JAYNE M., AMAZON REVIEW

Once I started reading this book I couldn't put it down. It was a thrill seeker with many heroes in this book. Makes you want to thank our soldiers for protecting our country. –HECTOR H., AMAZON REVIEW

Vivid and extremely entertaining! Couldn't put it down! – RUDY, AMAZON REVIEW

Great Book! I couldn't get it away from my husband - he usually doesn't have time to read, but he would not put Protect Hero down! –JILL K. AMAZON REVIEW

THANK YOU

My gracious and humble thanks go out to my father, brother, nephew, cousins, and all the men and women who have proudly served and those who currently serve this great nation of ours, the United States of America. I also thank my wife and kids, my mother, sister and my other brothers for always believing in me and supporting me. Thank you to all my family and friends that read the different edits of Protect Hero. I thank God for allowing all things to be possible.

PREFACE

Although the events and persons in this book may resemble those known to some, they are fictional.

PROLOGUE

MY FUCKUPS

I fucked up. I'm pretty sure all of us have said that at least once in our lifetime. For me, my fuckups were usually caused by falling unconscious behind a bottle's barrel while dealing with bad memories from my past. This time, however, was different, as my fuckup involved my family. As I've learned, it only takes one incident to change a lifetime.

If you are like me, you might often ask yourself what if? What if that suspicious person sitting next to you in a movie theater is counting the minutes until he unleashes his fury? What if that packed subway has some crazy fucker that is counting the days until he blows up the fucking thing? My "what ifs" always revolve around my family and my team.

It's been four years, and I'm grateful I decided to do everything I did. I'm not perfect. I have my flaws although I will deny them. I am a recovering alcoholic and my chronic pain from years of physical, military abuse keeps me craving pain medications. My inner mental demons fuck with me everyday. I'm lucky in many ways. I learned more about my life, desires, ambitions, and my family from the events that took place.

I served my country for twenty-four years in the Navy. I came from a Navy family. My great-grandfather, grandfather, and father were all in the Navy. I was essentially born into the Navy. My father was a Navy SEAL. He has always been my role model and my antimodel. I witnessed first hand through him how using alcohol to suppress mental anguish is never the answer. He taught me the most about being an imperfect man, a father, a husband, and a leader.

I was a commanding officer of the Navy's elite Naval Special Warfare Development Group, also known as DEVGRU, or to some, as Seal Team Six. Although the official Seal Team Six was dissolved in 1987, to us, it always survived as just Seal Team Six. We existed under the command of the Joint Special Operations Command.

We have always been the best of the best—America's team for when it was on the line. I fought for our country during wars in Iraq, Afghanistan, and other parts of the world. I saw men killed viciously in battle. I helped save men from dying in battle. I continue to struggle with the badness that survives from the evils I have seen. The crazy thing is, I never thought I'd have to use all my skills and resources to save my own family right here in the United States of America. I'm Retired US Navy SEAL Commanding Officer of the Naval Special Warfare Development Group, Seal Team Six, Captain Ryan Williams, and here is my story as I best remember it.

CARTEL LANDING

Second week of November

Our battle torn helicopter arrived at the military base outside Bogota, Colombia, which was staked in the middle of a lush green valley surrounded by cattle and farms. We moved quickly as we couldn't predict if the cartel would mount another attack. Emma's breathing improved, but she was still struggling. Her pulse was fragile and ghostly weak. Her chest expansions shallowed with less air movement. My little five-year-old girl was fighting for her life.

We boarded the US Air Force's C-130J-30 airlifter plane with urgency, as Emma's blood soaked her stretcher and flowed over the edges. The stretcher's wheels squeaked in unison as her faintly dying body rolled onto the plane. The plane's ramp matched a murder scene from fresh blood being tracked and trailing everywhere. The plane's cargo space was crammed with a make shift mini-hospital operating room packed right in the middle. The plane's roaring engines and fuel smell overwhelmed my senses.

The surgical team consisted of a flight surgeon and two nurses. The surgeon's overgrown, graying beard and surgical mask helped hide his pale face when he realized his patient was only five years old. I sensed the medical team had kids of their own, as they couldn't control their tears from soaking their paper surgical masks.

They started working on Emma frantically. Her blood pressure was 65/40 and her pulse rate was 120; both were very abnormal. Her oxygen saturation was 87%; also abnormal. Sensor alarms screamed saying, "hey this patient is in shock and dying!" I looked at my little girl in prayer and desperation, as bright red blood dripped out of her mouth and abdomen. She had to live even though she had already died.

They placed two large bore IVs in her tiny collapsed veins, and she moved only with extension to the needle's pain. The nurse's fingernails whitened from her forceful grips on the plastic lined bags that stored vital IV fluids and blood. Her blood pressure bumped up briefly with the rapid infusion of IV fluids, blood, and pressor medications. Her entry flank wound resembled four connected quarters while her abdominal exit wound was bigger than my fist. Her belly distended uncontrollably like a helium balloon being blown up from the increasing volume of her own blood.

The pilot of the plane yelped over the loud speaker, "Team Williams we are ready for take off. Please strap down and get ready. We are urgent for flight to Houston, Texas."

I refused to leave Emma's side. I stayed next to her even though my own abdomen kept expanding. I knew I had something wrong internally, but I didn't want to divert any medical care away from my little girl. I played off my wounds as scrapes, so I could avoid any medical attention until I knew Emma was stable. I fought my body's desire to crash. I had to fight my own need to die, so Emma could receive all the blood and care that was available.

Emma was waning. She no longer responded to my voice. She no longer grasped my hand. I couldn't help but cry and pray. My eight-year-old son, Jaxon, was watching his younger sister and father die slowly. Although his face was colorless, he remained strong, as he was healthy and without injury. He brushed Emma's hair with his bruise battered hands, and he cleaned all of the blood off of her. He wept until his eyes dried from not having any more tears left.

"Captain Williams, I have your wife on our transmission. Sir, she has not been made aware of Emma's condition," said one of the pilots as he handed me the transmitter.

"Natalie, we are ok," I said with confused reassurance.

"Ryan, how are you and the kids?" she asked.

"Honey, Emma was shot while we were trying to escape. She is sick, my love. She is getting all the care she can right now, but she was injured badly," I said while crying.

"Ryan, please hold her for me and don't let her go. I can't live without my little girl. Please promise me, Ryan, that she is going to be ok, please, Ryan, I beg you!" she cried.

I paused. I knew how grave the situation was for Emma. The trauma surgeon felt she was too unstable to operate on until she was in Houston. He was afraid she could possibly bleed to death on the C-130's make shift operating room. I was afraid he was right. We just had to wait until we landed.

"Natalie, I promise you that I will never let her go. I will never let her go." I had no other words.

"Ryan, let me speak to Jaxon, please."

I handed the transmitter to Jaxon. He was shaking uncontrollably while holding the transmitter.

"Momma, is that you?" Jaxon asked.

"Yes, my love, it's your momma. I miss you honey. I'm praying for all of you. You give your sister hugs and kisses for me ok?" Natalie requested.

"Yes, momma. I can't wait to see you. I miss you."

"Jaxon, you, your sister and your dad will be home soon. I just know in my heart my love. I always had faith in your dad to bring you both home safely, and I refuse to give up on that. Let me talk to your daddy ok."

"Ryan, your mother and I are scheduled to arrive in Houston shortly after you arrive. Congressman Herrera called me and said he arranged to have two air Marshalls on board to help protect us. He even helped arrange a local police escort for us. I will let them know that we need to be taken directly from the airport to the hospital where they will be taking Emma. You hold onto my little girl, you hear that Ryan? You don't let her go!" Natalie exclaimed while she was crying uncontrollably.

"Roger that, my love. I will never let her go. I will see you soon. I love you," I said.

"I love you too, more than anything in the world," she said.

I couldn't let her go. My heart and soul felt like they had died when I realized she had been shot.

The pain I felt in my heart was overwhelming. She was too young and too innocent to leave us at five years of age. I knew in my heart and with all my faith and belief that she would pull through this.

"Beep, beep, beep, beeeeeppp!" the monitor alarm screamed.

No, I thought to myself. Not again. NO! Please Lord DO NOT take my little girl. Take me, but DO NOT take my little girl.

"I lost her pulse, prepare to shock!" the surgeon exclaimed.

"Fuck, no pulse, no activity, I don't have breath sounds. Giving Epi now," he shouted.

"Charge...ready...shock! the defibrillator shouted.

It was too familiar to me. I felt faint. I heard voices in my head. What or who was talking to me?

"Don't give up, my son, don't give up," the voice said.

It was my father's voice. I felt myself fading. I heard the sound again.

"Charge...ready...shock! the defibrillator shouted.

No response. I prayed.

"Charge...ready...shock! the defibrillator shouted.

"I have a rhythm. I have a pulse, prepare to intubate."

Emma was barely alive.

"Captain Williams, we are maxed at 400 mph. We are praying for Emma, Sir. We have one more hour to go. They are ready for us at the airport. They have air transport for Emma, Jaxon, and you to get to the Texas Children's hospital right away. We are praying," explained the pilot.

It would take six hours to fly from Bogota, Colombia to Houston. It was a painstaking flight. Emma was dying, but still fighting. The surgeon provided CPR twice to Emma as her vitals signs crashed despite all of the IV fluids, blood, and pressor medications. The surgeon had run out of blood. He was maxed on her IV fluids and medications to keep her little life supported. I knew it would take a miracle to save her life. I asked God to take my life in exchange to save hers. She didn't deserve to die. I fucked up. My fuck up was worth my own life, which I wished I could give up for Emma. My inner demons were winning.

2

Denial

I have found that the hardest human admission is submitting to correcting what is wrong with us. How the fuck did I get to this point? How I did I fuck up so badly? I kept asking myself that I should have listened that day. I was just too drunk to act accordingly.

I received the call just two weeks ago. Somehow the call was more vivid now. I wonder why. I was sober and not on narcs or alcohol or some fucked up combination.

I remember how annoyed I was by my fucking phone ringing while I was trying to finish my first bottle of Jack for the day.

"Hello," I said.

"Ryan, hey man, how you doing?" Daniel asked.

"Hey, Dan, I'm ok, I'm better than yesterday."

I wasn't lying. I was better than yesterday. At this same time yesterday, I was already into my second bottle of Jack and about four oxys down. Now I was only halfway through my first and I hadn't popped my oxy cap yet. By the way, what the fuck was the CIA calling me?

"Ryan, how's your drinking, you leaving that shit alone?"

"Dan, say man, what can I help you with, I know the CIA doesn't call just to check on my sobriety."

"Ryan, we intercepted some chatter on lines that included your name. You're right. I wouldn't be calling you otherwise, and I'm sorry. I should call an old friend of mine more often."

"Wait, no worries on calling, but what the fuck do you mean about my name?"

"Ryan, I'm not supposed to be sharing this shit with you, but the fucking Mexican cartel has a price on your head."

"Fuck them. What the fuck are they going to do to me that I've not done to myself already?"

I did mean this. I couldn't make it through a day without hitting a bottle of Jack, popping oxycodone pills for my "chronic pain syndrome," having flashbacks of hell, forgetting I was married and had two kids, and a bunch of other fucked up things. What was I going to do, be scared now?

"Ryan, say man, this shit is real. The chatter talks about not only wanting your head, but wanting your family. This is some serious shit, Ryan, you have to take precautions."

"Dan, thanks for the call, I do appreciate you breaking all that protocol bullshit. For me, I can take care of my own."

I hung up the phone. At first, I didn't care what Dan said. After I sobered a bit, I found myself wanting to call him back to find out more details. I knew he wouldn't take my call at this point. I shouldn't have hung up on him. Just another fuck up added to my list. I should have called him back. I should have put the Jack down, put my head on, and made a plan.

3

Jack, Narcs, and Afghan

During one of our missions, I jumped from a wall about 12 feet high. When I cradled and rolled, my back didn't cooperate, and I broke my back. They called it compression fractures of my lumbar spine. I was supposed to rest for 3-4 months to let it heal while I wore a fucking brace, but I couldn't stand the fucking thing and it made me feel like a mummy. Fast forward five years later, and now I had unhealed lumbar spine fractures that just killed me. The pain eats my core. My only treatment for the pain was to stay comfortably numb with alcohol and/or pain medications.

Even though I was next to my dying daughter, my craving for Jack and pain meds was exploding. I wanted to put myself out of my miscry by not waking up the next morning. Finding my numbness from some Jack and Oxys sounded perfect right now. I felt my soul wanting to give in to the madness of my mental demons.

Alcohol shared similarities to a gun for me. I knew each time I gave into alcohol that I was playing with a loaded gun to my head. I always imagined my Post-Traumatic Stress Disorder (PTSD), as a knife and my addiction to alcohol as a gun. Each time I lost myself in appalling nightmares or frightful daydreams, I envisioned a knife's sharp point twisting and cutting up my soul. Not enough to kill me, but enough to injure me.

Of all my missions, our last mission almost killed me mentally and physically. We were outnumbered. The terrorists had us at an initial highpoint advantage in the building we entered. I felt our impending death. The smell of blood and guts was everywhere with urine and shit oozing from killed terrorists.

Although things were improving, I still couldn't sleep as the thought of the grenade under me keeps lingering with me. I was dead or at least I should have been. I prayed for an end to my nightmares and visions. I tried to ignore it while trying to be happy at home, but my PTSD was worse now than it had ever been prior and my craving for alcohol and narcotics was irrepressible.

My mind kept reverting back to that last night when we killed the core of terrorists that tried to kill our president and how my life could have ended. I will never forget those last few seconds that I thought my life was about to end. It had all flashed in front of me. My confusions made the matter even more challenging to recollect.

Flashback to three weeks prior.

We were coming in hot. I could tell we were getting close to our drop-off as our ride starting slowing down. We were somewhere in the middle of Afghanistan or what

I would call hell without luxury. This was my 77th mission with the Navy, and I knew it had the biggest price tag. Two fucking years of intel and previously failed attempts had me believing that this mission was our country's time.

"Captain Williams we are 5 Mikes to drop, over," said the pilot of our aircraft. We were a team of eight Navy SEALS riding on a MH-47 Special Operations Aircraft from the Army Special Operations' Command. My men and I readied our equipment and turned on our left eye night-vision monocular powered with white phosphorous to see in the pitch darkness. Right eye stays clear for any low light, sudden light or an up close subject.

Whenever I heard the five Mikes warning, I entered a super focused state of mind. I was responsible for the lives of my men and their families depended on my leadership skills to bring them all home. This feeling of responsibility is one that few people on this earth can ever understand.

I had lost men in battle and that is something that I can never forget. My past memories haunted me day and night. My mental demons ache me most at night.

The five minutes passed like five seconds.

"Drop site, ready ropes, time to go men, I bid you Godspeed," said the pilot. "Copy that," I said. We had to fastrope down from our ride. With about 60 pounds of equipment and our firearms, it was amazing how fast you could drop from the sky. We all pounded ground. Hammers hit steel softer than when we hit the ground from a fastrope with such heavy equipment.

We were 4 clicks away from our targets, and we knew we had tough terrain to cover both by vegetation and by insurgents. We had to make a lot of ground quickly in case our entry was noticed. Four clicks could take us anywhere from 40 minutes to 4 hours depending on what we encountered along the way, and we always encountered something along the way.

We all carried a variety of weapons. Most of us carried either HK 417s or FN SCAR MK17s that shot the bigger 7.62 mm round. Our team had made the switch to a heavier punch with the 7.62 mm from the 5.56 mm, as we needed to defeat anything that came our way. We had learned that these weapons were most reliable in the middle of nowhere especially in sand and water. We always had the interiors sealed to make them salt water and sand proof for at least 1000 hours. We could come shoot them while being submerged under water and even while coming out of sand, which is why we had to chosen them over other previous assault rifles used in the past.

Our sidearms were Sig's P226 MK25s, which I considered the most reliable sidearm I had ever had to shoot in battle. We were loaded with other weaponry as well as we had to be prepared to fight any type of small war in the middle of nowhere.

"Zulu, Zulu, come in, Zulu, Zulu, come in. This is Alpha King from Heaven, Over," said the pilot's voice from through the static.

"Yes, Alpha, this is Zulu. We copy. Over," I said.

"Zulu, we have you on infrared from the sky. You are clear to target, you are now 2 clicks away, Over," said the voice.

"Roger that, moving with boom," I said.

My team kept moving as fast as we could, as we knew that the insurgents had the tendency to move locations in the middle of the night. I knew that our intel was from an informant that spotted the insurgents in their compound twenty-four hours prior.

"Captain, there are armed insurgents in the road just up ahead of us, what should we do?" asked Special Warfare Operator, First Class (SO1), Jake Gomez.

"Alpha King, we have insurgents in planned path, can we assume Plan B path to avoid, over," I asked before we made our final move toward the insurgent's compound.

"Zulu, assume Path B, through yards of homes prior to compound, beware of dogs in home next to compound, 2 dogs sleeping now, but I am sure they will awaken on your arrival, over," said Alpha King.

"Copy that, Alpha, I hope you boys like dog for breakfast," I said jokingly. I knew that we would have to sacrifice the dogs if they awoke during our pounce through their backyard.

"Zulu, you are two Mikes out, one house to go," said Alpha King.

"Copy that, nearing preliminary, initiate radio silence to our end, out," I said.

"Jake, take spot," I said.

"Yes, sir," said Special Warfare Operator, First Class (SO1) Jake Gomez.

US Navy SEAL Team Six moved among the broken-down homes, there was evidence of insurgent gunfire everywhere we looked, as many of the homes had been run down likely from insurgent attacks. The air was like a dry cement pavement in 120-degree heat, the kind that would burn your feet if you walked on it barefoot. The air was filled with gunfire smoke and the smell of gasoline. The homes all around us were inhabitable although people lived in them anyway.

Jake jumped into the backyard of the house right before the insurgent's compound. Sure enough, both dogs woke up and started barking up a shit storm. Jake used his dog whistle to try to calm them down. He also came prepared with dog snacks as our intel had let us know that house before compound had two dogs. I didn't think either would work, but to my amazement, both dogs went silent with their dog treats and the whistle. Jake lifted his hand up signaling us to come forward over the wall of the house. Seal Team Six was now in view of the insurgent's compound.

We were moving in on our targets. They were to be taken dead or alive. We had been on this mission for over two years. To me, it had seemed a lot longer as I had not been home during this mission's time period.

Our reward would be a successful mission, with all our brothers coming home. We'd been working on this mission for too long to not finish it successfully.

"Sir, ground targets confirmed with infrared and thermographic sites. Over," said SO2 Gomez.

"How many targets verified? Over," I said.

"Fourteen verified, 4 outside, and 10 inside, others unknown. Over."

"Unknown?" I asked. "Unknown? Please estimate unknowns. Over." How the hell are we going to win if they have thirty unknowns I asked myself?

"Alpha, Zulu here, we spot 14 insurgents, any more by your sights? I asked.

"Negative, Zulu, we have 14 as well. Unless they have specially lined walls, we only see 14 insurgents, with 4 outside and 10 inside. Party invitation golden, you are cleared to proceed, sir, over," said Alpha King.

"Invitation to party accepted, please accept our reservation, over," I said.

"Zulu, Zulu, invitation accepted. Party safely; turn on the lights when the party is over. Over," said the voice on the radio.

"Copy that, Zulu out," I said.

My heart raced. My pupils dilated. My sweat dripped from my helmet. It was go time.

SEAL Team Six moved with precision. Our weapons were hot. We all had our night-vision goggles on and ready. The darkness then appeared as sunrise, with our night vision activated. Our target was a two-level outward, broken-down house with confirmed targets at all areas of the house, including the first floor, second floor, outside vicinity, basement, and what appeared as an outside bunker with tunnels in and out of house.

This was our intel, based on an informant that had reported to be delivering food and water to the terrorists that were hiding in the compound. Cash was still king in Afghanistan as informants would often provide intel for cash. We didn't offer cash to anyone; instead, we would only offer to those informants that we thought would best provide us with valuable information that we knew was of benefit.

Only God knew the specs. Only God knew the outcome. Only God knew if we would make it out alive.

"Let's roll, men," I said. "Godspeed."

At that, eight men with their orders to protect breached three regions, including the front and back entrance and the bunker. The mini explosions from breaching the doors sounded off in perfect unison.

"Clear," said SOCS "Loco" Moreno, as we cleared the main entrance. "Targets front. Go hot, go hot!" he said.

The gunfight started. Chaos filled the air. Our weapons' infrared lasers found their targets with surgical accuracy. Weapons controlled by the best men ever trained hit their targets. The sounds from insurgent assault rifles were piercing. The insurgents fired their automatic weapons at any peep or movement. Their continuous, automatic weapon fire proved their combat inexperience. For us, we preferred one-shot kills and two shots for good measure.

Our weapons were stocked with suppressors to decrease our sound footprints, as well as reducing the recoil from our assault rifles. The heavy black smoke from weapons blazing on both ends contaminated our lungs. Our targets were hit with precision, accuracy and without hesitation.

"Three down in bunker," said Lieutenant Green. "Bunker secured. East perimeter secured. Over."

Shots could still be heard every few seconds.

"Back side, seven down. South clear," said SO2 Bell.

"North, four targets down, north cleared. Over," said Lieutenant Green.

"Captain, Green and I can go in to clear," said SOCS "Loco" Moreno.

"Bullshit, Loco," I said. "I may have these bars, but you're my boys—I'm coming in. Down space, moving in, keep your sites secured. Over."

Then I noticed movement. "Targets," I said.

The firefight started again. There were three SEALs and eleven insurgents in the middle of a two-story compound. We were at a disadvantage not just in numbers, but also, in positions. We were in a low spot and some of the insurgents were in a high position firing down at us. We sat in what we called the "fucked" position.

"Roll, roll, support. Over," I said. Three other SEALs came in behind us. My men threw grenades up high to take out the insurgents in high positions. All I could hear was explosions and assault rifle fire everywhere.

A few of my men were loaded with FN40 grenade launchers on their FN SCAR MK17s. They were mounted on the lower rail of their rifles for additional firepower. The grenades worked as the insurgents firing from high positions stopped.

The smoke was so heavy and blackening that I could barely see out of my night-vision goggles. The smell of blood, bodily fluids, and intestines spoiled the air everywhere. The smoke from the firefight and from debris was so blinding that the only things to distinguish insurgents from SEALs were their reflections from our embedded US flags that were used to identify SEALs to other SEALs with night vision.

I heard the dreaded roll on the ground.

"Grenade, grenade!" I yelled as I jumped forward onto a grenade that an insurgent threw from some hidden position. I leaped onto the grenade to protect my seven fellow SEALs behind me. It was the longest two seconds ever recorded in my lifetime. My mental demons showed up to question whatever the hell was happening. Was this real? Was I recalling a past event?

The silence made time stay still. I pondered to myself. Although I knew I needed to seek real help, I had self-diagnosed myself with a combination of PTSD and a form of dementia. I believe I suffered from dementia pugilista, which likely developed from the many concussions I suffered in my lifetime from playing football, doing martial arts, and pounding my head many other ways while being a Navy Seal. I knew I had to see a doctor at some point, but I dreaded being told by someone that I had to retire from being a Navy Seal. Retirement was one of my biggest nightmares especially if it was not on my terms.

I had to get it together. With my mental illnesses, I would often time confuse real situations with past situations or even dreamt situations. It is hard to explain and hard to understand, but I always compared it to déjà vu. I simply could not tell the difference between the now and then and some random time points. I had realized that both illnesses seemed to be worsening especially over the last two years. I also had increasing difficulty with focus, spelling, and simple tasks. These issues became even worse if I was drinking.

The lives of my men were depending on me. I took slow breaths. I looked around and concentrated. I saw my team. I knew it was real. I quickly reestablished myself. I knew I was in battle, and I was lying on a fucking grenade.

My fellow SEALs backed for cover while firing at the insurgents. I killed the last insurgent while I lay on the grenade. Two more seconds passed, which felt like two hours.

All my fellow SEALs moved back. Two more seconds passed again. While I was lying on the grenade and waiting to die, images of my family ran through my head. Was this the end? Did I sacrifice my life to protect my men? Would my wife and two kids remember me? Would they ever understand why my brothers meant more to me than my own life? Would I die or be mutilated and scarred forever? Two more seconds passed.

"Captain, I'm coming to get you, don't move," said Loco.

"Bullshit, stay back, it can still go off! Tell my family I love them," I said with a cried crackle in my voice to the SEALs at a distance behind me.

Two more seconds passed.

"Captain, I'm going to roll you slowly; can you feel the grenade underneath you?" said Loco, as he tried to help me.

"Loco, get the fuck out of here!" I said. "That's an order. This thing can go off at any time and there is no way I'm going to let you get killed here in this shithole." Two more seconds passed.

"I have my order, and it is from God: to save your ass, Captain" said Loco. "Now can you feel the grenade? And can you let me get to it?"

Two more seconds passed.

"Yes, it's under my left hip," I said.

Loco put his hand on my shoulder.

"On the count of three, when I say roll out, then roll out. I'm going to cover the grenade with my armor shield. If we die from the blast so be it, as I can't think of a better man to die with, Captain" said Loco.

Two more seconds passed.

"Loco, no way man, get back, you follow my order and follow Lieutenant Green back to the rendezvous point. There can be more insurgents coming at any second, and I am commanding you to fall back now!" I said.

"Sir, with all do respect, fuck you and roll the fuck over, so we can get the fuck out of here! You can fire me later for not following an order," said Loco.

"OK, Loco, you crazy motherfucker—you always earn your name."

Two more seconds passed.

"One, two, three, roll out," said Loco.

I rolled out. The grenade was covered in a microsecond, as we both scrambled away. There was no blast. We took cover and waited for a delayed explosion. Nothing happened. Both of us got to a safe distance. We were all alive!

The grenade pin was never pulled; stupid ass terrorists I thought. Incompetent bastards. As my mentors always said, better be lucky than good. This time I was lucky.

All twenty-six insurgents were killed, including our main target, the elusive leader of the terrorist group that tried to assassinate the president of the United States on American soil.

Two years of work. Two years of pain. Two years of sacrifice and confusion. Two years of being away from our families. It paid off as we killed the bastard who tried to take out our commander-in-chief.

We moved away from the grenade area. We still had to take photos and video of our raid and all of the insurgents that we killed. We had to provide evidence to the United States of America that we had accomplished our mission that required two years of our lives.

Most of our mission was captured through video on one of our QuadEye night goggles, so Washington D. C. could often watch our missions live. I wasn't always crazy about the idea, but it was what we were ordered to do. I just loaded the trucks and got paid for it.

My priority was getting what evidence we needed to get the hell out of there. I wanted to get my men to safety. I knew how important collecting evidence was for the cause, but I also knew that at any moment insurgents could come and that we could face another firefight.

"Alpha, Alpha, the party is over. Please send our ride home," I said.

"Zulu, Zulu, anyone left at the prom without a date?" said the voice.

"Negative, Alpha. All the folks at the party had their last dance. The asshole is dead and packaged. All SEALs are alive and accounted, for God and country. Over," I said.

"Copy that, Sir, dead package. Zulu, ride in route. out," said Alpha.

All the SEALs started their trek back to the rendez-vous point with careful scanning of the area going back. We were back on the road that led us to finding the terrorist leader that tried to have our president killed. He was the terrorist leader often referred to as the current Osama Bin Laden. He was the most wanted man by the US government as well as every other country in the world.

We had to carry his dead body back with us as proof to the world that we had accomplished our mission. Dead bodies are always heavier than live bodies. Not sure why, but it always seemed that way. Or maybe my adrenaline rushed and made me stronger when carrying injured men in battle.

We knew that the insurgent's assault rifle shots could be heard for a long distance and that insurgents staying close by could easily hear the firefight. I knew that carrying the terrorist back would slow us down, but we had our orders whether I liked it or not.

"Zulu, team of insurgents one click from your tail, double time it to rendezvous point. We visualize heavy weaponry on insurgents with possible surface to air capabilities, over," said Alpha King.

"Alpha, copy that, we are on moving like lightning," I said in response to moving as fast as we could. I knew our lives were at risk if the insurgents had surface to air missiles such as RPGs.

"Zulu, proceed to rendezvous point B, we are now visualizing insurgents in vehicles believed to be armed with RPGs. They are half a click behind you. Zulu Cobra, Eagleviper, in route, 12 Mikes out. We are 4 Mikes out, but we will have to scramble until we have cover from Eagleviper, over," said Alpha King.

"Copy that, Alpha, we will head to point B," I said.

Fuck, I thought to myself, as I knew point B was 2 more clicks away from point A, and we had heavily armed insurgents on our tails. I knew we were about to get into another fight, as they would be on us very soon.

"Loco, we have insurgents in a vehicle believed to have RPGs, we have to proceed to point B, which is 2 clicks away. You ready up with the LAW?" I asked.

"Copy that, Sir, LAW dog ready to go, I will fall back to light up the sky and bring the fucking rain on these fucks," said Loco.

Seal Team Six kept moving toward point B. I could hear the vehicle approaching us. The insurgents starting firing their AK-47s at us from their vehicle in aimless, automatic fashion. We took cover. We were stuck in a pit until Eagleviper arrived with the rainstorm.

"Eagleviper, Zulu here, we are engaged with insurgents on the road, 4 Mikes away from point B, what is your ETA?" I asked.

"Zulu, copy that, Eagleviper in route, 6 Mikes out," Eagleviper pilot said.

"Loco, do you have eyes on vehicle," I asked.

"Yes, LAW dog ready to go," Loco said.

"Proceed to enforce the LAW," I said.

We called the LAW our Light Anti-tank weapon, which should be able to take out the vehicle.

"Copy that, the LAW is up and ready, and bringing hell with it," said Loco.

We could hear the explosion and see the fire from the Anti-tank weapon hitting the vehicle. I thought we were in the clear, but I could hear two more vehicles approaching at a high rate of speed. We only had one LAW rocket. We would have to push to point B and try to bunker down until our help from the sky arrived.

"Zulu, Eagleviper, one Mike out, take cover, we are bringing the rain," Eagleviper pilot said.

"Eagleviper, Zulu Team Six is at Point B, we are protected, green smokescreen in air," I said.

"Eagleviper engaged, see you fuckers," Eagleviper pilot said.

We could hear the sound of the Viper's Gatling cannon engaging the insurgents. There is no other sound like it. We always called the Gatling cannon the Shredder. It plowed and shredded matter with ease.

We could also hear the Hellfire air-to-surface missiles take out the two vehicles. We waited and stayed still. Terrorist moans and groans filled the air for a couple of seconds. We knew they were close. Smoke now filled the air.

The terrorists couldn't survive the power magnitude from the air strike that just sliced their anatomies into pieces. Their body's stench from the reaper contaminated the air we had to breath. The worst smells I ever encountered were those from dead men. Shit, urine and blood never makes a good mix.

"Zulu, all clear, Alpha King is on its way to bring you boys home, Eagleviper out," Eagleviper pilot said.

"Copy that, thanks for making it rain," I said.

We could see Alpha King, a MH-47 Chinook, approaching us. A Blackhawk helicopter also came to pick up the terrorist's body. We helped load his body into the Blackhawk. After we took photos of their dead bodies, we really didn't care about the other terrorists.

We all then boarded Alpha King. The helicopters began to fly away. We could see the shitstorm that we started. We could see fires from the compound from a few miles away as well as the remaining fires from the three vehicles that were destroyed.

We accomplished our mission that took two years to plan and finalize. Two years of missions without the successful outcome we had today. All men were accounted for and all survived. All had a story to tell.

4

IN FLIGHT TERROR

Emma wasn't doing any better. I think the flight surgeon wanted to disconnect her from her life support and pressors. I knew he couldn't do it in front of me.

Jaxon fell asleep somehow in the chaos. I didn't blame him. He had just been through his worst hell. I wish I could wake up from the terror. I knew his terror was far worse than any of mine. I really didn't think I was going to make the six hours on a plane while watching Emma die. A sober six hours for me at this point almost killed me.

Unfortunately, my haunts at night are oftentimes from past missions when I lost men. I remember all of my missions in detail. I've tried various techniques in trying not to think a lot about most of them. I've found that the recollections of a lot of the events caused me to suffer from nightmares and loss of memory in live situations. It was too easy to allow oneself to become consumed with the thoughts of training and/or missions, so I tried my best to finish tasks/missions and to move onto my next mission or home if it was time for me to be home.

Some of my men also struggled with post-traumatic stress disorder or some other undefined mental entity. There were times when I would wake up in the middle of the night next to my wife in a cold sweat and some state of shock or paranoia.

During our first years of marriage, my wife struggled with my nightmares, but she eventually adjusted well to realizing that I was in my own little world and that I couldn't necessarily share things even my nightmares with her. I was able to hide my addiction to alcohol when we were first married, but it didn't take long before she found out that I tried to deal with my mental demons and pain through the use of a bottle and oxys.

Even while thinking about my past missions, I would often redirect my thoughts to my family and my days and nights being home with them. By doing this, I was better able to balance my life than when I would slide into the bad thoughts of my past missions.

I rose up the ranks while being a part of the Navy SEALs. I became the captain of SEAL Team Six after being a part of the team for seven years. Before my retirement, I was the longest active commanding officer of SEAL Team Six as well as any Seal unit in the United States Navy. I guess I loved my job as a Seal. Seemingly, I had loved my job as Seal since I was seven years old.

My superiors had often asked me if I wanted to retire from being a Seal to move up the ranks to Rear Admiral. Although the thought of being an Admiral was intriguing to me, I just loved the "juice" too much of being in training and battle with my fellow SEALS.

My wife thought I was crazy after I would show her notices from the Navy to apply for the next level of command, which would mean that I would no longer be able to be an active Navy Seal allowed to serve on Seal missions and battles.

It meant a lot to me to serve with my men. It meant a lot to me that they had always protected me and that I had always done my best to protect them. The hardest thing about being a part of the military was losing men in battle. I made it a point to visit all the families of any of my men when they were injured or killed in action.

The biggest challenge of being the captain of SEAL Team Six was knowing that any mission we embarked on involved the highest risks to our team and the highest risks of losing one or all of my men.

After our mission to kill the terrorists that had tried to kill the president, I had a feeling that I was getting close to retiring from the SEALs. It was not something I really wanted to do, but it was something I felt I had to do for my family.

When I jumped on the grenade, my entire life summarized itself in a couple of seconds. In those seconds, the only things I thought of were my wife, kids, and parents. I felt that it was my wake-up call, in some ways.

I felt that my kids were growing up and that I barely knew them. I knew that if I felt that way, my kids must have too. I had a lot of thinking to do on my long flights home. I knew that the Navy meant everything to me, but I also knew that even the Navy would understand if I had to take some time with my family after this last mission. It's hard to say, but the flash of my life while lying on that grenade changed me in several ways. Now my grenade was my little girl dying right in from of me from my own fuckup.

5

CAUSE AND EFFECT

When I left for my last mission, Emma, was only 3 years old. Although she would always say "Daddy" to me when she saw me on the computer screen, I worried that she really didn't remember me. Jaxon was older when I left, but I hadn't been there to help him much with school, sports, or life in general. I prayed that my kids would forgive me for being gone for so long as two years to me seemed like a month, but for two young kids, two years is a real long time.

As I went in and out of consciousness from exhaustion, a bunch of memories ran through my mind. I remembered the last time I'd seen my wife, kids, and our home. I struggled trying to compartmentalize my own personal life from that of my missions. My PTSD and addictions seemed to always win control of my thoughts. Even though I was dead exhausted, I kept flashing back to undesirable memories. I shot a terrorist on American soil when two terrorists tried to assassinate our president. It was on my watch, and my mind battled with my near epic failure.

To make matters worse, I was under the influence of Oxys. I thought it was going to be another babysitting session while we held our heavy guns and tactical gear. I was wrong. I'll get back to me being under influence while on mission.

When the assassination attempt took place on our commander-in-chief, it shook the world. It was unexpected. I guess nobody expects an assassination attempt on the President of the United States. The same terrorist group that we had just killed had tried to take out the president two years prior.

My unit became involved as we had heavy intel that the terrorist group was planning on taking out the president while he was giving a speech in San Diego, California. Ironically, The president's speech was on winning the war on terrorists.

Generally, the Secret Service handled all Presidential security reconnaissance and protection, but terrorists had become much more aggressive both abroad and in the United States. My unit started working with the Secret Service three years prior to the assassination attempt when the current President was the Vice President, and he was visiting the troops in Afghanistan.

The president wanted to go into an Afgan village to see the conditions, but also, to show support to our troops that were helping build diplomatic relations with the Afghan military forces.

We advised the current president that it was not a wise idea to visit an unprotected village. Well, to put it mildly, he was on his own mission, and I didn't blame him. He is definitely a people person. He always struck me as the type of president that wanted to do good things for Americans and countries that we were assisting.

When we did combine our forces with the Secret Service, it was run under my command. I wouldn't have allowed it to be any other way. My unit knew the terrain and we knew the enemies and their evil ways. The Secret Service was very understanding to the fact that when we combined services that I was in the commanding officer and commanding unit. We enjoyed working with the Secret Service, as we understood the single goal of keeping our Commander in Chief safe at all times and at all costs.

When we received intel about the upcoming assassination attempt on the president in San Diego, we thought it was a hoax. It just couldn't happen especially on American soil. Were the terrorists just that stupid to pick a fight in our own Seal backyard, San Diego?

Our intel had also included facts that terrorists were using coyote type groups to smuggle terrorists into the United States through Mexico. What we didn't know was if the Mexican cartel groups, South American cartels or other non-cartel gangs were taking large cash payments to help smuggle Taliban or other Middle Eastern terrorists groups into the United States.

Our intel suggested that the South American cartel had a deal with the Mexican cartels to allow them to pass terrorists through Mexico. It was told that the Mexican cartels didn't care as they were getting paid to help assist the South American cartel get the terrorists into Mexico and into the

United States. We also had intel that the South American cartel and Mexican cartels may have joined criminal fronts.

On the day the terrorist group tried to kill the president, my unit joined up with the Secret Service. Our intel pointed to a long range sniper attempt on the president.

We had secured any high point for 3 miles outwards from the president's speech, which was scheduled to be outside. Even though we had done what I thought was a great job securing both high and low points for a 3-mile radius, I had an odd feeling in my gut that the terrorists were there. It was an instinctual feeling that came natural after years of training. You could feel it in your gut that something was not right.

My unit and the Secret Service had a combined manpower of forty-two men. We also had assistance from the Air force with a few drones that were flying around scanning the crowds, streets and buildings. I felt confident in our layers of surveillance and protection.

As we were doing routine checks of the streets and buildings, I saw a shine coming from a crane high up in the sky. Luckily, I had seen the terrorist's sniper rifle scope glass shine in the sunlight, which served as our only warning to where the terrorists were hiding.

Two of the terrorists were hiding in a crane depot that was on top of a building that was under construction. We had checked the crane the day before, and we had instructed the company to lock it down the day prior to the president's speech. We also ordered the construction company to lower the crane to the ground. The construction company either allowed someone to steal a key. They were given cash for a key or the fucking terrorists broke into the crane depot in the early morning hours.

I hated to admit it, but it was exactly what my sniper, Special Warfare Operator, First Class (SO1) Jake Gomez, would have done if he were taking out a high priced target. Jake had kills outward to 2,200 meters while using his McMillan Tac-50 Mk 15 .50 cal. Jake was always on the hunt for breaking the longest confirmed kill held by a UK sniper, which was at 2,475 meters (2,707 yards). Jake was so crazy that he had a tattoo on his shoulder that read "2500." He always liked when people would ask him what "2500" meant. He would say, "it doesn't mean anything until it gets underlined."

The shine from the riflescope glass happened just moments before the president was on the stage. My unit and the secret service moved in to where the terrorists were staging their assassination. We didn't have time to get up to the crane depot, as we knew that the President of the United States (POTUS) was on stage.

I shot first when we localized the terrorists. I fired my HK 417 at the terrorist when I noticed the shine. Despite my shots, the sniper was able to get a shot off just as the president walked onto the stage. The sniper's bullet missed the president by just a couple of feet. I killed the sniper with one of my shots and Gomez was able to take out the terrorist spotter with his sniper rifle while we were standing. I never had a doubt, as Gomez was the best sniper I had ever seen.

The video showing the assassination attempt was played by the media over and over for several days. The YouTube video got over a hundred million views, which was the most views any video had ever received in its history. I found myself watching the video online as well as having flashbacks of our part that was not on YouTube, but in our heads.

If we had been even two seconds late, they would have killed the new president. The president had only been in office for a couple of months when the assassination attempt took place. Ironically, he was giving a speech on taking an even more aggressive stance on terrorist threats when the attempt occurred.

I struggled with the attempt, as it shouldn't have come that close. The president's assassination attempt troubled me tremendously. Of all the flashbacks that always ran through my head, the attempt was the worst. It was my detail. I was in charge.

I knew the crane depot was a risk. I knew it was a high point that had to be eliminated. Although the secret service didn't think it was a risk as they thought the distance was unreachable, I knew that with the right shooter, rifle and ballistics that an experienced shooter could make the hit.

Regardless of the realization, I knew that it was too close for comfort. I knew that if I hadn't seen the rifle-scope shine that the president would have been killed. It would have been my fault. Instead of a hero, I would have lost my position.

(Flashback to day of attempt).

"We need to make to our way toward the outposts to ensure nothing is high. We have sealed all near points and all teams are in position within immediate reach distance to the president," I said.

"Sir, look the crane depot is still up. Wasn't that supposed to be taken down by the construction company?" SO1 Jake Gomez said.

"Fuck, yes, that was supposed to be taken down yesterday at 1400 hours. Shit, it is 3 clicks away and reachable to POTUS," I said.

"Sir, with all due respect, there is no fucking way anyone can make that shot at that distance and trajectory," Secret Service agent said.

"You fucking kidding me? That is perfect site, all day for me," SO1 Jake Gomez said.

"Call the fucking company now and tell them to take it fucking down!" I exclaimed.

"Sir, negative, they took day off to listen to the president's speech," Secret Service agent said.

"Fuck it, we will have to bring it down ourselves," I said.

I will never forget our walk towards the crane depot. Things didn't feel right. My heartbeat raced, and my stomach felt ill. Then it happened.

"Glare, glare, flash glare!" I yelled.

I took the shot. I knew it had to be a shooter aiming for the president. There was no time for confirmation. If I was wrong, I would have been sent to jail for the rest of my life. If I were late, I would have cost the president's life.

"Shooter, shooter, take POTUS, take POTUS!" I screamed.

"Shot fired, shot fired! Take POTUS!" heard over radio from secret service agent.

Gomez fired another shot at the second terrorist. His precise accuracy killed him immediately.

I could hear the screams over the radio. Fuck, I thought. The president was dead. I failed. I fucked up.

"Report, report? Over," I asked.

Radio silence.

"Report, Report! Over," I asked even louder.

Nothing.

"Agent report, was POTUS hit? I repeat was POTUS hit, over!" I asked.

Still nothing.

"Was POTUS hit? Is POTUS injured? I kept repeating.

"Negative, no contact. No contact. POTUS in transport to safe spot A, rendezvous for immediate pickup by Marine ONE. Eagles immediate wheels up for flight pattern blue. Repeat Eagles immediate wheels up for flight pattern blue, out," the secret service agent ordered.

Gomez climbed up the crane to the control box. We had no idea how to operate the crane. We had to bring down the crane depot in order to confirm the shooters were killed.

"Gomez keep lock on crane depot in case these fuckers are still alive. We will maneuver the crane downward to confirm kills," I ordered.

"Team B contain the stage and area, ensure no other shooters present. Screen for anything suspicious as they could have left secondary threats, over" I commanded.

"Team C localize immediately to crane 3 clicks to your south. We need to guarantee that their terrorists have not laid down other shooters or secondary threats, over," I asked.

"Roger that, Sir, Team B will cover POTUS grounds and Team C is heading your way," Loco said.

We lowered the crane. I could see the rifle shot explosions through the glass. I could smell their dead flesh burnt from the high-powered rifle shots. Dark red blood dripped everywhere. Two shooters confirmed dead. We examined their hardware.

"Fucking A chief. They had a McMillan loaded with Barrett .416 armor piercing ammo. We don't even have this round. Check out their scope, it's a fucking tracking point scope. An amateur could have hit the president with this firepower and tracking point. You just plug in the ballistics, humidity, wind pressure and aim a dot at your target. Boom, job done. Sir, these were well-funded terrorists. You think Taliban or ISIS?" Gomez asked.

"I don't know Gomez, look at their tattoos. One terrorist's tattoos are in Arabic while the other terrorist's tattoos are in Spanish. Weird. We will have to get the FBI and CIA in on this to help us figure it out," I said.

I should have made sure the crane was taking down first thing in the morning. I should have double-checked that it wasn't accessible. I should have done so much more. Instead, I allowed our president to be two feet from being killed. I allowed the president to be the ridiculed by other countries on how closed he came to being killed on his own soil.

We scattered after the shooting to look for other terrorists. The part nobody knew about was my confrontation with one of the terrorists. I ran into one of them. He was young. He didn't look Middle Eastern. He spoke good English, but with a Spanish type accent. He was scared, but so was I. I had him dead to rights, as he begged for his life. I took it. I had to take him out. I couldn't imagine some bullshit trial with a terrorist that had just attempted to kill our president. My fury and influence pulled the trigger while we stood alone. I know now that I made the wrong decision, as my killing put Emma on this fucking plane.

The memories burned in my head. At this point, I just wanted to finish up the clean up, get our evidence, and head the fuck back to base. I also wanted to get home, as I felt ill from the near successful attempt on the president.

Since there was an assassination attempt, we all had to piss in a cup for standard protocol drug and alcohol testing. It was the Secret Service's protocol since some of their agents were found to be drunk on a previous presidential detail that had some complications. Not as complicated as an assassination attempt. It was more like they drove the wrong way home.

I was fucked, and I knew it. I had no choice. I would have to deal with the consequences. All my hard work down the drain. My fucking back was killing me that morning, and I had to take a couple of Oxys even though I knew it was forbidden during any mission. I was under influence while on mission, and I knew the potential consequences.

The Navy chose not to report my positive drug test. They said it was too high of a risk to national security to be reported. What the fuck I thought? I guess since I spotted the shooter and took out two of the terrorists out that the story of Navy Seal under influence while on a mission was a threat to national security. I wasn't going to complain. I was lucky, and I knew it. I also knew I couldn't do that shit again.

Despite our near shortcoming and after the assassination attempt, the president invited our team to the White House. I didn't know what to expect at the time, but when we met with the president and some of his cabinet I did feel their sincere gratefulness. I was not always the biggest fan of some of our politicians, but I did like our commander in chief and our secretary of defense. They shot straight and didn't bullshit you.

The president pulled me away from everyone at some point during our visit. He was told that I'd killed the sniper who was pointing his rifle at him. The sniper was actually about a mile from the president, so it would have been an incredible shot if he had made it. We were able to take out both the sniper and his spotter. When we investigated the setup, we knew that even though the target was over a mile away, the terrorists had the right rifle setup to be able to hit what he was aiming at.

I will never forget the president's words. "Thank you for serving your country. Thank you for putting your life on the line. Thank you for saving my life and letting me be the father to my children, husband to my wife, and commander-in-chief of the greatest military in the world. What is your cell-phone number, so I can have it in case I need to call you sometime?"

I will never forget how puzzled I was when he asked for my cell number. I gave it to him without hesitation, and he called me back while I was standing in front of him. I answered the phone at that time. I was still puzzled, as I was not sure what was going on at the moment.

It was then that the president said, "Here you go. This is my personal cell-phone number that only my wife, two kids, and a handful of my best friends in the world have.

My wife bought me this phone at some mall store or something. It's cheap, and even the secret service doesn't know I have it. I wanted a phone I could use to talk to my family and closest friends without always being recorded and followed. Anyhow, you can call me for anything, anytime. I'll be happy to help you with anything, as you have helped our country and me so much more than you can imagine. I know in my heart that I can trust you with this number without hesitation. You saved my life, and I'm indebted to you. I'll never forget you and what your men have done for me, so please remember how grateful I am to be alive."

His words repeated in my mind frequently. I wonder if he would have thought of me differently if he knew I pissed positive. Of all the missions Seal team 6 had completed with some not always to our personal approval, I enjoyed protecting the president. He was a self-made person who understood the common person. He also seemed to tell it how it was instead of loading the podium with bullshit rhetoric.

Shortly thereafter and by executive order, my unit, SEAL team 6, reported for the task of killing the terrorist group who tried to kill the president. When I received the order, I had no idea that it would change my life for not only two years, but also forever.

There were a bunch of leads at the time regarding the responsible terrorists. Since we had killed the two terrorists in the crane depot, we didn't have a direct source to question. The two terrorists in the crane depot didn't have any identification on them or really anything else aside from their rifle and spotting scope. They had cut off their fingerprints, so we could not identify them through the FBI or Interpol. Their DNA analysis did not come up with any matches to either terrorist.

The odd thing was that two were definitely Middle Eastern and the other appeared to be Mexican. The Mexican appearing terrorist had tattoos with all Spanish language and marking consistent with the cartel. The Middle Eastern appearing terrorists had tattoos in the Arabic alphabet. The combination of both nationalities provided us with more insight that the Mexican cartels were definitely involved.

There were leads also suggesting it was a Taliban group, a North Korean radical group, or a group led out of Iran. It seemed that our side actually had no idea of how the terrorists had gotten so close to killing the president in San Diego. Our intel kept pointing toward some mechanism for the terrorists to move into the US while crossing over from the Mexican border.

We were promised an extended mission time of only three months, but we all knew it would take, as long it had to take. We were all motivated to find the terrorist group, as he was a new president who was very well liked by the people. In fact, he had won the largest popular vote ever for a president of the United States.

I felt in my heart that I would help find the terrorist group, but wanting to be home with my family also tore me. I missed seeing my kids and my wife. I oftentimes felt that I was in two battles in my life. One battle was to serve my country with full sacrifice and without questions while battling my own mental devils and my cravings for Jack. The other battle was to put my family on hold, as I had done for too many years already.

At this point, I knew my nightmares were far from being over, as I kept watching Emma trying to die. I was so fucking exhausted at this point. Every time I stood up to check on Emma, I became dizzy.

My abdomen was jacked. I stopped looking at my expanding belly, as I knew it was likely filling with blood. I had to keep an eye on Emma, but my body begged for medical attention. Dark red blood ran down my legs and out of my pants when I walked. I used paper towels from the restroom to try to hide the obvious. My time for rest was coming. Six hours of flight time, fuck I need a drink. I was in and out of consciousness during the flight. I couldn't die on this plane. I couldn't leave Emma and Jaxon stranded on a plane. If Emma died, Jaxon would be alone. Sleep brought me equal horror. My eyes were too heavy to keep open.

6

El Jefe (Head of the Colombian and Mexican Cartel)

"**J**efe, I don't know what happened. We did everything Hector assigned us to do, Jefe, please believe me, please, I beg you!" Juanito (El Jefe's second in command) exclaimed.

"Fucking bullshit! I trusted you with Hector's life! How the fuck did you let him be killed by an Americano? I (El Jefe) demanded.

"Jefe, we had the perfect plan. Hector decided to be on the ground under the shooters at the last minute. He wanted to tell you he killed the American president. Jefe, please believe me, he wasn't supposed to be there. I would never have put him in harms way. We had no idea the fucking Seals were going to be there. You have to believe me, Jefe, please, for my children I beg of you don't do this to me. Hector was like my son as well. When he was killed, I lost my son as did you," Juanito begged for his life.

You motherfuckers have no idea what it took me to get here. Mexico is my country. I love my fucking country and I loved my son more than anything else in my life.

You all think I was born into the cartel and that I have had it easy my entire life don't you? Fuck you for thinking that. I left my family to run away from all the bullshit my father was doing running the Colombian and Mexican cartels. He did everything he could to kill me for betraying him.

He had me found. He had me abused. His second in command tried to kill me when I was only twelve years old. You know what I did to him? I fucking burned him to death and sent his body parts to my father!

From the age of fourteen, I was running drugs, killing and doing anything for money. It wasn't until my own cartel started competing with my fathers that he asked me to join him. I still hate him to this day for what he did to me, but in some fucked up way I knew he had to challenge me to make sure I could survive this fucked up cartel life.

My actions earned me the respect to lead this predatorily business organization. Now I was done. I told my only son that I was done. I told him to take money and run away to some fucking isolated island and to never look back. I told him to get the fuck away from this fucking life, so what does he do? He does exactly what I told him not to do… to stay the fuck away from the devil's world. I was retired, happy and worth over five billions dollars.

Fuck this, I've had a great life. Yes, I've killed, stole, kidnapped, and did anything else that was illegal to make my living, but I've also given back to the poor. That should equal out my sins. I was fucking ready for retirement before the shit went down and I lost my son. The chaos and pressures of competing in the illegal cartel world wore me out, so why did I come back? I was forced to reengage. What the fuck was I going to do now? I knew I had to set an example by beheading Juanito. If I didn't, I would be seen as vulnerable and penetrable. Fuck…Juanito was fucked.

"Juanito, have you seen Hector's last video? El Jefe asked.

"No, Jefe, sorry I have not," as Juanito cried for his life.

"Well, fucking watch it now! Watch as that fucking Americano Seal asshole kills him. He was fucking unarmed. He fucking killed him in cold blood! He empties his fucking clip into my son's young body while he begged for his life. He kicks him in the face after he is dead! Do you get that? He fucking executed him! Watch it before I fucking kill you, so you know the pain I must live with now because of your failure! El Jefe exclaimed.

"No, Jefe, please I don't want to watch it, just fucking kill me!" Juanito begs for his life.

I played the video for him from Hector's cell phone. Hector recorded the video and sent it livestream to me as he died. I guess he wanted me to see who was capturing him. I don't think Hector thought he was about to die. Fucking Seal will pay.

I hit play for Juanito to watch Hector die. I'd watched the video too many times now. It was the last time I saw Hector breathing.

"No, please, please don't shoot! I'm unarmed, I'm unarmed!" Hector yelled.

"Fuck you, fuck you! Get the fuck down! I saw what you did. You just tried to kill the president! Welcome to the

United States asshole! I'm Captain Williams. You fucked with the wrong team today! No arrest, no jail, no jury, just the death from my cold, hard steel!" Captain Williams yells.

"No, please no, I have kids! I did nothing, I just ran from the gun fire!" Hector begs.

"Fuck you and die! I saw you run from the scene, I repeat fuck you and die!" Captain Williams shouts. His shouts are followed by loud gunfire.

"Juanito, tell me why I should spare your life? You let Hector die under your watch. Hector was son and successor. He owned my empire. You just ignored his safety. For your failure, I will not forgive you," I told him directly to his crying face.

"Jefe, Hector was a son to me. I told him he wasn't supposed to be with the shooter. I told him! I swear it!

"Juanito, you fucked up! I'm not sorry for this, I'm sorry for your family and the family of that fucking Americano. Taking his life will be too easy. He will watch his kids and wife be killed in front of him. I don't have time to waste with you anymore."

I sharpened my machete to a finer edge than a razor blade. The machete's swing pierced the air as it took off his head. His ignorance begged for my punishment. He knew he was to protect Hector. He knew the consequences as all knew. I didn't want to do this.

I retired from this bullshit. I had too many years of breaking and killing people that crossed me. Being the leader of the cartel wasn't something I dreamed of growing up. It was just the life I created out of necessity. It was my life. I wanted to leave, but now this fucking Americano brought me back in. I had to find him now. His head and those of his kin were mine. His seed would end.

7

EL JEFE'S CARTEL

Why the fuck did I let Hector go? I was done with this fucking life. A billion dollars of mine are buried all over Mexico. I had had enough of the fucking killing, kidnapping, drug running, and watching over my shoulder. How the fuck did I let him talk me into dealing with terrorists now? Sure the money was good, and it was easier than running drugs across the border, but now my only son was gone.

I was born into the Cartel life. I grew up knowing my father did something illegal. We had an amazing life from a money perspective, but I knew early on that it was from the evils of man. My sister ran away when I was a kid. She told me she resented my father as he killed innocent people for a living. I was too young to understand, but I hurt as my only sibling left me. Her last words promised me that she would come back for me. She fucking lied.

The other cartels tried to rise after my retirement. I think Hector hated the fact that I was no longer to be the King of the cartels. I think he felt that he had to prove himself in order to take my reign. I couldn't blame him as I felt the same way when my father died. My father came from nothing. He rose up the ranks in the Colombian cartel and was smart enough to realize that the future growth and ease of expansion came from gaining reign in Mexico.

My father combined the Colombian cartel with the Mexican cartel to become the most powerful organization in the world. You think the United States is powerful? Fuck that, our cartel had no rules and more power than most presidents. We ruled the world because we had no borders. The United States feared us and loved us. We provided the world with billions of dollars worth of drugs, prostitution, adopted kids, mercenaries for hire, and everything else that broke a law.

Desensitizing oneself to the cartel life is likely the hardest thing to do. You have to adjust to rapid death. Your friend could be right next to you, but if he fucked up you would have to kill him. Fuck, I had to kill some of my own cousins as I rose up the ranks. The harder you acted the harder you had to be. If you flinched, you died.

Losing Hector meant only one thing. My short-term retirement was over. If I didn't react to Hector's murder, I would be seen as weak. I had a lot of enemies and they would love to know that I was now penetrable. My own head would be hung from being displayed in the middle of Mexico City. I knew my head would have a price on it if I didn't prove that I was still in the game.

I thought I was done, but Hector's death was the rebirth of my reign. I had to find the fucker that killed him. He didn't have to die. He was murdered in cold bold by that fucking seal. I would do the same to him. I would fuck his wife and kill his kids as he bled from his balls hanging in his mouth. Revenge was now mine. I hadn't been this pissed since my father killed my own mother. Yes, I just said that. Fuck it, I kind of missed the action. It kept me alive!

8

THE FLIGHT HOME

My eyes were wide shut. I had to check on Emma. Two hours passed now. She was still on pressors. She was still technically alive, but I knew she was not in good shape. The doc kept telling me that she was going to be all right once we arrived in Texas. I was too tired to argue.

I kept fading in and out of consciousness. Same bullshit. Same nightmares and fucked up recalls. I remembered when I had just returned home. The flight from hell I called it. Fuck it took forever to get home from the Middle East.

Flashback to three weeks prior.

I was finally boarding my final plane for the last leg home from hell. I flew from Afghanistan to Kuwait to London to New York to Phoenix. I had a twelve-hour layover in Kuwait, a four-hour layover in London, followed by another eight-hour layover in New York. All without being able to shower. I smelled so bad that I knew I smelled bad. I just couldn't wait to have a shower in my own home. It had been so long. I was still in the same clothes as when I left Afghanistan. I felt bad for the people on the plane next to me.

As I was boarding the plane, a nice gentleman in first class offered me his seat for the flight from New York to Phoenix. He was well dressed and had a fine, U.S. flag pin on his lapel. All he said was, "Sir, I saved this seat for you and your journey home. Thank you for serving our country, young man. Please enjoy a cold one on me. Can I take your seat?"

I was in my field uniform flying home. I immediately told him no, of course, but then he said the following words that I will never forget: "Please take my seat, because the safety of my children, grandchildren, and their children means more to me than any luxury in the world. I'd be honored to give up my seat for a man who seems to have traveled a long way to get home. Please young man take my seat and enjoy some comfort and a beer on me."

It was my first time in first class. It was nice to be able to put my head down for a while. I had a middle seat in coach, so I was kind of happy that my stench didn't have to ruin the flight for two innocent individuals.

I felt obliged to have at least one beer per the nice gentleman's request, so I asked for a non-alcoholic beer. I knew I had to stay away from Jack as if I opened that door I would stay inside until they carried me off the plane.

I don't know what it was, but for some reason the beer I had on the flight in first class was the coldest and best I had ever had even if it was non-alcoholic. I could barely contain myself, as I constantly thought of being home with my family. I felt closer as each minute passed on my watch.

My heart was going a mile a minute. I couldn't wait to see my family. I couldn't wait to hold my wife and kids. It is always the best feeling when I was coming home, and I could picture myself being in the arms of my lovely wife and kids.

After the flight attendant handed me my second, non-alcoholic beer, I asked her to please tell the nice man thank you for letting me sit in first class.

She nodded. "Yes, I'll make sure I tell Congressman Herrera that you said thank you. It will be my pleasure."

I was stunned to hear that he was a US congressman. His demeanor was true and caring. It was later I found out that he was a former Navy man, as was his father. Ironically, God allowed us to interact that day for a couple of reasons that would become apparent later, but Congressman Herrera was going to hear from me again in the near future.

I was blessed to be alive and on a plane, flying home to see my family. I thought I had a bigger challenge ahead of me anyhow, and that was making peace with my wife. I could tell from our phone conversations that she missed her husband and the father of her children.

I also knew that she had wanted to have another child. With my being away for two years, our window was closing soon; we were getting older. I imagined that it had to be very stressful for her to know that any phone call or knock on the front door could be notification that I was not coming home alive. I wanted peace in my life and with my family at this time, and I couldn't wait to see them soon.

My kids were getting older now, and I would often think to myself that they would not understand why I was always gone. I was especially worried, as I had been gone for 2 years straight without seeing them in person.

I knew I had to get some rest. My physical and mental exhaustion crippled me at this point. I was enjoying my ice-cold, non-alcoholic beer, and I tried to focus my thoughts on seeing my family soon. As I continued to try to relax and heed off my streaming flashbacks, I realized that something was wrong in the first-class cabin. I didn't think much of it at first, but it appeared that a man was shouting at the flight attendant. I had my headphones on when I first noticed it.

Crap I thought. Was I dreaming or was I imagining something unreal? I only had two, non-alcoholic beers, so I wasn't drunk. I thought shit maybe the flight attendant gave me two real beers, and now I was under the influence. I struggled with fatigue at this point and mentally I kept struggling with past, real and fictional dreams.

I concentrated and focused on him at this point. To my amazement, the man was not only shouting at the flight attendant, but he also began to point at other passengers in the first-class cabin with gestures that appeared threatening. I was in the last row of the first-class cabin, so he really didn't point at me, maybe because of the distance between us.

I kept thinking I was dreaming. As a Seal just coming from a battle with terrorists in hell, I couldn't believe that I was watching some crazy man threatening passengers in the first class cabin. What the hell?

Before I could react to his misbehavior, he grabbed the flight attendant's arm and put it behind her back. I dropped my headphones and phone. I immediately took action. It was my natural reaction. I asked the passenger to let the flight attendant's arm go. He looked at me with such derangement that I knew something was wrong with him.

I asked him again to let her go. Then he tried to swing at me. I knew that I had to do something at this point, even though it felt awkward being on a plane, in my Seal uniform fatigues.

He was intoxicated and/or high on some type of stimulant. His eyes looked glazed and abnormal. He pulled a knife from his meal tray in front of him. It was one of the first-class silver knives. I was still in disbelief that this was happening. I questioned myself as I was exhausted, and sometimes my PTSD created false realities.

His knife caressed her pounding veins in her silk white neck. She cried for her life. Her death felt imminent. I opened my eyes as wide as I could. I was desperate to grasp the reality. The past two years slowed my reactions.

I filled my lungs with air and I leapt toward the crazed man. I pulled the flight attendant away from him, I hadn't slept in over forty-eight hours, so I kept questioning whether I was dreaming or if this was really happening.

He lunged at me with the knife, and I ducked away. He grabbed another female in the front row of first class and put the knife to her throat as the other female. Although I had no doubt that I would soon gain control of the situation, part of me seemed to question the fact that I was about to either kill or really hurt this fucking asshole right in the first class cabin.

He was paranoid. He told me to sit down or he would kill the female passenger. He still had the knife pressed against her anterior neck. I knew his intentions were real. At this time, the entire plane knew something was wrong. The captain came over the speakers and shouted to the man to drop the knife immediately or the captain would shoot him.

The man shouted back to the captain to shut the fuck up or he would kill her as well as other passengers. I knew I had to act fast, as he seemed to be getting unstable by the second. I kept inching closer to him. He kept backing away from me.

It was time to roll. I was tired, and I just wanted to finish my fucking beer before it got warm. This asshole had no idea that a highly trained Navy SEAL with a fifth dan black belt in ninjutsu was about to make his day go from bad to nightmare whether I was at full coherence or not.

I inched closer to him. I noticed that he had a wedding ring on his finger. I asked him to think about his wife. He didn't respond. I asked him if he had kids. He seemed to sadden at this question. I'm sure he felt remorse about what he was doing at this point. I asked him again if he had kids. I said that if he did, he should think about them and put the knife down before things got worse. I instructed to put the knife down, to let the flight attendant go, and to take his seat back in first class and that everything was going to be alright again just like nothing happened and that he was going to be fine.

He responded to my question by doing what I had hoped he would do. He looked down, as most people will do when they feel guilt or remorse. It was then that I took the knife away. I pulled him down to the ground by using a wristlock. By the way he went down and with the agony he was showing in his face, I was pretty sure that I had broken his wrist. He was crying in agony as I kept him on the ground.

I restrained the passenger. As I kept him on the floor, I asked the flight attendant to get something to lock him up with. We were still about an hour away from Phoenix.

The captain opened the cockpit door at this point. He pointed a small handgun at the passenger. I told him that it would not be necessary as I had complete control of the passenger.

I asked the captain if he had some form of handcuffs or restraints, so we could secure the crazed man. He went back into the cockpit for a brief period. He came out with plastic zip ties. Perfect I thought.

We brought the passenger over to a secure post in the first-class cabin that I figured out later was designed specifically to secure a belligerent passenger. We zip tied the crazed passenger to the metal post. There was a slide-out seat next to the post that came out of the wall. It appeared especially designed for the maintenance of restrained passengers. It had a quad based shoulder and waist type seatbelt restraint that could be put around the passenger while he or she was still secured to the metal post.

The captain later told me that after 9/11, all new planes were required to have special passenger restraints as well as a solid metal post to secure passengers during these type of situations. It hadn't occurred to me, but the first class cabin had 4 of these metal posts that then had small seats pull out in order to kept passengers restrained if needed. Well, the seat and restraints certainly worked in this situation.

The madman was restrained appropriately. I exchanged seats from the last row in first class to the front row, so I could keep an eye on him in case he acted out again. I think he realized how much he had fucked up at this point. He just kept crying the entire time. It was a long hour flight after the incident, hearing this asshole cry the entire time.

When I finally had a chance, I asked the flight attendant who'd had the conflict with the passenger about what had happened. She pulled me aside and said he became very upset after she refused to give him another drink. She said he had already had five drinks, which was the airline's limit on domestic flights.

I was dumbfounded. Here was an apparently successful businessman who was married and had three kids, and he was transformed into a man that was soon going to be taken into federal custody upon landing in Phoenix. Even though I identified with his alcoholism, I didn't feel sorry for him.

We'd had a chance to divert and land in El Paso, Texas immediately after the situation as it was the closest airport after the incident. I felt a little selfish, because the captain actually asked me if it was OK to divert to El Paso to land since we had a situation. I'd looked the captain in the eye and told him that I hadn't slept in probably four to five days and that I hadn't showered in over two days. I told him that I would personally watch and take care of the deranged passenger.

I guaranteed him that if this mad motherfucker made a bad move; I personally would take care of him. I told him honestly that I just wanted to get home to see my family that I hadn't seen in two years. Also I think the crazed passenger had realized the error in his judgment that he wasn't going to do anything else wrong.

"Sir," said the captain. "No worries. I have all the confidence in the world that you won't let him do anything else. There's nothing in the world I want more than to land this plane safely, so you can embrace your family and go to the home that you deserve more than anyone else on this plane. Thank you for serving, and thank you for saving all of us in this mayhem. I appreciate your service and I will forever be indebted to you for saving my plane today without having anyone injured."

What could I say at that point. "Yes, sir. I'm glad God put me in first class today, because I'm not sure what may have happened otherwise."

We finally landed in Phoenix. I was exhausted. The captain briefed the entire plane that we would have to wait in our seats with our seatbelts on while the Phoenix police and FBI took the deranged passenger off the plane.

The captain came up to me once again and asked me to secure the passenger after landing until the authorities could escort him off the plane. I gladly agreed, because I just wanted to get off the plane. I wanted this chapter over, so I could run into my family's arms.

When we pulled up to the tarmac, I could see the heavy police and FBI presence. Even before we landed, all the passengers were watching CNN on their individual seat

TVs. The news broadcasted the story on our emergency landing with a possible terrorist who had threatened the passengers and plane. I thought about how the media had put such a spin on the actual events. Again, I didn't care, as I just wanted to get off the plane. I was used to the media's spin on stories to make them sound more enticing to their audiences.

The police and FBI opened the front door to the plane. There were about twelve police and four FBI agents, all heavily armed and with heavy protective gear. I guess they couldn't take any chances.

They all came onto the plane and then they handcuffed the crazy businessman and hauled him away. As they hauled him away, the man turned to me and said thanks for not letting him hurt anyone. I am sure he realized that if he had hurt the flight attendant that his judged outcome would have been much worse.

When they escorted the man away, I felt bad for his wife and kids. During that long hour, he had talked about his family. He had a seventeen-year-old boy and two ten-year-old twin girls. Although I tried to never judge people, I thought to myself what a mess over a drink of alcohol. Unfortunately, I knew the evils of alcoholism and how powerful its influences could be.

Their dad was going to be in a federal prison for a long time, and it was all because he had wanted another drink. Alcoholism's grip shatters lives as it just did this man. He told me that his son was going to college on a full baseball scholarship. I actually felt bad for him and his family. I prayed for the man's family.

I'm just grateful that Congressman Herrera switched seats with me, as I was able to control a situation that could have easily ended up with a bad ending.

Overall, it was a terrible situation for all parties involved.

In my line of work, the emotions of certain situation had to be easily released. I knew that the madman could easily have killed a passenger on the plane before I got to him. I felt God had intervened at that point to have me switch seats into first class.

THE NEWS INTERVIEW

We were finally allowed to get off the plane. The FBI kept us on the plane for about forty-five minutes, as they took down all our names and information. They asked the crew, some of the passengers, and me a bunch of questions about what had happened. They then told us that they would contact us again in a few days for more questioning. All of us cooperated.

After we left the plane, we walked through a large crowd of people standing around our gate. I kept walking as fast as I could, as I just wanted to see my family.

Before I could reach the end of the terminal, one of the airline's representatives asked me if I could meet with their vice president of airline affairs. Although I was not in the mood to cooperate, I agreed.

We met in one of their private offices. They were all very friendly and grateful that I was able to defuse the situation and save one of their crew from a potentially life-threatening injury. I was amazed when the vice president then told me they would provide my family and me with free round-trip tickets to anywhere they flew not just once, but once a year for the next ten years. I was taken aback by the offer. I told him that I had to think about it, and that I just wanted to see my family at this point.

I left the airline's private office. I kept walking as fast as I could down the terminal to the end, where I had hoped my family would still be standing. I was so exhausted.

I was walking up the ramp and leaving the airport terminal when I saw my wife and two kids. I couldn't believe it. Jaxon and Emma were so big. My family was just a few yards away from me now, as compared to being almost eight thousand miles away just a couple of days prior.

I couldn't hold it in. Tears ran down my face as I approached them. I was so happy to be home. There is no other feeling like it. I reflected on that night during the raid when I dove onto the grenade, and I thanked God for giving my men and me a second chance. I thanked my dad for watching my six. I knew he was there with me. He always was there for me despite his own flaws.

I was a man who rarely cried. It was driven into me to never show emotion, but at this point it was my true emotion. I was not a man who had just saved a plane. I was a husband and father who hadn't seen his family in over two years.

I didn't think I had been this choked up since my daughter Emma was born. I ran to my family over the last bit of distance that separated us. All of us embraced. I didn't want to let go. My tears soaked their clothes.

All I could hear was the sound of cameras going off all around us. I hadn't noticed really, but there was a crowd of photographers and news reporters from every known news station. I didn't care at this point. I was in a state of complete, pure joy to be holding my beautiful wife and kids. I was not going to let go for anyone or anything.

Time stood still. I looked into Natalie's beautiful green eyes and almost fell to the floor from pure loving disbelief that I was home with my family. Natalie and I met randomly while in line getting coffee at the hospital where she worked. I was getting coffee before I gave a talk to a group of doctors and nurses on military response during a disaster. The military had a working relationship with one of the trauma centers in San Diego, and our seal team would often be present during the hospital's disaster talks and drills. Natalie saw me in line for coffee while I was struggling. I think I was up late the night prior drinking a little bit.

I remember it like yesterday *(in a flashback)*.

"Rough night last night, sailor?" Natalie asked.

"Um, you could say that," I replied.

"Here is a tip, sailor, you should brush your teeth to help hide the smell of the fucking alcohol." She said.

What a nag from a person I hadn't met, but her smile was so magical and her body rocked. I knew then that I had to marry her right then, but I couldn't let her have the lead in this exchange.

"Well, you see, I have diabetes and sometimes when my sugars are low I emit a alcohol like smell from my diabetic ketoacidosis. That is why I'm in line to get something to eat," I said lying through my teeth as I didn't have diabetes.

"Oh, shit, I'm so sorry, I feel like an asshole now."

"You should, aren't you a nurse? A caregiver?"

"Yes, I am. I'm so sorry. Gosh, I'm such an ass." Her face blushed full red.

"No worries, I think I can forgive you if you let me buy you a drink?"

"What? You are still fucked up aren't you, sailor?"

"I meant a drink of coffee, sweetheart. What did you think I meant?"

"Ok, I think I should get to work as I feel like an ass once again."

"Aren't you going to get your coffee?"

"Yes, that is my problem, I haven't had my fucking coffee yet."

"Wow, you have been around too many sailors with that sailor mouth."

"Large black coffee please, thank you."

"I got it. I haven't had this much fun since playing hide and seek as a kid." I said.

Ah, what a memory. Little did I know that Natalie was going to my talk. I was likely still fucked up from hitting Jack the night before, but I couldn't let her know that.

During my entire talk, I kept staring at Natalie. She blew me away. A woman that cussed as much as I did was somehow the turn-on that I hadn't realized in the past. Aside from that, she looked so damn hot in her hospital scrubs.

Immediately after I finished my talk, I rushed up to Natalie. I felt a little cocky at this point as I felt I had won our "coffee talk" exchange.

"Well, what did you think?" I asked.

"Impressive. Sorry I didn't know Captain Bad Ass was in the coffee line with me," Natalie said.

Wow I thought. Again the language and vulgarity. What was she protecting I thought.

"Well, with all due respect, thanks for your service. Sorry if I offended you in the coffee line. I have to start my shift," Natalie said.

"Hey, can we grab a cup of coffee or play field hockey sometime?" I asked sarcastically.

"Ha, ha, how did you find out I used to play field hockey? She asked.

"Reconnaissance. Very key to knowing your future date."

"Recon, huh, ok, tell you what. I will agree to meet you out on a field hockey date. I play on a coed recreational team. You come to one of our scrimmages, and if you score a goal on me while I'm playing goalie, I will let you take me out to dinner."

"Deal. What does one wear to play field hockey?"

"A cup to protect your boys, sailor. You see if I get the hockey ball I'm going to aim for them."

"Tough woman. I get it. Ok deal. What if I score multiple goals? What do I get?"

"Don't push your luck. Your lucky enough to score a chance, sailor."

"Ma'am, I prefer Frogman if it is all the same to you," I referenced.

"Sorry, I don't know all the symbol differences on your uniform or the ranks," she apologized.

I scored four goals during the scrimmage. I also scored with Natalie on the fourth date. She denies it had any relation to the four goals I scored. We joke about it all the time.

In all honesty, Natalie put up a front during our first encounters. She acted tough, but she was the sweetest thing ever once you peeled back her durable layers. For instance, she cries during comedies. She had to have way too many lights on at night, as she feared the dark. She puked after her first shot of tequila on our third date.

I am not going to lie. She always found a way to beat me whenever we went on runs on the weekends. She was probably in better shape than me when we started dating or at least she made it look that way.

I fell in love with her in the coffee line. Her smile. Her vulgar tongue. Her sexy body in her scrubs. So many reasons. She always brought out a person inside of me that I hadn't known existed. She calmed my volcanoes.

It wasn't long after we started dating that I knew I wanted to marry her. It also wasn't very long after we started dating that we knew we were going to have little Jaxon.

After I let go of my family, I felt a gentleman tap me on the shoulder. He had tears in his eyes that appeared to be as genuine as mine. He kindly asked me if I would answer any questions for the media. I looked at Natalie for her approval, since I didn't want to lose the moment of being home with my family. She nodded a kind yes. She knew she would still have me home soon. I was no longer eight thousand miles away.

Even though it was hard to do, I stepped away from my family. I kept them close and I prefaced the interview by saying that I would only answer questions for two minutes because I hadn't seen my family in over two years and hadn't showered in two days. I guess my stench let the media know that I wasn't kidding.

I stood in front of about ten to twelve cameras and about twenty phones and microphones. They asked me questions about what happened, if I knew the passenger, if the crew reacted correctly, what the captain did, and what I did. I gave only brief explanations. I didn't want to get dragged into in-depth questions and explanations. Finally, I said I wasn't going to answer any more questions. There was silence for about three to five seconds, and then one reported asked what seemed to be an odd question at that moment. I will never forget it. I often wonder how things may have been different if I'd answered him differently.

He asked if I liked professional football and if I had a favorite team.

I thought for a second, because, again, it seemed out of context. Yes, of course," I finally said. "I like the Professional Football League, or PFL. I can't wait to watch games tomorrow with my family."

The same reporter then asked me who my favorite team in the PFL was.

Again I thought it was an odd question following a possible hijacking of a airliner. After another brief hesitation, I said, "Well, of course I have a favorite team. I was born in Arizona, and my favorite team has always been, and will always be, the Phoenix Troopers."

Immediately after I made the final statement, the entire terminal went wild and began cheering. The entire situation was surreal.

My family and I collected my suitcase and duffel bag, and we didn't look back. We rode off onto the highway and trekked back home.

10

THE ARGUMENT

Although the car ride home was only 20 minutes, it was the longest part of my journey. I just wanted to be home. It was one in the afternoon. I couldn't wait to get in the shower and change into regular clothes. I was going to be a civilian once again, at least for the time being. I had just enough energy to get into the shower before hitting the bed. I had to stay up just for a while longer to spend time with my family. The whole process of being home felt dreamlike.

My first sleep at home was challenging. I kept waking to nightmares of all that had just happened. I knew it would take a while for me to normalize once again.

For that night's dinner, Natalie ordered our favorite pizza from a local pizzeria. The pizza's smell filled our home. We sat down to eat in front of the TV. I hadn't watched regular TV in about two years. It was Sunday, and that meant football was on, and I was a big football fan.

What better thing could there be than to finally be home with my family, eating our favorite pizza, and watching the

Phoenix Troopers professional football team? My son and daughter were wearing the jersey of their favorite player's jersey, number 11, Marcus Jackson.

I watched them absorbed by the entire game. I couldn't believe my eyes. They had gotten so big since I had last seen them. I'd missed so much while being away for the last two years. I'd lost the last two years with them. Where did it go? I wished I could have it back, just for a while, at least.

The kids went to sleep, as it was late. Natalie and I stayed up after the kids went to sleep. We were outside in our backyard, just talking. I missed her beautiful green eyes. I kept staring at her like we'd just met, and I was falling in love with her all over again. Even though I craved a drink, I pushed my alcoholic cravings as far away as I could.

I could tell she wanted to talk about having another baby. It was the topic of our last conversations when I was came home two years ago. I could hear it in her voice that she yearned for another child. I decided to ask her if she wanted to have another baby. I guessed that she would want to talk about it sooner or later, and I figured it was best if I opened up the discussion.

She got angry and started yelling at me. "Ryan, you know I'm thirty-six years old now; you know I'm too old to have another baby at this age!"

"Honey, I know we're both older now, but couples have babies into their forties," I said.

"I know that. I'm too old now, and I don't want to talk about it again. I have made up my mind."

She walked back into our house and slammed the back door right behind her. I was confused by her response as I figured she would have been happy and not angry. My first instinct was to hang out with Jack, as it seemed a perfect time to become comfortably numb.

I was happy to be back, but I could tell that being away had hurt my family more than I probably knew. I would make it better this time. I knew I had to be a father and husband now and not a Navy SEAL captain. I stayed outside for a while longer as I had to figure out how best to approach the topic again with Natalie.

I would have to speak with Natalie once again when things calmed down. I could understand why she was a bit testy or at least sensitive about the topic. We had talked about it for the last five years.

I did want to have another child, and we had planned on it two years ago. Unfortunately, the last two years were unlike anything I could have expected. My service time was extended, and I hadn't had any time to be home. Each time I thought my time was close to returning home, our mission was extended as Seal Team 6 had the most intelligence and experience with dealing with the terrorist that were our latest targets.

Since the day I first met Natalie, she always wanted to have three kids. We were blessed to have two kids, Jaxon and Emma. Each of them had their own distinct personalities, but they also shared so many similarities.

Jaxon always displayed a certain positive attitude that made him likable by other kids and parents. He likes computer games and playing sports. I've tried not to tell him, but sometimes he is too giving to others. I would say his biggest strength and weakness were almost the same quality of being generous. I'm not sure why that bothered me, but it sometimes made me feel uncomfortable that he could be taken advantage of for always thinking of others.

He was a funny kid in some ways. Although he was already an advanced belt in the deadly martial art of Ninjutsu, he couldn't watch a scary movie to save his life. Natalie and I made the mistake once of watching a movie that had a scary movie trailer before the actual movie. Jaxon didn't sleep for two weeks. He still has to sleep with the lights on sometimes, as he gets scared when he thinks about the scary movie trailer.

Pretty routinely, Jaxon would sleep in Emma's room. The next morning he would say she was scared, so he would sleep on her floor to help make it through the night. Natalie and I knew it was probably a combination of both of them helping each other dealing with their own nighttime fright.

When Jaxon was five years old, I returned home from one of my worst missions in my career. We lost 2 SEALS and 3 Marines. One of the SEALS was my best friend. The loss of men troubled me more than anything I had experienced. The loss of my best friend still haunts me from day to day.

Shortly after blowing out his birthday cake candles for his fifth birthday, I was lost behind a bottle of Jack while exposed in the pouring rain. I went outside to be alone, so my family would not see me drinking. I tried to hide my addiction from my kids. Natalie knew I had an issue with alcohol and narcs, as did my mom since she saw my father spiral downwards from his alcoholism.

Jaxon came outside fully dressed for the rain. He popped open an umbrella to cover my drenched body. He whispered in my ear and said the following words that still crush me, "Daddy, my birthday wish is that you find peace in your heart. Thanks for coming home for my birthday. I love you, Daddy." As I said, he was much too giving for his young age, and his words inspired me to try to stop drinking.

Jaxon and Emma were natural swimmers. Natalie and I started both of them swimming at a very young age. My mother used to tell the story of how she started yelling at my father for putting me in the pool at six weeks. She said he literally let me go to see how I would respond. I guess I actually starting moving my arms and legs like I was trying to swim. My dad always teared up when my mom told that story, as I am sure there was some part of it that was true.

He swore he saw me swim that day. He always told his Navy buddies that his son walked at nine months and swam at six weeks. I used to love to hear that when he told it to his friends in front of me. It meant a lot to me to hear him speak so highly of me as a kid. My dad was always the person I looked up to as I cherished his love and loyalty to us and to the USA.

The son of bitch was hard on us—and hard on us all the time, not just some of the time. He believed in being true to your values and beliefs. He always spoke like he was a preacher.

My father also battled his own demons as he suffered from alcoholism. I remember the first time I realized what alcohol was, as it was when my dad took me to a professional baseball spring training game. I was between 5-6 years old.

We went into the restroom. He went into a stall. I followed right into the next stall. As I was taking a piss, I heard a loud clank on the floor followed by a "son of a bitch! I looked down and saw his flask spilling on the floor. As a curious kid, I asked him what the flask was. He answered, "Devil's juice, it adds flavor to my soda."

I had no idea what to think.

After the game, I made the mistake of telling my mom that my dad was drinking devil's juice at the game. My dad didn't talk to me for a few days, as my mom lectured him and pretty much came close to kicking his ass for drinking in front of me and driving us home while under the influence of alcohol.

It is hard as a kid to know what is wrong when a parent drinks alcohol too much. I loved my dad very much, but it was painful for me to see him suffer and be dependent on alcohol to survive his nights. It wasn't until I was a teenager that I started to try to understand why my dad suffered from the disease.

There were many times when he had been drinking that he would storm around the house barking orders to us to "hit the ground," or "incoming." When I was a boy,

I oftentimes thought he was playing around with us. As I grew older, I knew that he was not playing around and that he was dealing with the many repercussions of war.

He was a closet alcoholic to everyone except us. Whenever we went to family or friendly parties, he wouldn't even have a drink. He might have a beer with his seal buddies every now and then, but he always gave the appearance that he didn't drink alcohol at all.

In retrospect, I didn't blame him for his weaknesses in giving in to the bottle. His drinking helped him deal with his demons and depression, and now after my own life experiences, I understood the challenges he suffered.

Unfortunately, I wish I hadn't followed in all of his footsteps. Alcohol had been my vice for dealing with my own depression, PTSD, and body pain. I started drinking heavily after my first few missions as a Seal. Don't get me wrong, I drank some in college and so forth, but it was more of a social thing of drinking with the boys. The suffering I witnessed and inflicted was just too much sometimes for my brothers and me to handle.

After I injured my back, alcohol and oxys numbed the pain and helped me cope. Too many nights I found myself in unbearable pain. I thought I had high tolerance to pain from years of military training and missions, but my back pain could put me over the top a moment's notice. My peace came from Jack's repression of my mental demons and oxys' soothing of the physical pain.

My father prepared us for the worst and always gave us his best. My father always lived in the red zone. I swear

I never saw him relax. He was a perfectionist. When he was sober, his mind was always clicking on how he could make processes or things better and more efficient. He was definitely one of a kind. Despite my fathers' flaws, he was my role model in my life.

He passed away when I was last home. I was able to come home for a few days, as I was given notice he was dying from cirrhosis of his liver from all of his years of heavy drinking. The Navy and the Red Cross had a special program for military members that allowed them immediate travel home when a family member was dying. I was grateful to them for allowing me to be at his bedside when he died.

I always thought my father would die while serving in the Navy. I actually think he wanted it that way, but he survived crazy missions against all odds. He will always be a hero to me as well as to many of his men and to our country. Ultimately, I think the time serving killed him. I have realized that it is almost impossible to have the mental mind to survive when you have seen your own men die. Alcohol ruined my father's life, and it was doing the same to mine.

Even so, my dad was my mentor. He basically raised me to be a Navy SEAL, even though he always said he didn't want me to follow in his footsteps. I had no choice. The Navy was all I knew growing up. It was all I wanted to know. My father was and will always be my team leader. To this day, I feel him standing behind me on missions. He is always there: guiding me, praising me, critiquing me, pushing me, and praying for me.

My dad would always race me in the pool. I think he let me win one time when I was four years old, just so I could taste victory. From then on, he raced me to the finish line each time, pushing me to be faster. Oftentimes, we would go swimming at Lake Pleasant, Arizona as it allowed us to swim for long distances. I had swum from one end to the other several times.

Lake Pleasant was our family's favorite place to go boating, swimming, and fishing. My two kids loved going there. While I was away, they always talked about Lake Pleasant each time I talked to them on the telephone.

For ten long years, I tried my hardest to beat my dad at swimming. When I finally did, he told me I got lucky. He also told me to always swim my hardest and that life was always a competition. He was right. I carry his words with me all the time.

After high school, I was blessed and lucky enough to get into the US Naval Academy. I kept swimming there and found that it was probably the thing I was best at in my life. I had a blast swimming for the Navy. I met so many great friends, and I was able to travel all over the United States and the world competing for the Navy.

Swimming is what kept me the most balanced out of all the things in my life. Even today, when I feel stress or I feel I need an out, I go swimming to keep me away from drinking. Swimming always kept me centered and focused on major tasks at hand.

I always envisioned myself trying to rescue someone when I was swimming. I'm not sure why, but it gave me an inspiration to swim faster than anyone else.

I once swam for eight hours straight. Why? I have no idea. I kept swimming, thinking I had to rescue someone far out in the ocean, and the only way I could save this person was if I could swim while carrying him or her for miles. I'm not sure how far I actually swam in those eight hours, but I assume it must have been several miles as eight hours at my pace covers a lot of distance.

If I ever lost a race, I would tell myself that it was the equivalent of losing one of my men or a civilian I was responsible for rescuing. It was crazy to think that way, but it kept the thought in my mind that my skills and speed in swimming would make me a better SEAL.

It was just the way I was. It was the way my father had trained me while growing up. He always said to me that God gave me the speed in swimming so that one day I could use it to save someone or to save my team. He would also say that God let me swim at six weeks for a reason, and the reason was to be a SEAL.

They tell me my records still stand for the naval academy's fastest times in the 100 and 200 meters. I'm not sure, because I've lost touch with that world.

My mother held on to all my medals, certificates, and newspaper clippings from my swimming events. She always said that she would share them with my kids one day, so that they could see another part of me aside from being away serving in the Navy. I guess she meant well. All mothers do.

Whenever I was home, I would hit the swimming pool and pretend my dad was right next to me, still trying to beat me. I could hear his voice saying, "I'm going to catch you. I'm going to catch you." After I turned fourteen, he never did catch me again, and to this day I didn't know if he was just letting me win, or if I was finally faster than my old man.

I always told him he should have competed in race competitions for his age group, as he was almost as fast as I was, and he was in his sixties. His answer was always, "God taught me how to swim fast to save the brave men of my country, not to beat other men in a competition."

He would always smile after he said that. The funny thing is that I knew he could beat anyone in the water. He was just the fiercest competitor I ever met.

I will never forget the time I did beat him for the first time. He got out of the pool, stood up straight, and looked right down on me. He then said, "Stay swimming. I will be right back."

He disappeared for about fifteen minutes. I didn't think much about it, but then he came back to the swimming pool with his Navy Seal pack with him. He told me to get out of the pool and to put on his pack.

At that age, I barely weighed about 115 pounds. His pack weighed about 60 pounds. He told me put his pack on and to swim 10 laps. He then said that when I was done with the 10 laps that I could get out of the pool.

At first, I thought he was crazy as I could barely lift the 60-pound pack. As he watched me struggle to put the pack on my back, he then said to me the following words, which

I often tell my men before tough drills or even before battles.

These were my father's words on the day, "Love the water so you can save your men. Love the water so you can remember that if you believe in yourself and God that you will swim faster than the enemy. You will swim for your freedom. You will swim to defend those that need your protection, and that no matter what body of water you may be in, remember this, water is water, swimming is swimming, and God is God, so swim today like you have never swam in your lifetime."

With that in mind, I jumped into the pool with the 60-pound pack. I could barely swim back up to the surface. When I did finally surface, my dad was gone. My first thought was to just get out of the pool, but I knew my dad was testing me. It took me about 2 hours to swim the 10 laps with the pack. Ten laps usually only took me a few minutes to complete.

I was determined to do the 10 laps, and I had no idea that it had taken me so long to finish them. When I walked into the house, my dad asked me with a sarcastic tone, "how was your swim?"

I immediately answered my dad by saying, "water is water, swimming is swimming, and God is God, so I swam today like I've never swam in my lifetime." My dad walked up to me and gave me the longest and tightest hug he had ever given me. I saw a tear in his eye although I know he would have never admitted it to anyone.

I have to give him credit, though, because he was always just an arms length behind me as I grew up. I miss him so much. I feel I never really had the time a kid deserved with his father. I think that is also why I loved swimming so much, as my best memories were always about my dad and me swimming in the pool.

When I was next to my dad during his last breaths, he said three things to me. "You ever wonder if you would have won gold in the Olympics?" he asked. He was pissed off at me for the longest time that I didn't take my invitation to try out for the US Olympic swimming team. He was pissed that I chose the Navy, because he didn't really want me following in his footsteps.

He always brought up the fact that the man who won gold for the United States was a man I beat during a college race. I know in his heart he was equally as proud that I wore the gold Navy SEAL emblem, as he would have been if I'd worn the Olympic gold medal.

The second thing he said to me was, "You may not know what your true mission in life is—it may not even be a mission you serve in the Navy—but whatever it is, embrace it. Your heart and soul will let you know when it's the right mission in your life."

And I'll never forget last thing he said to me, which was, "Love your family, and always protect them just like you do for your country—your country won't hold you when you are most in need, but your family will. Don't ever forget that, my son. I'll watch your six from Heaven."

That time with him was the most I think I had spent with him my entire life. I held his hand for hours, even after he passed away. His entire body was yellow from his cirrhotic jaundiced state. He had been sober for the last 3 months, which was likely his longest time without a drink. It didn't matter though as his liver disease was too advanced. He gave up drinking too late in his life. I always wished he had given it up much sooner, so he could lived longer.

The men from his Seal unit stayed in my father's room as he passed. They were all brothers, and they had been together through thick and thin.

I didn't want to leave my father's side. The hospital staff finally had to ask me to let go of his hand, so the physician could pronounce him as being officially dead.

I just couldn't let him go. I felt for once in my life that he was human and not the machine I'd always thought he was. I also felt that for once I had my father to myself, and I wasn't sharing him with the rest of the country and the Navy.

He was always away serving, protecting. He was my hero, but most of all he was my father and the grandfather to my kids. He was the man above all men. He was my protector and the role model above all role models!

When I lost him, I lost a part of my life, but I gained the encouragement that I would always try to be there more for my kids. I always had to remind myself that one day I would be able to be home with my kids and that I couldn't die without spending more time with them.

My mom was even tougher than my dad. She had to be, because she had to deal with my brother and me all the time. My dad was gone most of the time while serving, so my mom really was the one who was always around.

She was born in Mexico, and she came to the United States when she was a child. She didn't tell us much about her childhood, but my brother and I always assumed it had been rough, as she did not have much when they came to the United States.

Of the little information that my mom would share with us about her past, she talked mostly about her younger brother and how they were inseparable. She didn't have any pictures of her family, but she wore a pendant on her necklace that had a picture of her and her younger brother. I knew it was painful for her as she always said she had to leave to try to find a better life for herself. She would always tell my brother, Adrian, and I how one of her dreams would be to reunite with her brother and her parents one day. As her son, I always promised her that I would help her find them one day even though I didn't know what that meant.

My dad would often tell us how he met my mom. She worked as a waitress at a local diner near my dad's naval base. He always said he fell in love with her the first time he saw her at the diner. He told my brother and me how he would sometimes go to the diner twice in a day just to see her.

She knew he was a Navy SEAL, and she always told him to stay safe. My dad would always tell us that her words kept him warm at night when he was away on missions in cold environments.

My mom was such a strong and intelligent women. She worked full time at the diner and put herself through college. She received her bachelor's degree in finance from the University of San Diego.

She then went on to receive her MBA. She worked in private industry for a short time before she had my brother and me. She then became our mom, and she dedicated her life to us.

She raised us to love and care. She helped offset my dad's obsession with teaching us how to win and survive and his battle with alcoholism. I couldn't wait to see her again when I came home. She raised us by speaking to us in both English and Spanish. To this day, I am grateful that she did as I used the Spanish language quite often. Seemingly, I didn't know that by knowing Spanish that I would actually help myself in a future situation.

11

BEING HOME

A few days passed since I had returned home. I was taking my kids to school and picking them up each day. I felt like a regular person, although I really didn't know what being a regular person felt like on a day-to-day basis.

It was the biggest joy for me to be involved with my children's lives again. I could get used to doing just being with them every day.

Natalie was still upset, but we kept talking our way through it. I could tell she'd kept it bottled up inside her for the last two years. We had talked about her dream of having three kids since we started dating. It was my dream as well. I remembered our wedding night, and I promised her that I would always do everything to make her dreams come true.

Finally that night after dinner, Natalie and I made love for the first time since I'd been home. I was actually nervous in some ways.

We shared a nice dinner as a family. The kids went to sleep early, and the rest of the night was ours. Her anger towards me had dissipated in some ways by making love that night. I also felt that we were strong again and almost getting back on track.

Our night felt like a romantic movie, as we had not been together in so long. It just felt right again. Our night was filled with passion, almost as if we had just started dating. We made love a couple of times that night. It was a night that I knew I would always remember.

When I woke up the next morning, I told Natalie about a dream I had. It wasn't a nightmare this time, but a magical dream. In my dream, Natalie was pregnant with a baby girl. In the dream, we named our little girl Bella. Natalie smiled with tears in her eyes.

Natalie took the next day off from work, so we could just spend the day together. Natalie and I took the kids to school together. She had such a twinkle in her eyes and a "just very happy" smile on her face. I hadn't seen her smile like that in a long time.

After we dropped off the kids at school, we came back home and made love again. I felt like we were newlyweds again. We held each other in bed for a long time. Not having an agenda for the day was new to me. I accepted the pleasure without guilt.

We decided to go out for lunch. I hadn't had real Mexican food in a long time, so we decided to head to my favorite Mexican restaurant. I was a big fan of their enchiladas with a fried egg on top. This was the closest enchiladas I had come across that resembled my mother's cooking.

My mother had been an amazing cook. Each bite took me back to my childhood home where the aroma of the chiles and spices would permeate through the house. I used to love to sit in the kitchen with my mother and watch her make handmade tortillas.

After lunch, Natalie and I went to a movie. She picked the movie. Some romance movie believe it or not. The type of movie didn't matter, as I was just so excited to be with Natalie. We had a remarkable night, morning, and day. I really didn't want it to end.

The movie brought tears to Natalie's eyes. We both enjoyed it. She always was the hopeless romantic. We hadn't been to a movie together in years, so it was a special moment.

I swore that I was going to spend more time with my family, as I'd taken their love for granted too long. I wanted to be home. I wanted to be with my wife and kids. I felt I'd sacrificed enough for my country and the Navy for so long that I forgot about my family and how special they were to me.

After the movie ended, we headed to the kids' school as it was time to pick them up. Getting my kids at school was now my favorite activity. Just being able to watch my little girl come to me with her pigtails and little legs running as fast as they could meant the world to me. I recorded her running toward me every day, and I swore I would never forget how special it was to have her run into my arms.

We hustled home because Emma had soccer practice, and she had to change into her uniform. I hadn't seen her play yet, as she had started to play while I was away. Excitement ruled my world right now in being able to watch her. Natalie said she was a natural. Emma was fast, tough, and crazily competitive.

After she changed and came out of her room, I couldn't believe my eyes. She looked so freaking cute. She had her black and pink soccer cleats, her black and pink shin guards, pink soccer shorts, and a shirt that said, "Girls kick balls hard." The shirt's message received many laughs. Instead of eye black under her eyes, she had eye pink. She was seriously decked out for doing some damage on the field.

We drove Jaxon and Emma to the park for her practice. Jaxon brought his bike so he could cruise around while Emma practiced. It was 79 degrees outside, and just a picturesque day.

Emma was truly a natural at playing soccer and being an athlete. Natalie said she hadn't even seen a soccer game or practiced, but she excelled at her first practice session. I couldn't believe my eyes. This little girl had talent and skills.

It seemed like she had the skills of an older player already. She was dribbling around everyone without difficulty. Her kicks had power behind them, and she was super fast, with an amazing stamina. I was so impressed. I could have watched her for hours. Pure joy for a dad especially since I hadn't seen her play.

She was also so dammed cute in her little outfit, pigtails, and eye pink. I was so proud to be her father. I took a million pictures that day—at least it seemed like it. A part of me was just so captivated with the moment that I didn't want to let it go.

It always seemed that these moments were too short, or I missed too many of them. I knew I had to change that part of my life, and I felt that I had to make a change at some point. I just didn't know how at this time, but I felt God would help me sort things out sooner or later. I felt in my heart that my family needed me more now than ever.

After her practice, Emma held me so tightly. She looked up at me with tears in her eyes and said, the following words to me that I will never forget: "Dad, today is the happiest day of my life. I loved having you at my practice. I felt like I had special powers. I was so happy having you there. Please promise me that you will always be at my practices and games. Please, Daddy."

My heart was so heavy after hearing her say those words. I had to look her in the eyes. I held her tight, and I told her that I would always be watching her, now and forever. Emma was so humble.

We drove home after Emma's practice. All I could do while driving home was talk about how awesome she was on the practice field. I couldn't wait to see her play in a game. I couldn't wait to watch the video that I took of her practicing.

Emma competes with Jaxon in everything. She acts tougher than her age. I guess most little sisters likely have to be tough when they have an older brother.

Emma's biggest strength was her loyalty to her brother and mother. She struggled sometimes warming up to me. I couldn't blame her as I blamed it mostly on the fact that I was gone for more than half her life.

Unfortunately, Emma demonstrated bouts of anger at times. Natalie would tell me how she would often throw things at Jaxon and lock herself in her room. It might sound like an occasional normal behavior for a kid her age, but she seemed to act out more than Jaxon did when he was her age. Her school counselor mentioned that my absence might cause her to be angry with me, which might cause her to be angry in general. I didn't know what to do aside from loving her when I was away and home. Anytime at home was difficult for me to separate between battle time and family time.

With my time in the Navy and serving on some fucked up missions, it was only natural that I was paranoid with certain things while back at home especially if my kids were with me. The loud sound of a car's tires peeling out would send me into a crouched stance. If someone was walking extraordinary fast toward my kids and I, I would shove them behind me. Fireworks. Fuck firework shows really fucked with me. Blaring sounds, bright lights, or any other unnatural occurrences left me ready to grab my sidearm. Hard habit to break even when at home relaxing.

We took our kids on vacation to New York City about three years ago. Talk about a trip of paranoia. I had not been there since prior to 9/11, so I had no idea of the landscape. I prepped Jaxon and Emma for something way more than just visiting a major city. I reviewed more than the "don't talk to strangers" speech.

One of the more difficult things for me is being in large crowds. Being in a large crowd is just so hard to gain control if a situation arises. Most people especially those in tourist mode are accustomed to being in the white zone. No awareness, just the complete opposite. No awareness generally equals panic if a situation occurs. As I have learned from my life experience, you can't control panic.

Anyhow prior to visiting NYC, I instructed Jaxon and Emma of being totally aware of exit doors, evacuation routes, suspicious persons, strangers asking for money, etc. I even reviewed what to do if they were kidnapped. Nothing to complicated just some basics. Call 911 if able. Leave your cell phone on, yes, Jaxon had a cell phone at a young age only so Natalie and I could utilize it more as a tracking device than for him to use it for social reasons. Fight until you can't fight anymore.

I also reviewed some other tips and tricks concerning being held captive. For instance, ask for information. Where are you taking us? What direction are you taking us? What do you want? Who are you working for?

Gain as much visual and audio information about the kidnappers. What is their height? Any major scars and/or tattoos? Any accents or foreign languages spoken? Memorize everything.

If held in a home or building, leave any clues available from the information gained. For example, if the kidnappers describe direction or destination try to etch a number in ground or wall with 1-North, 2-South, 3-West, and 4-East. Ask to use the bathroom in privacy. Insist on door being closed since you are a kid I would tell them. Leave a message under the toilet lid. No pen or marker available? Make a cut in your mouth or hidden area and use blood to leave a message. Crazy thoughts I realize for a five to six year old or even a three to four year old, but I refused to not try to train my kids from an early age to be ready for anything that might come there way. I think Emma thought I was crazy when I gave them instructions on self-protection, but Jaxon seemed to get it at a early age at least I had hoped he did.

We were sitting at the dinner table as a family. It was Wednesday night. Natalie made the best lasagna—at least, I thought it was the best. It was always a treat for us when she made it. She learned how to make it from her mother. I usually ate way too much of it.

It was lasagna, TV, and then off to bed. It was a simple routine for us—a simple lifestyle, but addicting to someone who never seemed to have a routine in a daily life. My routine seemed to be just staying alive and making sure my men stayed alive. I was glad to be home. For some reason, I had more thoughts of staying home for good this time as I felt my time in the Navy SEALS was coming to an end at some point sooner rather than later. My battle with my change in memory recall, nightmares, and difficulty with separating the past and present all kept intensifying. I understood that my time in a doctor's office rang soon.

12

THE INVITE

I received a call that night. I couldn't believe who it was on the phone. I thought it was a joke at first. The voice asked, "May I please speak with Captain Williams?"

I thought, "Who the hell is this? Nobody calls my house asking for Captain Williams." Our phone number was a private telephone number. We had caller ID, and it didn't identify the caller's telephone number correctly. Were my boys playing a trick on me?

"Yes, this is he," I replied.

"Ryan, this is Marcus Jackson from the Phoenix Troopers. I heard you like football on the news. Is that right?"

"Wait a second, who is this and how did you get my number?" I asked in disbelief.

"Sir, it is Marcus Jackson, #11, from the Phoenix Troopers professional football team. My agent had to cash in many favors to try to get your number, sir," Marcus Jackson said.

"That's funny. How do I know it's really you?" I asked.

But little did I know that on the phone was one of the baddest wide receivers of all time. It was number 11, Marcus Jackson, from the Phoenix Troopers. He was calling me to thank me for serving and for doing what I did on the plane. Somehow he made the conversation flow around my family and me. I wasn't sure where or why he was calling me, to be honest.

He mentioned that the Troopers were having a game on Thursday night on national TV. The PFL was celebrating the armed services, and he asked me to bring my family to watch the game from the owner's box suite.

What the hell? Was this real? Man, I was a big football fan. My dad and I always watched the PFL games. I went to a game only once, when I was eighteen. The tickets were a birthday present. My dad got us seats on the forty-yard line of the home team. We had such a blast. I remembered it like it was yesterday.

Marcus said we could be on the field before and during halftime for a special thank-you to those who served or were serving in the military.

I didn't know what to say, at first. Again, I thought it was a joke that one of my Navy buddies was playing on me. We always pranked each other. They all knew I was a big football fan, so I wouldn't have been surprised if they actually did try to pull a fast one on me.

My first response was to say no. I'm not the type to celebrate my service, but at this time my kids knew something was up. They could hear me asking about whom it was, details about the game, and so forth.

I had to say yes for them, and, well, for me too. I felt my men would have wanted me to go. They would have wanted me to share their lives in spirit.

"Hey, everyone, guess who was on the phone?" I asked my wife and kids.

"Who was it, Daddy? Who was it?" asked Emma.

"Marcus Jackson—you know, of the Troopers—number 11, the best wide receiver of all time," I said with full excitement and continued disbelief.

"He's invited all of us to tomorrow night's game. We're going to be able to be on the field before the game and during halftime. We'll also get to sit in the owner's box during the game. They'll have free food in the box, and we get to meet some of the retired players. Can you believe that?" I asked.

I was still mesmerized by the thought. Kind of hard to believe, I know, but I did think back to the one game I went to with my father and how special it was for me.

"Natalie, you won't believe what else he's done for us. Guess what? Marcus arranged a special dinner for us that includes having our kids stay at some place called Momma's Place, where they watch our kids while we go on our dinner date. Have you ever heard of it? He said there's a location right next to the restaurant where he's treating us to dinner."

"Yes, of course," she said. "They always have commercials on Momma's Place on TV. It looks so cool, but I hear it is expensive. They have food, games, crafts, face painting—wow, I sound like the commercial."

I turned on the TV to see if there were any commercials about it, so I could understand what the place was and the concept behind it. Sure enough, after two channels, I found the Momma's Place commercial. Oddly enough, the commercial ended by saying never an accident or incident. What was that all about?

The place did look awesome. They had certified sitters, entertainment, and food for the kids. It had to be a fabulous time for the kids, plus I could actually have a peaceful dinner with my wife. Natalie and I might even be able to relax while being out on a date. We hadn't been on a dinner date in what seemed like ages.

In fact, I couldn't remember the last time we actually went out to dinner without our kids or even with our kids. My wife was an extraordinary cook, so I actually preferred just staying home with my family and enjoying her delicious dinners. Just the thought of Natalie and I being out on a date seemed more exciting to me than the actual football game.

13

THE GAME

We went to the game the following night. I had to have my standard fiver round of Jack. I couldn't relax unless I took the edge off. I had mastered driving while under the sauce. It didn't make any fucking sense, but it was the only way I could make it in a public setting anymore. Five hits of Jack was just enough for me to calm my nightmare storms. The last sip in the fifth took the longest to down, as I knew I would not have another one for a long while.

Jaxon and Emma wore their number 11 jerseys. Jaxon had on eye black and Emma had on her eye pink. We took several pictures at home before we left for the game. Marcus and the PFL had asked me to wear my Navy uniform because they were celebrating the armed services, so I did. I hadn't worn my dress uniform in a long time, so I had to get it laundered the day prior.

I can't explain how happy I was to see my kids meet the players before the game. I thought my wife was going to pass out when she met Marcus Jackson. It was too funny.

We took a bunch of pictures with Marcus and many of the other players and coaches.

Marcus made me cover him during the pregame, while they were running pregame plays. I guess he heard I played defensive back while in high school. I had skills back then, but certainly not good enough to cover him. I did get an interception on one play, although I'm sure they planned it that way. I didn't care—it was marvelous to be on the field and acting like a kid, while my kids watched their dad having a great time.

My kids had a blast. They received autographs from several players and the head coach. We felt like celebrities.

Emma asked the owner if we could come to every game and sit in the owner's suite. It was the only way to watch a game. She always said what was on her mind. She was five, so most of the time it was very cute. She was a brave five-year-old.

The owner was smart in his reply. "Of course. But it's up to your mother and father, so ask them first."

Marcus signed a jersey for me, thanking me for my service and for saving everyone on the plane.

He saw my SEAL emblem on my uniform. He knew I was part of the team that had killed the terrorists. I could feel it by his look. I could also see it in his eyes just how genuine his thanks were to all of us who served. He seemed to be just a regular person that worked extremely hard in his profession and that it didn't come easy for him. I had a respect for those that gave 110% to their work, as we SEALS couldn't have it any other way.

The cool thing was that he gave me his cell phone number and told me to call him if I ever wanted tickets. The entire organization was grateful. I thought about my team and all my men and how I had no regrets jumping on that grenade. They would have done it for me, and I would do again if I had to do it to protect them. It was my job, and it was why I was so proud to be the captain of the best SEAL team ever.

I appreciated being home. I was thankful to be alive. I was indebted to my men to be with my family. For these moments, I thought to myself that I didn't want to leave my family again. I had missed so much, and I didn't want to miss any more. I would always cherish the time we had at the football game as the professional football organization allowed to have an experience that we would not otherwise ever experience. The look on my kids' eyes could not be replaced. They enjoyed every minute of it, and we were all very appreciative.

14

THE CAKE SURPRISE

My wife reminded me that my forty-second birthday was the following day. To be honest, I'd forgotten what the dates were lately. All the days had seemed to run together, especially for the last two years. Natalie asked me if I wanted to go pick out a cake for my birthday.

I didn't want to make a big deal about my birthday, but I was excited to be home and to actually get a chance to celebrate it with my family. Most of my birthdays were spent away from my family. In fact, my wife had reminded me that we hadn't been together for one of my birthdays in over four years.

Wow, I thought. It seems a little sad that I had no idea, but my wife remembered. She always had the best memory for things like that. She could always remember what we wore on our first dates, what we had for dinner on one of our dates or anniversaries, what the weather was like when we were together, and just about anything, for that matter. My memory sucked.

I always tried to forget those times that I was away from my family on their birthdays or holidays. It just sucked not to be with them for Christmas, Thanksgiving, or their birthdays. Sometimes I was able to call them on these special days, but a phone call can never replace being with your family, although I would take it any day of the week as compared to not being able to speak with them.

I could remember my missions and when they were and where they were, but it seemed that when it came to my own life, I struggled to remember exact details. I was lucky enough to be there when my kids were born, and those memories always repeated in my mind.

We stopped at our local grocery store to pick up my birthday cake. We were going to have a little lunch celebration the next day, as Natalie and I had our big dinner plans that Marcus Jackson had set up for us. We couldn't wait to be alone for a while. It had been too long.

When we pulled up to our house, I noticed the light I'd left on in the kitchen was off. I didn't think much of it at the moment. Maybe my wife or one of the kids had turned it off on their way out.

My next thoughts were those of suspicion, as my mind always questioned everything. I was always on target. I kind of lived in the red zone all the time, although I tried not to when I was at home, at least.

To my amazement, when I opened the front door, I was greeted by about twenty people shouting, "Surprise!" I was shocked.

I looked around the room, and I saw some of my Seal buddies and some of my family. My younger brother, Adrian, from Tucson, Arizona, and his wife were there. I hadn't seen them in about seven years. He was two years younger than I was, so we were not only close brothers, but also, best friends since he was born.

He was a Ranger in the army, and our tours were always at different times. We did serve together in Iraq in the '90s. I was able to see him for one night while we were both there. It was odd during these times to be so far away, yet I was able to see my brother while we were both on mission miles away from home.

During an argument one night, my dad told my brother that he would disown him if he joined the Navy. My dad's reasoning was that I'd already joined, and that he would be damned if he lost his both sons to the Navy.

Well, technically my brother did listen to my dad. He joined the army instead. In fact, he didn't just join the army; he joined one of their most elite forces. The Army Rangers were the army's most lethal and flexible force. They did most of the army's airborne and air assault operations. Ranger training, like Navy SEAL training, was always known as one of the toughest things to do in the military. Many men tried one or the other, and most failed. Our SEAL ethos was contained in the statement, "I will not fail."

We always gave shit to each other about how our own teams were better than the other's. We always said how we'd see each other when one of us was coming to rescue the other. It was simple pleasure in talking smack especially when we were in college during the Navy vs. army football games.

My brother was a smart guy. He did graduate at top of his class at West Point. He wasn't as good a swimmer as I was, but he excelled at baseball. He was captain of the baseball team for his last two years at West Point. The kid could have pitched with the pros. He threw a ninety-two-mile-per-hour fastball while in college. He had offers to enter the major league baseball draft after his service, but he turned them down. His dream was to be an Army Ranger.

We were inseparable when we were kids, as we were only two years apart. Our friendship was one of those that most people don't get to experience in their lifetimes. I was so grateful to see him.

My mother stood in front of me. My eyes gleamed. Her beautiful brown eyes and uplifting smile brought back so many memories to me in an instant. I stared at her locket that she wore on her neck ever since I could remember. Since my father passed, she had not been the same. She suffered from depression after his death and had withdrawn herself from her friends and family. She often blamed herself for not being more aggressive in trying to stop his drinking. Their love inspired many. I hugged her and held her tight as I could feel her pain.

The delight was in my eyes as I saw my family and friends, and I knew I wasn't about to ship off. It always seemed that the only times I was seeing them was right before ship-off time.

My heart didn't know what to do. It felt confused from previous reactions. I was going to enjoy this moment because I didn't know when it would be time for me to leave once again.

Natalie took several pictures of all of us including a family picture with my mother, brother and our kids. I stared at the photo for a long time, as it still was difficult for me to realize that my father was not in the picture anymore.

My mother's beauty shined as brightly as her treasured locket. My brother still had his childhood tendency of making funny faces in photos. My kids seemed to have grown up so much while I was gone. I couldn't help but stare at the photo as it represented the most important people in my life in addition to my wife. Natalie posted them on Facebook as well as a lot of other photos from the last few days.

I hadn't taken to the Facebook thing. I wasn't a big fan of sharing private information over the internet when I knew how accessible it could be to those that shouldn't have access to it. Whenever we gathered intel for certain missions, I was amazed how often social media postings could be utilized to gather more intelligence on terrorist threats or other. For these reasons, I had asked Natalie not to post stuff on Facebook. I guess she won that argument as she said she was tired of not having anything to post about me.

Each time I told her I didn't like the fact that she would post our kids' pictures on it for everyone to see, it seemed she would post another picture. We had different minds. I always saw the bad in people, and she oftentimes saw only the good. I guess we were like the yin-yang Chinese philosophy of being completely opposite in views in many ways, but still interconnected in all ways.

I always asked her to not post information on Facebook about our upcoming plans. To me, it opened up nothing but badness to televise upcoming plans to the world. Anyhow I lost that argument as Natalie did it anyway. I couldn't blame her excitement though as it was pure joy.

The surprise party went on for a while. When the party wound down, my SEAL buddies and my brother stayed through the night. We all pulled up some chairs around the TV and watched the sports channel. I kept seeing the commercials for Momma's House. I think our kids were just as excited to go there, and my wife and I were going to be able to have dinner together.

My buddies couldn't believe I had the chance to be on the field at the football game. I showed them some pictures of my family on the field and with Marcus Jackson. Pretty cool stuff, they all said.

It was amazing to all of us, I think, as just a few days ago we were in the middle of hell, and now we were sitting in my home. Wow, what a difference a few days made, and what a difference in scenery.

We kept watching TV. Adrian changed the channel to watch the news. I hated watching the news, especially the local news, as it always seemed all they showed was a series of murders, car accidents, or substance I just didn't care to hear. I'd seen enough bullshit overseas. I never could figure out why people wanted to know about who was murdered, who had their home burglarized, whose house was on fire, what politician was having an affair, and on and on.

One story did get us going, though, and it was how many kidnappings were occurring in the United States. It was hard to have a complete grasp on the graveness of the level of kidnappings, but the news story said more kidnappings had occurred in the last year than in the previous ten years. I couldn't believe it. Most of us in the room had kids, so we all were especially glued to the television at this point, as the story raised many concerns.

It appeared that the South American and Mexican cartels and their gangs had gotten into kidnapping as another way to make money, since marijuana had been legalized in the United States.

The cartels had lost billions of dollars when marijuana became legal in all states and at the federal level. It was estimated that it cost the cartel $7-9 billion a year in lost revenue from not being able to sell marijuana illegally anymore in the United States.

Apparently, the cartel tried to compete with the open market in the United States, but the cost of marijuana was similar to the cost of cigarettes at that point. The fines and prison terms for selling or buying illegal marijuana were so steep that it was not worth the risk anymore. In fact, you could walk into your local convenience store and buy marijuana, just like milk and cigarettes.

The news story was saying how the cartel gangs were kidnapping kids from the United States and selling them as work slaves, sex slaves, Internet porn slaves, and as kids for adoption to ultra wealthy foreigners in the Middle East, China, and Russia who wanted to have American kids. The Cartel also made money from ransoms paid by parents in the US. I think we were all floored by what was going on, and we had no fucking idea that this was such an issue.

My American blood raged. All this time there was a war occurring in our own backyard. It always seemed that we were fighting some fucking war thousands of miles away instead of fighting the horrible violence that was occurring here in the United States.

The cartels seemed to have more ruthless power in the United States than our government would admit. As a SEAL, I was privileged to some top-secret information, and the things on the cartels were insane. The cartel's networks and cash vaults were deeper than those of any other terrorist group we were trying to fight. I didn't understand it. It seemed like a solvable problem to take out the cartels just like any other terrorist group. The cartels lived in our own backyard, yet we fought terrorists 8,000 miles away. Anyway, it wasn't my fight—at least I didn't think it would ever be at that time.

After the news story, we all started talking. We were more bullshitting than anything. We all swore that if any of our kids were ever kidnapped we'd find the fuckers and cut off their heads just as they did to their own victims.

The energy in the room rivaled a nuclear power plant. Most of us had just returned from battle, and it seemed as if we were creating our own war in our heads, so we could get back into action.

The ideas kept flying back and forth. Finally, I decided to get some paper, and I started writing things down. At the beginning, it sounded like a bunch of bullshit, but after a while all the ideas and suggestions actually started coming together. They began to mesh into an actual plan.

I forgot that in this small room in my house were members of the Navy SEALS, my brother, the Army Ranger, and one of his Ranger team members. It was filled with a bunch of badasses who knew how to plan, organize, and survive.

At the end of the night, we had an entire plan, including how to organize a group whose chief service and sole objective were to be available to protect families and help them find their kids if they were kidnapped.

It seemed almost impossible at first, but we had accumulated so many contacts over the years and an insane ability to gather intelligence at a moment's notice, so that it made sense that we were talking about forming a new organization or company, whatever it was going to be.

Yes, we were very likely just bullshitting at the time, but isn't that how the CIA (Central Intelligence Agency) was formed at some point? I didn't know what Protect Hero would become, but I had a feeling we were building something that had a tremendous potential to help protect those most in need of protection.

They were all going to stay a few days as Natalie helped set up a family and friend fishing trip for us to go to Lake Pleasant, Arizona. Our kids loved Lake Pleasant. The lake was about forty-five minutes from our house, so it was convenient to go there for a day or weekend. We all loved fishing and swimming there. One of my favorite pictures in the entire world was of Jaxon and Emma standing on the pier looking out at Lake Pleasant while they held hands. I carried that picture in my wallet and in my chest shirt pocket wherever I went. It always reminded me of whom I was truly protecting.

15

THE DATES

Natalie was excited to be getting ready for our date. I have to say that I was also. We had not been on a dinner date since Emma was born. When I was away on mission, it always seemed as if time passed without the realization that my family's world still existed with or without me. I was glad that my wife now understood why I did what I did. When we first started dating, I'm not sure if she truly understood.

Our first dates included a visit to the zoo, dinners, a couple of movies, and some careful maneuvering of our busy schedules. A few of our dates included doing things as a group with some of her friends from work and some of my Seal buddies. At times, it was an eclectic scene to say the least.

Natalie seemed to accept that I was a Seal early on in our relationship. I was always very honest with her about what my job entailed. Our love for each other grew quickly, and the sparks started early in our relationship. I knew very early on that I had to marry her, as all I wanted day and night was to be with her. She always calmed my soul in all the bullshit and chaos that I had to balance in my life.

Natalie and I were inseparable in the beginning of our relationship. All was fine until one of my Seal buddies was killed in battle in Iraq. His death brought back the reality to what was a fantasyland for me at the time when I was falling in love with Natalie.

She came to his funeral with me. I knew then that she absorbed the Navy Seal life. She cried the entire time. After the funeral, I lost it to Jack. I hadn't had an issue with drinking while I was with Natalie in the beginning, but unfortunately, she witnessed first hand how bad my addiction to alcohol was after his death.

The first few nights after my friend's death, I drank pretty heavily. Natalie thought she was going to have to bring me to the hospital, as I had a bout of throwing up blood from such heavy alcohol intoxication. His death tore me apart as it did to my entire fellow SEALS. I struggled with his death and the possibility of losing Natalie at that time.

Natalie and I actually didn't talk for a few weeks after she witnessed my downward spiral. I didn't know why at first. I assumed she finally saw what could happen to me in my line of work and how I was an alcoholic.

She told me her worries after the funeral. She feared she would attend my funeral one day with our kids after I was killed in action or lost my battle to Jack. That night created a moment that I remember like yesterday. We stared at each other without saying a word. I felt she accepted that she could lose me one day whether it was being killed in battle or from old age. Whatever it was, she accepted my chosen lifestyle and me. She looked deep into my eyes and told me she loved me. I told her I loved her, and we never looked back again. I knew then that she understood who I was and what I stood for in being a seal. I also made a false promise to her that I would never drink again. I wish I kept that original promise.

I'd seen too many of my buddies not have a life outside the Navy, being addicted to alcohol, or struggle with PTSD. Too many times, when they did have a wife or significant other, it seemed short-lived as the other problems took control. Not many people understood the sacrifice of our time away and the high risks of what we did. My blessings included the fact that Natalie understood and accepted me. Although we hadn't been on a date in years, I hoped we could return to our first few dates and the magic we shared.

My wife was wearing a black dress that I'd bought her ten years ago. She still looked so amazing and beautiful in it. I couldn't believe my eyes when I saw her. I still remembered the day I bought it. I was so excited to buy it, and she was so mad, as it was expensive for our budget at that time in our life.

The entire past few days had been so surreal. In the back of my mind, I still felt as if I was still away on a mission. It was very hard for me to assimilate to the situation that I was home now, safe with my family. My nightmares calmed while I was at home. I believe being in an environment without active stress reduced the nightmares and confusion. Or maybe I was just confused about being confused?

I didn't know when my next mission was going to be, and for now I didn't care. I was home with my family, and I had to let the missions go. I had to be home and remember why I did everything I did.

We left the house for our date. The kids were just as excited as my wife and I. They had seen the Momma's House commercials, so they knew it looked like a lot of fun.

We pulled up to Momma's Place, which was right across the street from the sushi restaurant where we had reservations. I was impressed by how massive it was.

When we walked inside, the manager greeted us. She took us on a tour. She was nervously on target with all our questions and concerns. It was everything we saw on the commercials and more.

The manager already knew what we were most worried about when dropping off our kids. She showed us the play area that had special flooring, which was soft and helped prevent injuries. She showed us the clean café area, where the kids would eat dinner. They had nice bathrooms and washrooms for the kids to wash up before eating. Jaxon and Emma were excited to see the theater area where they were going to watch movies all night.

It was impressive even to me, but I needed to solidify its safety. As the manager seemed to know our concerns especially mine, she showed us their security system. They had cameras everywhere inside and outside that were recording everything to an offsite facility she said. I noticed one of the cameras didn't seem to be connected to its plug. When I asked her about it, she said the camera had an internal battery like a smoke alarm. I nodded, as it seemed believable. I noticed the alarm system keypad didn't have a working light. I asked her about it, and she said the security company was going to replace the light as it had burned out. I also asked why there was only one phone near the front entrance. I wondered what one would do if they were in the back and something happened and they needed to call 911. She answered with a little delay, "well, at least one person here has a cell phone, so I guess one of us would call from our cell phone."

They had only two entrances that allowed a self-lockdown if there were any issues. Nobody could come into the main area without a pass code that had to be entered to allow the security doors to be opened. The manager also showed us that the police and fire stations were only two minutes away.

Curious, I had to ask if they had ever had an incident at any of their facilities.

"Never," said the manager, with a confident smile.

She made me nervous about letting our kids stay there, but I didn't want to ruin what appeared to be a good time for our kids. I felt myself trying to leave the red zone and going into the white zone, at least for now. I didn't think I could ever be in the white zone for long.

The white zone was a term used for individuals who were unaware of their surroundings and were in a complete, ignorant bliss, not worrying about any bad situation or even considering the thought. Even as a kid, I was always checking my surroundings and looking over my shoulder, which always kept me in at some level of yellow, orange, or red zone.

We left the kids at Momma's Place. I'm not sure who was more excited—the kids or my wife and I. We crossed the street to the sushi restaurant.

My wife was a big sushi fan, and so was I. Unfortunately, on our salaries, and with our kids, a sushi dinner was pretty much out of the question most times. We tried to do it once a year, although I'd been absent the last two years, so I think it had been over three years.

Marcus had set us up with reservations at the best sushi place in town. We hadn't been there, as it was crazy expensive and well out of our budget. However, tonight was on Marcus, and he made me promise him that we would live it up at dinner and for our special night. It was not going to be a hard promise for me to keep.

We arrived at the sushi place. The co-owner and manager at the restaurant greeted us ecstatically. The staff started clapping for us when we entered. I guess they had some insight that we were coming, and I'm sure they were told we were guests of Marcus. We felt like celebrities once again.

I had no idea that Marcus actually co-owned the place. Pretty cool, I thought. He seemed like a responsible professional football player, as well as a serial entrepreneur, charitable person, and a true role model.

He helped his community with so many charitable efforts, including camps for underprivileged kids. He did everything from football camps to golf camps. He was a big golfer during the off-season.

We sat down for dinner. My wife ordered a martini. I didn't think I'd heard her order a martini since one of our first dates. I ordered a jack and soda. As an alco-holic, the hardest place to be is in a bar or near a bar as the strength to stay away from a drink weakens the most when directly exposed. I would try to keep to my five as I was carrying.

I had a concealed weapon's permit, so I pretty much always carried my weapon, as it was a hard habit to break. By Arizona concealed-weapon laws, I was OK to conceal my weapon in the restaurant as long as they didn't have a restau-rant restriction not to be able to carry a concealed weapon. I also wasn't supposed to be drinking, but I didn't give a fuck.

We looked at the menu in great anticipation. I couldn't believe the prices. I had been so isolated from most of the real world around me, and I was used to meals in a make shift mess hall.

I stopped looking at prices, as I'd sworn to Marcus that I would not look at the prices and that I would just enjoy an evening with my wife. True American blood ran through my arteries, so I had to keep my promise. I smiled at the thought of knowing I was having dinner with Natalie after so long.

My wife downed her first martini and ordered another while she still had the first glass in her hand. She looked so beautiful in her black dress. She had that twinkle in her eyes that I hadn't seen in years.

Out of curiosity, more than anything, I looked at my phone to make sure I hadn't had any calls. Even though I was home on leave, my command was always on call, so I always had to be checking my phone for any information.

My wife caught me looking at my phone. She grabbed my hand, and I looked into her beautiful green eyes. She melted me.

She asked gingerly, "Honey, please put your fucking phone down and spend the night with me. I have waited for our time together for so long. I need you tonight. Please don't make me share you with everyone else tonight. I want you all to myself tonight."

Her spirited words reminded me of time we met in the coffee line as she now rarely cussed especially with our kids around all the time.

I couldn't resist her eyes twinkling, and the touch of her hand gave me goose bumps from my body's need for hers. I turned my phone to vibrate, and I put it into my pocket with abandon. I felt twitchingly comfortable. I was trying to be in the white zone. I had my worries, but I was with my lovely wife. I had to try to rekindle our relationship and act like a normal person. I had to let go of the treacherous world I knew and focus on the love of my life for tonight. She had been so patiently waiting for me for so long that I knew I had to listen to her request.

16

THE DINNER AND
REALIZATION

"I'll have another martini, please," said Natalie. She had finished her second martini in fifteen minutes.

She was gulping her martinis like water, and she now had her third one coming. To my knowledge, she wasn't a heavy drinker, but maybe she drank while I was away to cope.

"I'm perfectly OK. I'm having a good time—I'm with my husband, we are at a nice restaurant that we don't have to pay the bill, and our kids are not here, so I'm drinking up," she said excitedly.

"Sir, do you know what you want to order?" the waiter asked.

"Yes, we do," I said.

We ordered way more food than two people could eat. I felt guilty at first, but I kept remembering my promise to Marcus. He made me promise to him that we would have a great time and that we would live it up while he covered the tab.

"Hey, I'm going to the restroom," I said.

"OK, hurry up; I'll keep your spot open, but just for a little while," Natalie said while laughing.

She was happily drunk already. She had the sensual smile on her face. I remembered it well; as it reminded me of the first time we made love. She gave me that same smile as if to say that I was going to get lucky that night.

I went into the restroom. It was a bad habit for me, but I checked my phone. I was surprised. I'd missed two calls somehow. I forgot I had my phone on vibrate, and I hadn't felt it in my front pocket. Both calls were from Jaxon, and he'd left voicemails. My first thought was that he was calling to give me a report and to let me know how much fun he and his sister were having. I couldn't wait to hear his voice to hear how much fun they were having.

I played the voicemail, and the rest of the moment changed my life...*forever*. I wished I had chosen something else to do that night with our kids such as staying at home to watch a movie. I wondered what if?

"Dad, Dad, we are being taken! We are being taken! Please come now. There are five guys in costumes. They just released gas. They are going to take us, Dad. *Emma!*"

I was in disbelief. I kept waiting for him to say, "Just kidding," but it never came. The voicemail kept playing. All I could hear was what sounded like chaos—chaos that I was not used to hearing, as now it involved my family. It was vastly different. I hesitated as my memory felt clouded. I struggled to remember where he was calling from for a moment. I challenged the reality with a nightmare that I didn't want to believe. I snapped out of my disbelief, as I had no other choice. I knew that every second counted from here on forward.

I ran to our table and grabbed Natalie by the arm with my phone in the other hand, and I yelled at her, saying we had to leave. I didn't expect any resistance, but she resisted and resisted heavily.

She yelled back at me. "*No*, we are not leaving. No, no, no, I don't care if the president of the United States is calling you—I don't care, we're not leaving. I haven't seen you in two years. I haven't been out with you in five years. I haven't had dinner with you in five years. No! Absolutely not; I am *not fucking leaving*!"

Everyone in the restaurant turned their heads at this point. Natalie was somewhat intoxicated and loud. The restaurant manager began walking our way, as it was now becoming a big scene.

"Natalie, we need to leave now, *right now*!" I exclaimed. She kept resisting. I hesitated for another second. I didn't know what to say for once in my life. I'd led men into battle. I'd saved lives in battle. I'd lost men in battle, but I NEVER lost my kids.

I yelled at her, "Extreme, *extreme*!" *Extreme* was our code word for an absolute emergency that didn't allow for questions. It was our word for getting the hell out of a situation. "Natalie, our kids have been kidnapped!" I yelled, in my own disbelief.

We had planned for everything. We had even trained with our kids for extreme situations as well as disaster training. I felt my job had forced me to be aware of the world and to try to relate that awareness to my family. We would do our disaster drills at least twice a year, so we could feel comfortable with our plan in case it had to be implemented.

Natalie's face dropped, and she let go of her chair. She looked to me as though she was about to faint, so I put my arms around her in an effort to catch her if she did faint and fall.

She now knew something was wrong. I yelled at the manager as we ran out of the restaurant. I told him to call 911 and to send the police to Momma's Place, which was just across the street. I wasn't sure if he would or not, as he seemed to care more about all the raucous that had occurred in his restaurant, and he didn't have the appearance that he was believing what I was saying. I had no choice. We had to get out of there in order to get across the street as fast as possible.

We ran across the street to Momma's Place. Natalie took off her high heels and kept up with me. She was an athlete in college, and it was clear that she was going to get there as fast as she possibly could. She was also calling 911. Through my confused head, I was running through all types of scenarios about what to do. We weren't there yet, so I couldn't know exactly what to do, as I had no idea what had happened and why Jaxon left such a terrible message.

We arrived at Momma's Place. We couldn't get through the door that secured the main entrance as it was locked. Natalie and I peeked through the windows to see if anybody was inside. I couldn't see jack shit. I could see what looked like a haze of smoke only, but I couldn't see any-body or anything else inside.

Since the door was locked, I had no choice but to break the glass in order to get inside. I grabbed a very large rock that was part of the landscape, and I threw it through the glass. Natalie and I then squeezed through the broken glass in order to make our way into Momma's place. We started yelling for Jaxon and Emma, but there was no answer.

After the main entrance, the only way to get inside the facility was through an electronically controlled entrance that stood about six feet tall. There was no way to get around it as it was purposely built as a fortress likely to make sure all the kids were secure.

I jumped what seemed to be about six feet in the air to try to get access to the top of the entry door. There was a small opening above the door that I was positive I could fit through. I failed at my first attempt, but I tried again, and I was able to reach the top and get through the door.

I tried to open the door for Natalie, but I didn't have the code to open it. There was not a real way to open it unless you entered an electronic code. I didn't know what to do as Natalie kept screaming at me to open the door as well as screaming Jaxon and Emma's names to see if they would answer.

I drew my subcompact handgun from my backside. I told Natalie to stand to the side, so I could blast the lock. I fired my handgun once, but it didn't work. I fired again, and the electronic door finally opened.

We ran around the entire facility, yelling, "Jaxon! Emma! Jaxon! Emma!" There was nobody there. There was no answer. We could see evidence of a struggle, as there was popcorn and spilt drinks everywhere. There were also several cell phones on the floor that had been crushed to make them incapacitated. I didn't see any evidence of Jaxon's cell phone, which gave me encouragement at the moment.

The *Avengers* movie blasted in the background. The entire moment felt surreal as though I was in a bad dream. Another nightmare for me, but this one included my own kids. I had to keep my shit together, as I knew that I had to act quickly as every second counted at this moment. I was confident this situation was real and not a nightmare.

The back door was closed. We ran through the back door to see if anyone or anything was outside. There was nobody there. There was an eerie silence. We saw large tire tracks on the street that seemed to be spread apart widely, but we didn't know what they meant. I assumed whoever took our kids was likely in a large vehicle such as a bus or an eighteen-wheeler. The tracks were still hot to the touch, which made me realize that the kidnappers had just left the scene of the crime.

Natalie was crying like I'd never seen her cry in the past. I was crying. The cruel reality hit me hard. I wished the grenade went off that day, as if it did, my kids would have not been there that night. I collapsed to my knees in front of my wife with unstoppable tears and emotions. I wanted to hit something. I wanted to kill someone. Why didn't I follow my instincts when we did the walk through the place? Why didn't I say something and pull my kids out of there? I knew I felt something wrong. I knew I shouldn't have left Jaxon and Emma there. I kept yelling to God, "Why, why? *Why*?"

I fucked up. This time I knew I really fucked up.

17

THE DISCOVERY

I didn't know what to do. I didn't know where to go. In the span of five minutes, I felt I'd lost a year. I felt helpless at the moment. We had to gather ourselves as every second counted.

The police pulled up with three squad cars, one after the other. They ran out with their guns out of their holsters and drawn to dead of rights. They came into the facility and asked us to put our hands up. I froze for a moment as I actually didn't know what to do or say. I was in the horrid black zone. The zone when you just panic and can't react. I'd never been in the black zone, so it was a new experience. My heart jumped out of my chest with an intense heartrate that I'd never felt in my life.

I yelled back at them, "We're parents of the kids. We called you!" I'd forgotten that I had my gun in my hand, so I must have looked suspicious to the police at first.

"Sir, drop your weapon and put your hands in the air. Now!" the officer yelled at me.

What the fuck I thought to myself. I felt a rage in my soul that I had to control. I was so pissed off that they were pointing their weapons at me. I had to gain control before I found myself in a bad situation.

I did what he said despite my desire to resist. Two officers came up to me, turned me around and asked me to drop to my knees. I knew it was standard procedure, but I felt such an enormous urge to resist at that time. They kicked out my right leg to force me to the ground.

It was getting harder for me now to keep myself in control.

The police officers then put me in handcuffs and asked me to stand up. It was my first time in official handcuffs. The fucking handcuffs were put on way too tight. I felt the cold steel piercing my skin and my hands began to go numb. In Seal training, it was very common to be placed into handcuffs or other restraints as part of our capture training during SERE training.

Natalie was yelling her lungs off at the police to take the handcuffs off of me. I was yelling at them as well as I couldn't understand why they thought I was a suspect.

"Sir, have you been drinking? The officer asked.

I was so fucked right now. I didn't know which way to roll. I had to keep my calm.

"No sir, I tried my wife's beer but that was it. I'm driving tonight, so I'm the designated driver," I lied.

I was in control as long as he didn't have me do a breath test.

Five more minutes passed. I controlled my urges. They ignored my request to loosen the cuffs. My hands were turning blue. The officers finally realized the situation and who we were as they looked through our identification. The

officers looked at my IDs including my US Navy identification card.

Finally, they uncuffed me. In just that short period of
time, my wrists had become flaming red with torn skin. Six
more police officers arrived at this time.

They discovered that our kids had been kidnapped. As
we all tried to figure out what had happened and what to
do, a million things had been running through my mind in
addition to the self-blame.

I remembered just the night before and what my
brother, my buddies, and I were all talking about at my
house. This was almost too real to be real. What was I saying—it *was* real. I wasn't confused about anything at this
point.

The perpetrators had kidnapped several kids including
our kids. This had just happened. Our kids were kidnapped.
We had no idea why, who, or how it had happened.

My wife and I stood outside the facility at the request
of the police. I felt helpless. I had no idea what to do. I
couldn't accept that—I couldn't accept—that I was not
going to do anything.

I called my brother, Adrian, as I knew I could depend
on him for help. My kids loved him, as he was their favorite and only uncle. I explained to him what had happened.
At first, he wouldn't believe me, as it couldn't be true.
Unfortunately, I had to assure him that it was true.

I told him we had to do something. Of course, he
agreed. He said we had to activate Protect Hero, which we
had just organized the night prior at my house. He said he
would call his Army Ranger buddies that lived in town. I

told him I would call my Navy SEAL buddies that were still in town for the weekend. I still didn't know what we were going to do, but I could feel the plan coming together quickly.

We stayed at the facility, just waiting for more information. But it didn't seem to be coming our way. One officer was putting up the yellow crime-scene "Caution, Police Area" tape everywhere to seal off the area. We stood there, still feeling useless while watching the yellow tape going around the crime scent. I went back inside the facility to try to get an update from the police officers, but to no avail.

The captain sat us down. He asked us several relevant questions. He asked us what Jaxon said on his voicemail. He asked when we received his call. He asked us what we were doing. He asked us if we had any suspicions about the place when we dropped off our kids.

Overall, he sounded as he knew what he was doing, and I had confidence in him that he would do everything he could to help get our kids back to us safely. He told us they were working on a plan to help get our kids back. He was very reassuring that we would get our kids back.

Natalie fell into my lap crying. I think she had some relief from his words, but she knew we were losing time. He asked us to go home and stay by the phone. He asked us to let the police do their job. At that moment, we really had no choice.

We decided to drive back home and try to make a plan. We had to put our heads together. I knew that with each passing second that we were losing ground on catching the perpetrators that took our kids. I knew that as every second passed that the chances of us catching them was decreasing. I had faith in God that I would see and hold my children once again no matter what it would take.

18

AMBER ALERT

We began our drive home, which felt longer than usual. Natalie turned on the radio. It blasted, "Amber alert, Amber alert—there have been several kidnappings from Momma's Place establishments. If you have any information, please contact your local police." The message kept repeating itself. Even after Natalie turned off the radio, it kept playing in my mind.

Our cell phones then starting alarming with a similar text stating, "Amber alert, Amber alert-there have been several kidnappings from Momma's Place establishments in Phoenix and surrounding areas."

I knew I had to be calm for my family at this time. My calmness began to allow me to have more rationale thoughts. I kept playing the events of the last half hour in my head, over and over.

I finally thought of things to do. I told Natalie to call the cell-phone company, so they could trace Jaxon's cell phone. She called and called, and nobody would answer Jaxon's phone or the cellular-phone company's customer service line. I could feel her frustration as she kept yelling at her phone like it was a person who could hear her.

Finally, the cell-phone company customer service representative answered. Natalie began yelling and explaining the situation in her state of hysteria. She begged them to do an immediate trace of the cell phone without taking the time to explain what had just happened. She put her cell phone on speaker, so I could hear what was being said by the customer service representative.

"No, ma'am, we can't do a trace of anyone's cell phone including your own family without police approval or a warrant from the court," the customer service representative said.

My wife kept yelling at her, "Please, please. Our kids have been kidnapped! You have to help us!"

The customer service agent kept saying the same thing, over and over, about how we couldn't get the trace without police approval or a warrant from the court.

Natalie asked to speak with her supervisor. She said he was on his dinner break at the moment. Natalie hung up the phone, but she kept calling back, trying to get someone else to help her. She also called the police captain to try to get him to get the trace on Jaxon's cell phone. She kept getting the captain's voicemail. She must have left a thousand messages for him in a short period of time. Of course, I didn't blame her.

We arrived at our house, and to my amazement, there were a bunch of vehicles parked in front of our home including my brother's vehicle. My brothers were all ready for our mission. It was time to activate Protect Hero.

It was time to find our kids. I had no doubt. I had helped my team and country find the fucking terrorist who tried to kill our commander-in-chief. We caught up with him in a shithole place in the middle of hell. And I knew deep in my heart that we would find the fuckers who took our kids. I knew in my heart that we would have our kids home again.

"Cap'n, sorry about the situation, sir," said Loco. "We're here to help you kill those fuckers and to get your kids home safely, sir! What is the plan, boss, we are all with you until the end?"

My men, my brother and some of his Ranger buddies were ready to go in an amazingly short time. We were ready for war. We were ready to find our kids. It was the unofficial beginning of Protect Hero. I didn't know it at that moment, but I later realized that the kidnappers had a plan, a specific plan that still rattles my cage in disbelief.

19

Emma's Wish

I woke up again. Fucking recalls of nothing good. My mind became so fuck filled with badness that I couldn't even dream of nice things. The floor beneath my feet was drenched in blood. I didn't know I could bleed that much and still be fucking alive and conscience.

The doctor woke me up and asked me if I was feeling ok. Ok I asked, what the fuck did that mean? My daughter was dying if not died right in front of my eyes, and I was not too far behind her. He gave me a shot of morphine for pain. Fuck, I should have just asked for more. I wanted to feel numb from the bottom of a bottle of Jack, but for now the morphine would do the job.

I couldn't stand anymore. My eyes feel to the back of my skull when I tried to stand. I sat with my hand holding Emma's hand. She didn't deserve this shit.

"Doc, more morphine please?" I begged.

Lights out again. Three more fucking hours until we would touchdown on US soil. Emma's last wish was to see her mother. I had to at least be alive to let her have her last wish. Numbness turned to black. I was out.

20

THE PLAN

We all assembled in the same room we were in the night before. Our notes from the previous night were still freshly placed on the table. I kept calling the police captain to discuss the matter with him and to try to get more information from him if I could. I was desperate at this point. Unfortunately, he was not answering my calls.

I knew at this point that we had to take things into our own hands. I knew we only had a few hours to try to find Jaxon and Emma before it was too late. We didn't know who was responsible at this point, but we assumed it was one of the cartel groups from either Mexico or South America as all the news stories implicated the cartels in the mass kidnappings across the United States.

We all rushed to sit down and coordinate our plan. All of us were familiar with making operative plans. We were all used to making plans and decisions with surgical precision with just a few minutes to spare. I grabbed a huge map of Arizona that I had in my office. I slammed it down on the table in our living room. I grabbed a bunch of pads of paper and some pens so we could make a plan as quickly as possible.

We had no idea where our kids were headed. With some of our Seal missions, we had to make our best educated guess on where the enemy might be heading and/or located. We had to make an educated guess that our kids were being taken to Mexico. The Mexican border was only about 160 miles away from Phoenix, so we knew we had only a small amount of time. They could also easily head to California to load the kids into international shipping boats, which meant about 350 miles of road travel. We also didn't know if they had a plane that they planned on using to fly the kids out of the country.

In the background was Natalie, crying uncontrollably. I couldn't blame her. I felt like doing the same thing. She kept calling the police captain, the owner of Momma's Place, and anyone else she could to try to get answers.

"Men, thank you for being here today," I said. "I have no words. I need your help more than ever. As you know, Jaxon and Emma were kidnapped an hour ago. We're already behind on our mission. As we saw on TV last night, the cartels are most likely responsible for the kidnappings that have occurred all over town. I don't know much about the cartels, but I know they're ruthless, dangerous, and have nothing to lose, as lives don't mean anything to them. Only money does. With that in mind, we need to prepare for war.

"The only difference is that this war may occur on our own soil. It may lead into Mexico or South America. It may lead us directly into the cartels' bosses. All of you have families. All of you have your own responsibilities. All of you know what is at stake.

Although I appreciate all of you being here, I will understand if you are not up to this mission. I can't guarantee success, nor can I compensate you in any way, aside from my soul's promise to all of you that I will always be indebted to you. I can't guarantee we may not lose one of our brothers in this war. What I can guarantee is that I will not stop fighting until I find my kids. I will not stop fighting until I can rest knowing all the kids are home safe once again. This is my life mission now. There is nothing else for me.

"You men know my brother and me better than your own families, and you know we would do the same thing for all of you. Do you all understand? Are you with me?"

"Hoorah!" they all said in unison.

"The first part of our plan needs to include knowing all escape routes from the facility. I need all possible major and minor routes out of town. I assume the cartel will be moving the kids out of the city and out of the country. This means we only have a little time.

If they head directly to the Mexican border, that means we have two hours to catch them, assuming they went straight there, and we're already an hour behind. If they're heading to California, then we may have more time. Either way, I have to assume they're not heading east.

Second, I'll have to call in some favors from the big brass. I figure they'll understand and want to help us. I'll tries calls to friends with the CIA, FBI, and NSA. By the time the police realize the significance of the situation and are able to assemble an appropriate plan, our kids might be out of the country and impossible to locate.

Third, we're going to need some firepower. I have a small armory of weapons, but I have to assume we'll need more. Any of you have anything available at short notice?" I said and asked.

"Cap'n, I have us covered," said Loco. "I brought my Batmobile, and it's ready for war. I'll show you shortly."

"Fourth, we need air support," I continued. "There's no way we have time to catch them on the ground. I'm hoping we can plug into the SOCOM Seal Satellite Link. I'm hoping we can get some help from our government that we love and work so hard to defend." I spoke with confidence as I prayed that I could depend on some assistance from the US government when I needed it most.

The men started mapping out the state and the Southwest in order to figure ways in and out. It was time for me to make the call to Rear Admiral Jennings. I hoped he could help me in my time of need.

We had not had much luck with getting hold of the police captain. I kept getting his voicemail. I think between Natalie and I, we had left about twenty voicemails. His out-going message now said that his voicemail box was full and could not take any more messages. Go figure. I couldn't blame him, though, as I'm sure he was scrambling to figure out a plan and to mobilize his own men.

Natalie kept trying to get hold of a supervisor with our cell-phone company in hopes of getting a trace on Jaxon's cell phone. No luck there either.

My brother and our team were making a plan. I called Rear Admiral Jennings through a secure phone line. I was praying he would understand the urgency of the issue and that he would help with our unfortunate situation.

"Admiral Jennings, sir, how are you?" I said. I was sure he could hear to urgency in my voice.

"Ryan, what's up? You OK? Aren't you home, son? Why the hell you calling this old man when you should be enjoying your family?" asked the admiral.

"Sir, yes, sir. I'm at home, but I need your help, sir."

"Copy that, Ryan, anything you need—you know that."

"Sir, my kids were kidnapped an hour ago right here in Phoenix. I have no leads. The police have no leads, and I need your help, sir." My voice cracked.

"Ryan, how can I help? I'll help in any way. I mean it!"

I wasted no time. I knew exactly what I needed. I needed eyes in the sky. I needed unrestricted access. I needed what I knew the government could offer only to those with access. I needed what I thought would qualify as a Homeland Security threat, which would open the door for me to gain otherwise restricted access without a presidential or congressional clearance.

"Sir, I need a trace on my son's cell phone, and I need SEAL's eye in the sky," I said.

"Ryan, you know I need to go through the standard approval process for both of these, which may take a few days, but I know you don't have a few days," the admiral said.

"Sir, I may only have a couple more hours before I may never see my kids again; I hate to ask, sir, but I need your help now."

"Ryan, you've served your country with such sacrifice, you have saved men in battle, and your courage and work ethic are unmatchable. You've never asked any questions, but rather you've always done the job that was asked of you for the protection of our great country. I'm going to exercise my authority to proceed based on the authority given to me to act in times of a threat to national security. I will worry about the details later. Ryan, I'll call the congressman who serves as the congressional oversight chief of the Homeland Security Committee, Congressman Herrera, who lives practically in your backyard, but you'll have to call him as well so he knows the extent of the urgent threat. He can give immediate clearance for this type of nonmilitary issue. Do you know him?"

"Sir, yes, I have met him. Ironically, I spoke to him only recently. He gave me his seat in first class when I was flying home from New York City. Do you have his contact number so I can call him immediately?" I asked.

"Yes, of course," said the admiral. "I just texted it to you. Call him in five minutes. I'll call him first to give him the lowdown. He's the only congressman I trust. He's a former Navy man, and he always tells the truth."

"Yes sir, I will," I said quickly.

The next five minutes seemed to take forever. I called Congressman Herrera. He answered after the first ring. "Captain Williams?" he said, to my disbelief.

"Yes sir," I said.

Before I could say anything else, the congressman said, "Son, I have four kids and seven grandkids. All I can say is please just get your kids back. You have my authority and clearance to proceed with using Navy intel for this mission. My father died while serving in the Navy, and I know he would not want me to hesitate in making such a lifesaving call right now. I'm at your service in any other way I can be. My prayers are with you and your family. I bid you Godspeed. Now go!"

I called Rear Admiral Jennings back right away. Even though his phone only rang three times before he answered his phone, it seemed to take forever of a lifetime.

"Ryan," he said. "I can't offer you interior intel at the moment, but I know you can do that on your own. I'll e-mail you the information for full access right now. You'll be able to get an immediate trace on your son's cell phone, but remember, if his phone is off, you will not be able to trace," Admiral Jennings said.

"Roger that Sir, I understand," I said.

"I will pray that Jaxon has his phone on. I can give you satellite access with reverse access for the past hour. You'll have SEAL satellite access for sky visualization at up to one-meter accuracy," Admiral Jennings said swiftly.

"You know I'll likely get some heat for this, right? Listen to me carefully. Whatever happens, remember one thing: your family is my family. I have fought for this country for exactly this reason, to protect our families.

If you need anything else, please let me know. If things get tough, and you need off-the-grid support, call me right away, and I will see what else we can do. Anyhow, I just sent you what you need. Godspeed, my son. I will always have your back," Admiral Jennings said.

"Sir, I'll die for my country, you know that," I said without hesitation. "Thank you for your help and understanding. I'll win this war, and we'll get our kids back and all the other kids that were taken today."

21

THE HOUSE

I logged on to the SEAL site. It was still too familiar to me, as I'd spent hours on it doing reconnaissance, research, and planning for several past missions. I went to the cell-phone trace site. Somehow even with my confused mind, I still remembered all my passwords and access codes. I was fresh from having time off from battle, but I felt that I was back in the thick of it at this point. The objective was different this time, and I knew there was absolutely no room for error. I refused to even think about not seeing Jaxon and Emma once again and having them home safe soon.

I entered Jaxon's cell-phone number, and I prayed he still had it on and that it had not been taken from him. The site loaded his cell-phone information. I was so inpatient. It seemed it was taking forever. I kept watching the "loading" message praying that it would turn into a hit on his phone.

The site finally hit where Jaxon's cell phone was located. He'd left it on, and it was moving, according to the site. The site showed a location on the highway just as we had suspected. I ran into the room where my brothers were. We had to move, and I knew we had to move right away.

We needed to make and finalize our plans as quickly as we could, as we didn't have much time left to afford.

"Guys, I can't explain everything right now, but we have SEAL eyes in the sky, and I have a trace on Jaxon's cell phone," I said quickly. "We have to move. Do you guys have a plan for isolation?"

"Cap'n," Loco said. "We have a plan to move toward all major exits out of Phoenix. We figure we're at least an hour behind them. Any vehicles that are moving kids are likely moving at legal speed limits to avoid looking suspicious, so that is our biggest advantage right now. We think we have a speed advantage if we can avoid police stops. We should be able to catch up to them if we move quickly."

"Loco, I agree. We have to move now. I don't know what we're up against, but our biggest enemy is time. I'm assuming that one of the cartels took my kids. You guys have seen what they're capable of doing. They're merciless. They may be worse than any enemy we have seen. They may be worse than anything we know about. They have limitless power and an almost infinite amount of money. We will have to be calculating. Loco, as far as firepower, step into my office," I said.

We walked into my garage, where I'd spent two years building an underground safe for my arsenal. It was my hobby I guess as I enjoyed being a marksman.

"Cap'n, what the fuck?" asked Loco. "Holy shit, this looks like our fucking SEAL arsenal—wait, what the fuck? This *is* our fucking SEAL arsenal!" Everyone laughed.

"Loco, who do you fucking think ordered all the badass shit we used in combat? Uncle Sam gave me the pen to order the best of the best to protect our country, and well, sometimes-extra units would arrive. When I met with the companies that made all this shit, I always told them that I needed a demo model to practice and ensure safety while back home. You know what I mean? Of course, I still paid for it all, so it is all legit," I said.

"We need to take everything here. Grab the two McMillan Mk 15 .50 cals with scopes and those red boxes labeled exploding tips, three HK 417s with Mark 8s, five M4 12 gauge shotguns, four FN SCAR MK17s with 25-round mags and ACOGs, eight Sig P226 handguns, four AK shotguns with 30-round mags, one LAW (Light anti-tank weapon) with one rocket, all night-vision goggles, and some badass C4 explosive shit. I assume you fuckers know how to use this shit," I said.

"I only have seven bulletproof vests, so you guys take them. I'll be OK. Load as much ammo as you can, as I have no idea where we'll be going, and I especially don't know when we'll be back. In case you are wondering, I do have a gun trust for all this badass shit and all of you guys are now on it not that it matters right now," I said.

"Cool, Cap'n," said Loco. "I've also got some toys in the Batmobile as well."

"Loco, what the fuck is the Batmobile?" my brother asked.

"I thought you'd never ask, come outside and check it out," said Loco.

We went outside to the front of my house. To our amazement, Loco had a black Hummer H1 fully decked out, military-style. He opened the back door, and we saw enough high-powered rifles and ammo to supply an entire unit. He even had a fucking RPG rocket launcher. I am not sure how he got that or where it came from, but I didn't care at the moment as we just might need it as well as the LAW.

"Loco, what the fuck?" I asked.

"Cap'n, you all have kids. These are my kids, and they've come to play tonight with whomever is fucking with us."

"Love you, my crazy brother," I said.

I went back to my computer to look for Jaxon's trace on his cell phone. It was working. We marked its location on our GPS. We were locked and loaded with enough fire-power to take on an army—at least, that's what we thought at that moment.

There were eight of us. We loaded into four vehicles. I took the lead. We sped toward the highway as fast as we could. Jaxon's cell phone was not moving, and it seemed to be at a house address outside Phoenix.

We were forty minutes away. We planned on making it in fifteen minutes. I prayed that Jaxon and Emma were safe. I prayed that we would find them unharmed. I prayed that I would hold my kids again. I promised God I would never let them go.

22

THE CHASE

We headed out into the night. It was almost ten o'clock now. I knew we had to move fast, as I was not sure how long they would stay close in town. A million thoughts ran through my mind. I felt my walls crumbling. I wouldn't be able to live with myself if I lost Jaxon and Emma. I felt so much pain, not knowing if I would see my kids again. I could feel them crying. I could feel their fright.

I was determined to keep myself from crying. I had to battle on and find them. My peace existed only in saving them and bringing them home where they belonged.

We flew through traffic like there was no tomorrow. We were on the highway going at speeds well over a hundred miles per hour. I prayed that we would not run into any police, as I knew we would likely get arrested, regardless of what we would tell them about us trying to find my kids. We had no choice, and we had to catch up to our kids.

I kept one eye on the road and the other eye on my trace on Jaxon's cell phone. It was still at the same spot. I was praying that they were held at a house for the night. It would help us scope out the area and try to rescue them. I still had no idea what to expect.

We made it to the zone where Jaxon's cell phone appeared to be. It was a rough neighborhood for sure. I knew it could be very dangerous for us, as we had no idea how many kidnappers there were. I also knew that if they were cartel, our work to rescue the kids was going to be very difficult. I didn't care at the moment as my kids were worth losing my life.

The trace led us to one house. I knew the accuracy of the trace was to about one meter, so I was confident that we had the right house. We pulled our vehicles close to the house. The house had a few lights on outside and inside, which was a good sign.

We all knew the plan. We had all done this too many times. The only difference this time was that we were now in the United States. We were on our own protected soil.

We got down from our vehicles. We had enough fire-power to wage a small war. I just hoped the kids were OK. We all knew the risks that we were about to take to rescue our kids. We knew the benefits also of saving my kids as well as other kids.

We used our standard setup to breach the house. Two of us split at all four sides of the house. Loco and I stayed at the front, so we could breach the front entrance.

On my command, Loco breached the door with a "Door Slammer" that he had in the Batmobile. We drew our firearms. I was carrying my favorite assault rifle. It was my Seal Issued HK 417. The same assault rifle I used to kill one of the terrorists in San Diego when they were trying to assassinate the president.

We ran into the house from the front. We had some of my brothers breach the backdoor. We cleared the living room, the kitchen, the hallway, the bathrooms, and the bedrooms—there was nobody in the house. We checked the basement. We checked the attic. We kept checking. We kept looking. Nothing. I kept searching. The signal for Jaxon's cell phone was stronger than ever. They had to be here.

"Cap'n, Cap'n—I found something, sir," said Loco.

23

THE BREAKDOWN

Loco brought me a cell phone. When it hit my hand, I dropped it. My hand weakened from the realization that it was Jaxon's cell phone. It was smashed and was not functioning. I opened the back to look for the trace chip. It was there. Miraculously, the trace chip had survived the smashing by the perpetrators I assumed.

It was Jaxon's cell phone. I couldn't breathe as I realized that his hand was holding it not too long ago. His little innocent hand had held it so many times. I lost it. I broke down and fell to the floor. I cried and cried as I felt myself losing all hope. I kept asking why and how did I lose my kids? How did I let this happen? I felt I fucked up so bad and the only person to blame was myself for allowing this to happen on my watch.

I couldn't stop crying.

I'd been through wars. I'd seen my own men die in battle. I'd put my life at risk so many times. Now I was hopeless, confused, and scared. I felt myself entering the dreading black zone where panic sets in and you body and mind freeze into helplessness.

I walked directly to my vehicle. I popped the trunk. I grabbed jack and starting chugging. There was no end until the bottle emptied. I gave up. I knew no other ending.

"Cap'n what the fuck?' Loco asked.

He knocked out the bottle from my tight grasped hand. The bottleneck broke in my hand, as my grasp was death tight. I didn't know what I was more pissed about and whether is the fact that Loco just bitched slapped a bottle of jack out of my hand or the fact that all of jack was now on the fucking ground.

Time stood still. Am I right to be pissed right now? My mind was so jacked that I was wondering what to do next.

I knew I had to gather myself, as it was important to save every second possible until we found our kids. My tears turned into anger. I was fucking really pissed off now. Fuck the tears. Fuck the cartel. Fuck this fucking world I thought, as I started shooting at the wall. I emptied my entire clip into the wall, reloaded and emptied another clip while I shot at the house. I didn't know what to do. I fucked up and I didn't know what to do. My tears kept falling as I lost my mind and soul.

"Sir, we will find them," said Loco with tears in his eyes. "I promise you we will search and search until we die. I promised you that when you saved my life in that shit-land, Afghanistan, it was so I could help you find your son and daughter. I know in my heart, sir. Please don't give up. You and your kids are my family, and I never let my family down, sir."

"Brother, keep faith in your heart as we have faith in you right now. We are here to help you find them. Those assholes are going to have to answer to all of us for taking my niece and nephew. I love you, brother, we will find them I promise you!" said Adrian.

They were right. I had to snap out of it. I started to remember everything I'd taught my kids about survival. Jaxon was smart enough to keep his cell phone on and on vibrate so we could trace its signal. I tried to remember what, if anything, might help us find them.

We paced around the house with a snail's pace. For the first time in my life, I felt completely defeated, as I didn't know what our next step was. I stared into the bright night outside a window, as there was a full moon that lit up the night. All I could do was pray at this moment. I prayed to God to give me a clue. I prayed to God to give me some sort of sign. I prayed to God to help me find my kids.

I felt in my heart that I was missing something. It hit me. I ran straight into the bathroom. All the men ran after me to see what I was doing. I checked one bathroom and looked behind the toilet lid cover that housed all the internal housing of the toilet. There was nothing there.

I ran to the other bathroom. I lifted the toilet lid once again, and there it was. Jaxon had written in what appeared to be his own blood, "LA HARBOR OK 4." I could barely make out the written message because it was written in blood, but we were all positive that that was what it said.

Jaxon remembered. I'd taught him and Emma about using the undersurface of the toilet lid to write a note of distress. It was an area the perpetrators would never look when he asked to use the restroom. The *4* was our shorthand for all four of us in the family and our love for each other. My training with my kids hopefully was going to pay off with Jaxon remembering what I had taught him. My tears stopped falling for now. God gave me the strength to keep pushing. I felt a strong presence of calmness that somehow reassured me that I would see Jaxon and Emma again.

We were back in business. We had to move and move fast to catch them and rescue our kids. I was hanging everything on Jaxon's message that they were heading to and out of Los Angeles Harbor, which meant we had about three hours before they got there by motor vehicle at least.

24

DON'T EVER GIVE UP

We ran back to our vehicles. We sped toward the highway again. We didn't have time to sit down and make a plan. We would have to develop the plan on the fly, as we drove to Los Angeles.

I logged on to the SEAL site from my wireless link with my cell phone. I wanted to see if we could get any satellite images of the highways and look for a bus or vehicles that seemed linked together. I'd assumed they were moving all the kids together and that the house was a meet point to change vehicles and to gather all the kids together.

The only problem with us not being on a live mission was that I didn't have access to a live feed. We would have to have another level of security clearance to have a live feed in the United States. The satellite feed was still good, even though it had a couple of minutes of delay.

The link would be able to tell us which highways they were taking and what part of the harbor they might be loading the kids. I assumed at this point they were going to take the kids and sell them to be slaves, prostitutes, or even be illegally adopted as kids to super wealthy families in the

Middle East, China, or Russia; they also would sell some of them back for ransoms.

It was a Saturday night, there would likely not be a lot of bus traffic on the highways—at least I hoped there wouldn't be. The SEAL site satellite link showed two buses behind each other on Interstate Highway 10. They were near Blythe, California. Blythe was just across the border from Arizona. I'd hoped to catch them in Arizona; because the gun laws in California did not allow us to have the weapons and/or assault rifles that we had, no matter what the circumstance was or who we were. Our large capacity rifle magazines were also illegal in California. Not to mention the rocket launchers we had. I didn't have many connections in California, so even a pullover by police would have landed us in prison for many years for having weapons that were illegal in California. It wouldn't matter what the scenario was or our desperation to save my kids.

I knew we were also dealing with the cartel and that they would be heavily armed—likely more heavily armed than we were. I knew we had to take our chances. We no longer had any other choices at this time if I wanted to see our kids again.

We were about forty-five minutes behind the buses by my rough estimate. I prayed that the buses we were trying to catch had our kids onboard. We were running out of time, and we all knew that.

We were on Highway 10 traveling at speeds in excess of 120 miles per hour. We had to catch them before they made it to a densely populated area, as I knew it would improve our chances of isolating them on the highway. It would also help prevent any casualties from being in the spread of crossfire if there was a gunfight.

The next SEAL satellite feed showed the buses stopped off the highway. The satellite image showed them at what appeared to be a small airport off the highway. It was called Chiriaco Summit Airport. I'd never heard of it, and I had no idea what it was.

As a family, we had driven from Phoenix to Los Angeles in the past, but I'd never noticed an airport. I wasn't sure if they were going to fly the kids out of the country. We were within five minutes of getting to the airport, and my heart was racing. The level of adrenaline pumping in my blood was the highest I had ever felt in my lifetime even more so than when I had been in heat of battle. Good thing Loco knocked the bottle of Jack, as I couldn't afford to be fucked up right now.

We pulled up to the airport slowly. We saw two buses in the parking lot. I was stunned and amazed, as there were kids inside. There were kids inside the bus! I couldn't believe my fucking eyes.

We calmly got out of our vehicles. We tried to avoid looking suspicious. We were loaded with as many weapons as we could hold.

Loco suggested he pull the old drunken-bum routine and walk up to the bus like a drunken bum begging for money. I agreed with him, as it was possibly the only way to approach the buses. We stayed close behind him, hiding behind cars.

It was pitch-dark outside now as the full moon had moved behind the cloud array, and it was no longer bright as day in the sky. It was if God was taking care of the skies for our benefit. The sky's blackness made it easier to conceal ourselves.

We could hear Loco talking. He did a good impression of a drunken bum—almost too good. Three men came out of the bus with guns at their sides. They told him, in Spanish, to leave several times.

Then the encounter escalated. The men surrounded Loco, and one pointed a gun at his head with a red laser activated and told him to leave, again, in Spanish. The man was saying he would shoot him in the head if he didn't leave. I knew we were about to get into a gunfight.

Loco starting yelling, "Fuck you, fuck you, fuck you cabrones!" It was his code for "Let's roll." Loco took out the cartel man as he forcefully broke his arm in an arm lock followed by a swift cut of his blade to the man's jugular. His blood splattered all over Loco. Loco then dropped and took cover, as he knew he was in the line of our fire.

We stormed out from behind the vehicles. Four more men jumped out of the other bus. The gunfight started. You could tell the cartels' gunfire as they shot their automatic weapons aimlessly. Inexperienced fuckers. Bullets hit the cars and the bus. Bullets screeched in every direction.

I could hear the kids in the bus crying and screaming for their lives. A car exploded next to the bus from a bullet penetrating the gas tank. The blast blew my hearing and lit up the parking lot. A loud ringing in my ears persisted. My balance was thrown a little bit. Images of Jaxon and Emma raced through my brain. I had to engage in the gunfight.

I aimed my weapon's laser at a cartel member. He had me in his sights dead to rights. He shot first. His shots struck the car that was protecting me. His shots missed me by a few inches at best. I felt the car's metal debris hit me after the bullets penetrated its shell.

He had me pinned down. My men were engaged in what appeared to be about 20-25 cartel members. They had us flanked in a matter of seconds as we were still trying to get better positions.

I knew I had to use my experience over his inexperience. I kept my rifle tipped above the car's hood, so he could see that I was still there. I dipped down lower beneath the car's engine block while still supporting my rifle's point at his view. I could see his leg and foot as he knelt down behind a car also. I drew my handgun. I knew I had to take him out as he also had a better position on my men. I shot. I hit his ankle. He fucking fell to the ground. He was still alive. I had to get some answers out of him.

"Where are my kids!" I demanded an answer from him.

"Fuck you, pendejo!" the cartel member said with a thick Spanish accent.

"Tell me now or I'm going to fucking kill you, you understand?"

"I'm already dead cabron, I'm already dead, so shoot me! El Jefe will chop my head off if I say anything. You're a dead man!"

I had to get some information from him, but he wasn't giving me shit. I hid him from the other cartel members and handcuffed him to a pole, so I could get back into the fight. I knew he was my only hope of getting more information on where our kids were taken.

Loco was trapped in between the cars that separated the cartel and us. I knew his position compromised his survival. I had to get to him somehow. He saved my life once before, and I knew his life now depended on us.

My men continued to take out the cartel's men. I sensed I had only one option to get to Loco. I got into his fucking crazy batmobile. He said the engine block and front end had armor on them that could hold back up to a .50 caliber bullet. I knew it was my only way to get to him at this point.

I revved up the engine. I pulled out while taking on heavy fire from cartel that were onto of a wall that surrounded the airport's entrance. I accelerated with my foot all the way down on the gas pedal. I went toward to wall. Bullets pierced through the windshield. I kept my head ducked underneath the dash and wheel hoping the batmobile's armor protected me. I aimed the vehicle in their path. I was confident my men would know that I was trying to both take out the men on the wall and divert the cartel's men away from Loco who was trapped in between the cars.

BOOM! I hit the wall at full speed. My door was stuck from the impact. I was a sitting duck. The wall collapsed, but I knew if they survived that the cartel's men would soon be right on me. My grip on my rifle tightened. I had to stay inside the vehicle, as I couldn't get out. Bullets swarmed the vehicle. I could feel the bullets power through the armor and into the dash. Fuck I was dead.

In a flash, Loco and my men overcame the cartel's men and firepower. No wasted shots. One and two shot kills were our standard. My men and my brother struck with complete and overwhelming precision. The perpetrators were no matches for US SEALS and Army Rangers even thought they had more men and better initial positions.

They took out the entire remaining cartel within what felt as a few seconds. I again saw my life flash in front of me. First, one of the cartel's members had me dead to rights and just missed me. Second, I was stranded in a vehicle in their direct line of sights. I was still breathing as his aim laid bullets just far enough from me to miss.

All my brothers were unharmed and untouched although it didn't seem like it at first. We knew we had just survived a gunfight that had us outnumbered. I knew I had to be running out of lives.

Once the gunfight was over, I ran back into one of the buses. There were about twenty kids on the bus. They were tied down to their seats. They were all crying and yelling frantically.

I looked and looked. I couldn't find Jaxon and Emma. I ran to the other bus. There were about fifteen kids on that bus. They were also all tied down to their seats. I checked seat by seat. I checked under each seat.

What happened? Where were Jaxon and Emma? I started to ask every kid on the bus if they had seen Jaxon and Emma. None of the kids were saying anything. I don't think the kids realized that we were the good guys.

I didn't know what to do. I pulled out my military ID to show the kids that I was in the Navy. I begged them to help me. I ran over to the other bus to try to get the other kids to tell me something. I showed them my Navy ID again. I had tears running down my face.

Finally one of the little girls on the bus opened her mouth. With tears in her eyes, she said, "The men said they were going to kill them. They said there were going to kill Jaxon and Emma, because Jaxon had a cell phone, and he was trying to call the police. They also said they were going to take them and shoot them because he said his dad was the Navy Seal that helped kill the terrorists. They took them off the bus when we stopped here. Please, please, help them, please."

I fell to my knees on the bus. My will had been shattered once again in the same fucking day. This day, this very evil day ruled my world. I felt all my tears of my lifetime falling on this day. I stood up with my hands shaking, as I knew I had to try to find them. I couldn't give up at this point. I had to find them, dead or alive, and I had to personally kill the motherfuckers who kidnapped my kids. My will was weak. I was broken once again. At that low point, my strength came from looking into the eyes of my men and my brother. Their will was not broken. Their will supported mine. Their will was not going to allow me to give up, not today, not on this fucking evil day.

I ran over to the cartel man that I handcuffed to the pole. His head was bent over his chest. He was dead. His fellow cartel members must have shot him dead to prevent him from talking. I felt for his carotid pulse. Nothing. The fucker was dead. A loud burst from a corporate jet jolted us as we saw it take off from the small airport's runway. My heart sank as I felt the presence of my kids.

25

I WILL FIND YOU

We ran inside the small airport. There was nobody inside, and the doors were all locked. "What the hell," I thought. My brother joined me as we scurried around the airport. We found a man walking out of the tower staircase. He started running from us. We caught him and started questioning him.

"Did you see two kids get onto that plane? Where was the plane headed?" I yelled at him.

"I don't know. I don't know!" the tower man said.

"Bullshit! Tell us now, or I'm going to kill your ass. My two kids might have been on that flight. Put yourself in my shoes man and help us out!" I said desperately.

"Yes, there were two kids on the plane. It was a Gulfstream. The little boy was about eight years old and the little girl was about five years old. They were heading to South America. Please don't hurt me. I'm just doing my job. I am telling you everything I know, I promise," the man said

"Who owned the plane? Was it the cartel?" I yelled at him.

"I don't know, sir. I just know the plane was owned by some corporation from Mexico. I know their flight plan was heading nonstop to Colombia. I'm sorry. I wish I could help you more."

"Damn it!" I said. "What are we going to do now? I need to save my kids."

"Ryan, we are going to find them, bro, I promise you," said my brother.

"Adrian, how the fuck are we going to get to Colombia? How the fuck do we know if this asshole is telling the truth? Damn, I fucked up, Adrian? I don't know what to do. Even if we get a flight to Colombia, how are we going to find them or even put up a fight to save Jaxon and Emma?" I asked in sheer horror of the situations' reality.

"Ryan, we are going to figure that shit out. We just need to think for a moment and put our heads together," said my brother, Adrian.

"Cap'n, you guys ok?" Loco asked short of breath.

"Loco, we just found out that the cartel took Jaxon and Emma to Colombia for who knows what," I stated with tears in my eyes.

"Cap'n we are still going to save them. We can call the admiral. We can ask for a favor. We can try to reach out to some of our black op friends in the private industry. I just we know we will figure it out man," Loco said confidently.

"Ryan, you remember that time you said the president told you to call him if you ever needed anything? Well, I think this would be the only time you're ever going to need something, my brother," Adrian said.

"Adrian, what's he going to do?" I asked in despair. "We have no ability to head into South America without some SEAL tactical force and executive orders. You know that."

"Ryan, we only have two options at this point. We either call him and ask him, or we call your admiral and beg him to give us assistance on this one. Either way—they are both long shots, I know. But we can't fly into South America on a commercial flight with any type of weapons and expect to save Jaxon and Emma from the fucking cartel in a foreign country. What are we going to do? Walk up to their front door and ask for them back? The clock is ticking, and every minute we waste time talking about it, those kids are going to be farther and farther from our reach. You know that bro, so call him now, damn it!"

My brother was right. He helped me remember the day I met the president of the United States. SEAL Team Six was invited to the White House as congratulations for our catching the terrorists that had tried to assassinate the president two years ago. My team had figured out secret transmissions that made us suspicious to the fact that there was an assassination terrorist threat on the president's life more so than the usual bullshit crap.

Although I struggle with my mental confusion and a lot of other unknown bullshit, I will never forget that day, as the terrorists had everything planned right. The only mistake they made was the shine from the riflescope that I saw from the distance. Every good sniper knows to never show their glass because of the reflection shine risk. We even used scope reflective devices, but you could still get a long-range reflection at the wrong angle. Luckily, the terrorist sniper was not the best sniper in the world as we were able to find him and prevent him from taking the president's life.

Adrian and Loco were right. I had no other choice at this point. I prayed the president would help. I knew if he didn't help us that I would never my kids again. My pain from the possible realization of not ever seeing them again pointed the barrel of my gun in the wrong direction. I wouldn't be able to live with myself if Jaxon and Emma were killed or lost to a ruthless world.

26

THE PRESIDENT

As I listened to my brother and I recalled the president's words, I realized I had no alternative at this time if I wanted to see my kids again.

It was past midnight in Washington, DC. I knew what I had to do. I had a small window for some type of miracle to happen.

I believed the president's sincerity when he spoke his words to me, so I felt he'd understand why I was calling him, even if he wasn't able to help us at the moment.

I pulled up the president's number on my cell phone. I saved his number under the name Ron Johnson as a disguise. I hit the dial button. The phone rang a few times. It kept ringing. I had no idea what to expect. I had no other option at this point, and I had nothing to lose.

"Hello, Ryan, is that you?" the president stated.

"Yes, sir, it is, Captain Ryan Williams from SEAL Team Six," I said.

"Yes, Ryan, how can I help you?"

"Sir, I don't know where to start, but I don't want to waste your time, and time is my biggest enemy right now,"

I said. "Sir, my son, Jaxon, who is eight, and my daughter, Emma, who's five, have been kidnapped by one of the cartels we suspect. We saved over thirty other kids tonight who were also kidnapped by the cartel. For some reason they took my two kids and flew to Bogota, Colombia in a Gulfstream registered to a Mexican corporation. I don't know their intentions, but they can't be good, Mr. President."

The phone line was quite. I could hear the president breathing and thinking. "Ryan, I'm sorry to hear what has happened to your kids. The cartels are bad. We've known that they've been trafficking kids all over the world to make money, as their drug businesses have slowed substantially. Since marijuana has been legalized in all states in the United States, the cartels have taking a big hit on their drug business, so they have been compensating by doing trafficking of kids.

Our intelligence also suggests that the cartels of South America and Mexico have joined forces somehow under one leader. We know they helped the terrorists that tried to take my life and that they are likely trying to regroup at another shot at me or trying some unthinkable terrorist act on American soil. Ryan, do you remember Operation Sol or what was going to be Operation Sol?"

"Yes, sir," I replied. "Operation Sol was the plan to have fifty operators enter into Mexico and Colombia to take out the three or four main cartels a few years ago. It was a combination of an effort between the US, Mexico and Colombia. I was asked to lead the operation. I can't forget it as I think all of us wanted to take out the cartels even back then. I also can't forget it as the operators were being offered $250,000 per job. From the little I reviewed, the operation was very aggressive with a complete plan to not just make a few hits, but to completely wipe out the cartel system and all of those involved. What I also remember was that it seemed like a very achievable task as the amount of intel was extensive. I believe the operation was squashed when the newly elected Mexican president took office. I recall he didn't want US operators in his backyard as he felt the Mexican government could handle the cartels."

"Yes, you are correct. We have been trying to reorganize the operation, but we keep hitting resistance from the current Mexican president," the president stated.

I didn't know what to say at that point. I wasn't sure what I expected him to do or say, but I was hoping for something—anything.

"Ryan, I have to run a lot of drills with the secret service once a month. The drills range from an assassination attempt to an attack on our entourage to the kidnapping of my wife and/or kids. With the scenario concerning the kidnapping of my family, I have to proceed with running the country without compromise for the millions of Americans we must still protect, as well as because I'm the leader of the free world. At the end of the drill, I'm to assume that I can't let my personal feelings get in way of running the country, and that I must assume that I will never see my wife and kids again, as we are not to negotiate with terrorists. Well, these thoughts keep me up at night many times. I say to myself all the time that I would have to focus and run the country without compromise, but then I realize that my family is my family, and that it's not that easy." He paused for a moment.

"Ryan, please tell me what you would need if you could have everything you needed to save your kids," the president asked.

I was shocked to hear his words. I was elated with some reserve, as I knew this might open our door to trying to rescue Jaxon and Emma.

I told him without hesitation, "Sir, I have all the men I need. Some of the men are part of Seal Team Six, and the others include my brother and a couple of his men, who are Army Rangers. I'm certain we can increase our chances if we had the following. We would need an airlift into Bogota, Colombia, with a stated flight plan for a humanitarian mission. We will need a weapons-supported helicopter lift within a three-mile range of the cartel's hideout. We will need satellite support, Coms support, and weapons support with a full green light for a full SEAL team mission. Sir, as you know, the only way we can do this is with an executive order."

"Ryan, I have to tell you the honest truth, OK? Shortly before I met you, and after I learned how you killed the terrorist who had a rifle pointed at my head, I had a dream—a dream for which I believe only God could be responsible to include in my memory.

"Ryan, I dreamed that one day you would call my personal cell phone and ask me for some help. In that dream I helped you, and you helped me for something that I will never mention and I hope will never happen, as the thought of my dream is horrifying. Ryan, that's why I gave you my personal cell phone number that day. Now you're calling me, as I dreamed, and now I'm going to help you. I'm going to text you the cell phone for General Fisher. I'll speak with him and provide the executive order based on a terrorist threat to our national security. We'll base the plan on a threat to my security when it all gets written up. Of course, as you know, this will all be top secret, and it will serve strictly as a black op mission."

"Yes, sir," I said.

"Hopefully, General Fisher will provide you with a ride and a weapons-supported lift. Tell him what weapons you'll need. Since it's an executive order based on a terrorist threat, you'll be able to get what you need. Ryan, may I suggest one thing to you?" the president asked.

"Yes, sir, of course."

"After you rescue your kids, please take out that fucking bastard who leads the cartels. Do it for our country and for our kids, so these cartels learn not to fuck with us on our own land or anywhere else in the world. This just gives us the incentive we needed to ensure they will not do business in our backyard. Your kids are about the same ages as my kids, and I will not rest until they're safe in bed, as my kids are tonight."

"Sir, I will promise you this: we will win. We always win!" I said with exhausted confidence.

27

General call

I called General Fisher on his cell phone. He answered his phone and said, "This is General Fisher."

"Sir, this is Captain Ryan Williams of Seal Team Six. I have an executive order from the president to proceed with Operation Sunshine, which is a little similar to a previous Operation called Operation Sol," I said.

"Yes, Ryan, the president gave me the details and told me what we need to do. In all honesty, I don't agree with allowing you to follow through with this operation?" General Fisher said sternly.

"Sir?" I asked.

"Ryan, you are putting the lives of our military men in harm's way without any care in the world. You have no plan. You have no preconceived idea of how difficult your crazy plan will be to even have a remote chance at success. I'm sorry, but even with an executive order, I can't authorize what I consider to be a fucking suicide military mission!" General Fisher said even more sternly.

"Sir, with all do respect, sir. I respect your opinion and I understand your dilemma. I assure you, sir, that my team and I understand the risks. I have served on 77 seal missions and with all honesty, sir, at least half of those were fucked up, had no tangible gain, and were more to almost appease some fucking politician that decided to get a little pissed off at some other country because their diplomat spilled some wine on them during some summit dinner." I replied with complete abandonment for any appropriateness concerning the military chain of command.

"Ryan, you must have the balls of a fucking tornado with longhorns, son. Fine, you have a fucking executive order. Good for you. I don't really fucking care. This is still a military based operation, and I don't believe you will be successful with a mission that has so much emotional ties to it. Do you understand my point?" General Fisher asked.

"Sir, I understand your point, so please try to understand mine. I have given my life for my country. I have done everything that was ever asked of me whether I had an agreement or disagreement with the goals or outcomes. To me, the cartel came into our own backyard and tried to kill our commander in chief. Now they came into our home and pissed on our floor while stealing our kids. I can't help but being a little emotional about it, sir. I pray that you never have to face a similar, personal situation, sir, as I believe you would agree with my intentions otherwise. Sir, if you say no, my wife and I will never see our kids again, and I am certain the cartel will continue to operate on American soil. Please, sir, please reconsider," I begged desperately.

"Ryan, ok, you have my agreement, but only barely. If you cost the lives of any of our men or even scratch any of the fucking hardware that I'm going to authorize to your person, I'm going to personally come find you and cut your fucking balls off. You still there? I would take my threat very seriously," General Fisher stated as he slammed the phone against the wall.

"Yes, sir, I understand. I am sure you understand sir that it is not only about saving my kids, but also, completing a task that should have been done years ago with Operation Sol," I replied.

"Ryan, when we get off the phone, I'll order a C130, two Stealth helicopters, a Blackhawk for pickup, an unmanned air droid, and some hardware for your mission. You need to get your asses to Desert Center Airport, which is to your east. You'll have rendezvous there with the C130 in two and half hours. Since this is an executive order, we have a STAT green light, so things will move very quickly. You'll have approval for a full SEAL team mission, so that means you'll be able to use live SOCOM satellite feeds, intel, and anything else you need. The president told me this is a war you have to win for our country, so although I am reluctant to help, I'll be providing you with anything you need. Just don't forget what I said about the consequence if you fuck up!" General Fisher exclaimed.

"Sir, thank you so much for your help," I said. "We will win this war!"

We blazed through the desert to rendezvous at the airport. My heart pounded. The images of my kids kept rolling through my head. My eyes ran dry out of tears. The last time I saw them was an image that was instilled in my memory over and over: the last time I placed my hand on their heads, as most parents do when they say, "I love you." My brain was working properly now although I still knew I would still need to seek medical attention at some point. My confidence was slowly building back up again.

28

EL JEFE'S CALL

I knew in my heart that we would save them. As we were driving, my cell phone rang. It was an unknown number. At first, I thought it was the police captain, and I was hoping he might have had some news. Any news would help.

"Hello, who's this?" I asked.

"Captain Williams? Is this Captain Williams?" the strange voice asked in a Spanish accent.

"Yes, this is Captain Williams. Who is this?"

"Señor, this is Garcia, military commander of the cartels. Do you know who we are, señor?"

"No, I have no idea who you are," I said. "What do you want?"

"Señor, it is not what we want, it is what you want. We have your children, and we want to make a deal. You understand?"

"Fuck you! I'm going to find you and kill you!" I couldn't hold back my tears and my voice was silenced by the reality. "They're too young and don't understand what's happening. Have you hurt them?"

"Señor, El Jefe will speak to you now. He is in command of the combined forces of the South American and Mexican cartels," the man said.

"Captain Williams," said a different voice. "It is so odd that our paths have crossed this way. I'm happy to say that your children are safe. They will not be harmed, but you must cooperate. Do you understand?"

"If my kids are safe, then let me speak with them." I said.

"Captain Williams, I will not hurt them, I promise you, but you'll have to cooperate with what we need. The funny thing is that you have no idea of what I'm speaking." He laughed.

"I know who you are Captain Williams. I know your team saved the president from the terrorist's bullet. I know your team—the famous SEAL Team Six, who everyone knows and fears—was responsible for killing the terrorist. That terrorist you killed paid us to help him gain entry into the US. The cartel has taken to other lucrative businesses since your country has legalized marijuana. We would have left things alone and stayed in the drug business, but your country's change in policies and laws made us change our business plans. How do you think the terrorists got into the United States? Who do you think helped them? It is nothing against the United States, you see, it is just business. When the terrorists are paying us millions to help them achieve their goal, it was too tempting to pass up," said El Jefe.

"Why the fuck are you telling me this. I don't fucking care. I just want my kids!" I exclaimed.

"Patience, Captain Williams, patience. You see one of the terrorists that was supposed to help with the assassination was caught in transport, so my son had to help them finish the job. You know what that means, Captain Williams?"

"I said I don't care! Just tell me where my kids are!"

"No, no, no, Captain Williams. You need to care. It was only business, as my son was helping the terrorists enter your country. You see when you killed the terrorist you also murdered my son! Do you remember that motherfucker? He was unarmed and gave himself up to you, but you fucking stared him in the eyes and killed him! I have the fucking video from his body camera that day. He surrendered to you! You were supposed to keep him alive, but instead you emptied your entire clip in him. You shot him with over 10 rounds. He was dead after the first bullet, but you executed him and then kicked him in the face after he was dead! You fucking murdered him while nobody was around you! I will avenge his death! You murdered my only son, motherfucker!"

"Fuck you! He tried to kill the president! He earned his death! Where are my kids asshole!"

"You are not fucking understanding me, Captain Williams. I have your kids, so you can see them murdered just as you murdered my son! Now, since your team has foiled our plans, killed my son, and has taken a major source of revenue, you'll pay for it. You understand yet, Captain Williams?" El Jefe asked.

"I don't follow you, and I have no idea how this has to do with my kids, so I don't understand."

"Señor Williams, you see, I have some other per-sonal news to share with you, but I must share with you in person. Also we will be assisting another group doing a mission in the United States. If you cooperate and the mission succeeds, I promise you I will return your chil-dren to you without questions. If you do not cooperate, I will personally behead your children and send you the video. Just you can watch it, as I had to watch my son's video of you killing him. I will then deliver their heads to your front door right before I kill you and your wife, cabrón. I will also make sure my men kill you and your family and everyone else you may know. Comprende, Señor Williams?"

"I'm afraid I don't understand," I said. "Nor can I negotiate with terrorists, by the governance of the United States! Just let me kids go before I find you and kill you, you fucking asshole."

"Daddy, Daddy, please, please help us," Emma screamed into the phone. "Please, Daddy, they are hurting me."

My heart stopped. I dropped the phone to the ground as I lost my will and my strength once again when I heard her five-year-old voice cry for me and for help. It was a tone of voice that I'd never heard from my little girl.

I picked up the phone. My voice crumbled as I spoke into the phone. I drowned quickly into the bottom of the abyss.

"OK, OK. I will do anything you say, but please do not hurt my kids. Just please tell me what you need me to do." I said in desperation after hearing my daughter crying in the background.

"Señor Williams, your mission for us will likely be the easiest you have ever done. We just need an escort for a very special group as they enter the United States from Mexico. If there were any trouble, I would expect you to be able to help our team circumvent the trouble. I cannot tell you what their mission is, Mr. Williams, and I say that for your own protection. However, I do think you are probably smart enough to figure out that their mission does not have the best of intentions for your country."

"Once our special group crosses into the United States, I will give you a time and place where you can pick up your children. If you try anything in retaliation, you and your family will be killed. Trust me, I never lose, and I will definitely not lose this mission once again. You understand, Señor Williams? I advise you to not think about coming after me, as I have more resources than any other country you have ever fought against, and I don't play by the rules. Also, I hate when people try to interrupt the cartel's business. We only care about making money, and we don't care about anything else.

You will receive a text with information on where you will be picked up. You get there right away and come by yourself or your kids will be killed."

I knew El Jefe was a ruthless piece of shit. I knew I couldn't take his words lightly and that he was not bluffing. When I had done some preliminary research for Operation Sol, I thought his rule and actions were equally as bad or worse than the terrorists we fought. I had watched a news special on the most dangerous person in the world, and it was not a terrorist from the Middle East. It was El Jefe.

The news special displayed images of what he had done including hundreds of public beheadings, killings of police and politicians, and killings of anyone who tried to get in their way. To the cartel, it was all about money and power. Their message was clear. If you got in their way, you would be killed and they would possibly come after your family as well.

Nobody actually knew El Jefe's real name aside from his reported boss, El General, who was thought to be the original leader of the South American cartel. His anonymity kept him safe. What I didn't know or what nobody knew at that point was that the South American and Mexican cartels merged into one cartel that was lead by El General. El General was presumed dead or in hiding, as he had not been heard of in a long time.

For some reason, the cartels' business did not always make the front page of our US newspapers or make the news headlines on TV. I didn't always understand how terrorist issues in the middle east always made the news headlines, but the cartels' dealings in our own backyard rarely made it. It wasn't until the number of kids being taken by the cartel escalated to such a high number that our media was finally starting to publicize the atrocious issues of human trafficking and child prostitution led by the cartels.

29

THE PLAN

What was I going to do? I kept thinking about my loyalty to my country as well as to my kids. I knew the mission would have some legal implications if it were found out what we were doing. I knew I risked so many lives and careers, as well as the exposure of the president of the United States. However, when I heard my daughter crying, my heart sank, and all I could think about was having my two kids safe and home again. I had no idea the president's assassination attempt had ties to the most dangerous cartel in the world.

We all met and reviewed our options. We had to piece together a plan that would allow me to be picked up by the cartel and my team to track my whereabouts. I knew we had to do something that would not give any trace of evidence to the cartel that I had a team in position ready to strike at any time. I knew I had to contact another government agency, since the means for what I needed was not going to be completely available to us, even with the army and Navy's help.

I placed a call to one of my buddies at the CIA. I remembered a conversation with him in the past about their use of undetectable cameras, GPS, and other technologies that I'd hoped I could gain access to for this mission. In a rush, I dialed his cell-phone number. It was eleven o'clock at night Arizona time. "Dan, sorry to bug you at this hour, but I really need to talk to you as I need your help."

"Ryan, my friend, don't ever worry about calling me. You've saved my ass way too many times. I owe you one of my kids. You know that. What can I do to help you?"

"Thanks, Dan. Sorry to be so blunt, but my two kids were kidnapped by the cartels. They are taking my kids to South America. The fucking cartel leader called me personally to dictate his dreadful plan to kill them if I don't cooperate. I'm desperate. They want to pick me up to help them with some fucked-up mission. Of course, I have different plans. Basically, I have a team in place consisting of some of my men from the SEALS, my brother and some of his US Ranger buddies. We have a plan that we know will work if we have the right support. What I need from you is an undetectable means of visual, audio, and/or positional advancement in real time."

"Wow," Dan said. He was silent for a moment before continuing. "Ryan, I'm sorry to hear your news. Of course I'll help you. We'll have to classify this project under a black-ops proposition with a threat to Homeland Security in order to get authorization for what you need. How much time do I have, so I can start working on it?"

"Dan, thank you. I actually have an executive order from the president for this mission based on special circumstances. Unfortunately, the cartel is picking me up in four hours, and I need a few things in place before they pick me up in Arizona."

"Ryan, I'm on it. I have an agent in Yuma, Arizona. Don't ask. I will have him on his way to you with some badass shit in twenty minutes. You'll have real-time tracking and audio. I don't think he has video on him. Where can he meet you?"

"Dan, thank you so much" I said. "I'll send you coordinates near the airport where they're picking me up. Dan, can we depend on the CIA for the tracking? Can we send/receive info to my SEAL team from the CIA?"

"Sure, we'll uplink live with your SEAL satellite."

I knew our time was limited. I received the cartel's text with the location of my pickup by them. We had to piece together our plan while on the road to the meet point for my pickup. I had no idea where they would be taking me. I just felt we were against the wall and had no choice.

The simple plan was to get picked up by the cartel at the airport they designated in their text. I would have our satellite track me in real time. My team's flight path would be unknown. They would have to track me and fly not too far behind. The one good thing was that I would have audio uplink; however, it would be limited to a small time period, as the battery for the audio device was limited to three to four hours max. I knew I would have to use it to help confirm when I found my kids and to provide any intel I could.

We arrived at the rendezvous spot with the CIA agent. His name was Scott. I hadn't met him in the past, but Dan said he was one of his best field agents. He went over the

GPS tracker and audio device. The audio device fit deep in my deep ear. I would have to have a doctor or someone pull it out once the mission was over. I could basically activate it by scratching my ear, as the device was activated by the pressure of my finger. The only problem was that I wouldn't be able to turn it on and off, so I knew I would have to use it when I thought our window for providing intel was best.

The GPS tracker was placed into a pill that I had to swallow. It was untraceable, and I would probably shit it out in two to four days. I just hoped I would have enough time to secure my kids and have our team come save us with these limited time options.

We left the rendezvous spot and headed straight to the airport. We were driving at 100 to 110 miles per hour the entire way. Once again, our biggest risk was getting pulled over by local law enforcement. Even though we had an executive order, it was a top-secret mission, and I knew we would not be able to afford any kind of hang-up or betrayal by local law enforcement that might be on the take with the cartel.

We arrived at the airport. We reviewed the plan as best as we could, not knowing exactly what was going to happen next.

Basically I would get captured and assume they would take me to where Jaxon and Emma were. I had hoped I would encounter El Jefe, as he was more secretive than any other figure in the world. He helped run a multibillion-dollar illegal business, and virtually no one knew who he was, what he looked like, where he was from, or anything else. Now we knew that El Jefe led the South American and Mexican cartels, which meant his power and wealth was almost untouchable.

I swallowed the pill. I waited for confirmation from the CIA satellite uplink that the GPS device was activated with the heat of my inner core. I received the signal that I was now live and able to be tracked.

I prayed with my brothers. We had been here many times before with a plan, and the knowledge that one or all of us may not make the next day. We knew what the odds were. We knew we had support, but we didn't have a bailout plan if we failed. It was all or nothing, and, for all of us, that was good enough as my brothers knew I would do the same for them if they needed my help.

My team drove away and waited for me to be picked up. A caravan of four black SUVS pulled up. Several men stepped out of the vehicles and were heavily armed. They all had full military outfits, including bulletproof chest vests and light body armor. I felt ready, as I knew my team was ready.

They had men take off all my clothes. They even checked my ass. They scanned all my clothes with a metal wand detector. All I had were the clothes on my back, a undetectable GPS pill somewhere in my gut, and an unde-tectable earpiece that I hoped worked when I needed it. Most of the cartel men approached me, while some stood and protected the perimeter. They seemed well trained, but I knew our team could take them without hesitation. I had no doubts.

"Señor Williams, we did not expect to see you here," said the cartel man. "We know you have some men nearby.

Our eyes in the sky are watching them, so I hope you did not have some crazy plan in place, because if so, we will kill you, them, and your kids. I will then personally deliver your kids' heads to your wife right before I rape and kill her. I have seen her pictures, and she is one hot bitch. Do you understand, Señor Williams?"

"Don't ever, ever call my wife a bitch you fucking asshole! I will make sure I kill you first for calling her that!" I shouted.

"Ok tough guy, we will see about that," the cartel man said.

"I just want to see my kids, and I'll do what you ask of me. I'm here for them and them only, so stop threatening me and let's get going, you understand, *asshole*?" I knew I could not show any weakness.

The asshole then hit the smack out of me with the butt of his handgun. It hurt like hell, but it wasn't anything I hadn't had done to me in the past. Blood and a couple of broken teeth exited my mouth from his smackdown.

They covered my head with a sheath. They took me out onto the tarmac. I could hear a plane in the background. It sounded like a fairly sizable private jet.

I then assumed that this plane would be taking me straight to Colombia. The plane took off. I could hear several men talking in Spanish in the background. The fucking assholes would hit me in the head, face, or abdomen each time they passed by me.

For a while, it took everything in me to not try to fight back, but I knew they could make things a lot worse for me. I kept thinking of Jaxon and Emma. I knew I was their only chance at rescue. Although our plan was not extravagant or based on weeks or months of intel research, I was confident that we would succeed. We had no other choice, and I knew my men dedicated their lives to our success.

After several hours of flying—and getting beat up—it felt like we were descending. I kept picturing Jaxon and Emma. I prayed that they were OK. The plane hit the runway smoothly. I hoped I was one step closer to seeing my kids. Once the plane stopped, the men stood me up.

30

FOREIGN LAND

I was exhausted, and I felt a bit drowsy from being beaten the entire flight. We deplaned finally. My adrenaline rushed. My physical bruising confused my mind. I hated it. I wasn't myself and now I felt my mind reverting into a confused state. I had to concentrate and pull myself together. My kids' lives depended on me being physically and mentally sharp.

They threw me into the back of a truck. It was raining. I actually liked being in the back of a truck, because I could hear my surroundings. This was a big mistake on their part. I was trained to picture my surroundings and track my path based on the road texture, sounds in the background, elevation changes, and basically anything else that could help me retrace my path in case our rendezvous exit was the same airport.

The rain soaked me at this point. It was a warm rain. The rain provided me with the only water I'd had in several hours. These stupid asses probably thought they were hurting me by having me in the back of a truck, but it actually provided me with peace and quiet to allow me time to gather my thoughts and piece together whatever plan I could. It also helped my mind position itself for a positive outcome.

"Oye, este es el pinche Americano. El es el padre de los ninos. Cuidado con este pinche Americano porque es un chingon. El es del SEAL Team Six, cabrónes. Ellos son los mas chingones de los marineros." said one of the cartel assholes.

Who would have thought that growing up speaking Spanish would now pay off? I could understand everything they were saying. They just assumed that I was some gringo who didn't understand Spanish. They didn't know my own mother was from Mexico. Their Spanish sounded Mexican, so I assumed El Jefe surrounded himself with his own Mexican men since he was from Mexico.

The cartel man had basically said that I was the father of the kids, which probably meant that my kids were close. Otherwise what would the guys at this location know about them. I took any clue I could.

They walked me on a path that seemed about a half mile from where our truck had stopped. I could hear about six to eight men walking beside me. By the sound of their gear, I assumed they were all very heavily armed. "Lleve este cabrón a la casa de El Jefe," the cartel man said. Another clue for me: he had said to take me to the house of El Jefe.

The men taking me then started saying in Spanish how El Jefe wanted to use me for a mission, and that the mission was classified. They also made it very clear that I had killed El Jefe's son when his son was helping the sniper who was trying to assassinate the president.

They made it sound like the mission was to help bring "special soldiers" to the United States. Were these guys that fucking stupid? I wasn't going to argue, as each clue as to my whereabouts was what was going to help me rescue my kids and get the hell out of there.

We walked up several stairs. We were still outside, so I assumed the stairs led to the front of the house. I felt like I was freaking climbing a pyramid or something. My wife and I had climbed the Mayan ruins in Mexico once, and it felt as the same type of steps. The steps were small, and the slope was pretty vertical. This motherfucker probably had his house built on some fucking pyramid to help protect him. It made sense to have a high vantage point in case he was ever attacked.

We stopped. The ground did not feel level, so we must have arrived at the front of the house or whatever it was. It was quiet. A door opened.

"Este es el Americano?" a voice said behind the door.

"Sí, este es el chingon Navy SEAL," said the man who was holding my arm. "El Jefe está aquí?" He was basically asking him if El Jefe was at the house now.

This was it. I was ready to meet El Jefe.

The man behind the door took me inside. I could hear Spanish music in the background. Since my mother was from Mexico, I grew up hearing some of her Mexican music. This music sounded familiar. Eerily familiar.

I could also hear only one man walking next to me, and he didn't sound like he was heavily armed. We walked up more stairs. He sat me down next to him.

He took off my head cover. I was now staring at a man in his fifties. He had a gray beard and a full head of hair. He was well dressed. He had a sidearm on him. We sat in silence and just stared at each other.

I think he was trying to feel me out, while I tried to assess my situation. From the room I was in, I could see the house and its surroundings. Sure enough, the place was high on a hill, and I could see the many steps I'd climbed to get to the top. Whoever owned this house sure went through a lot of trouble to build it on a high-ass spot. I knew that would later be a factor in our rescue as it is always difficult to attack someone at a high point.

31

MY FAMILY SECRET

The strange man opened his mouth. "Congratulations, Señor Williams. You are now sitting across from one of the most powerful men in the world. How does that make you feel?"

I thought, "What the fuck?" It was the same voice I'd heard on the phone. I knew then that I was sitting across from El Jefe, who was one of the most mysterious and crazy fuckers the world knew. He was worse than any terrorist, as he actually led an army and was wealthy, powerful, and greedy as shit. Now he led both the South American and Mexican cartels. The other thing was he was a mystery, as nobody actually knew his real name or what he looked like.

"Excuse me, I don't understand?" I asked in a stupid voice, knowing damn well who the fuck he was.

"I'm the man who runs your world right now!" he said. "I'm the one who you fucked out of millions of dollars by being at the wrong place at the wrong time, fifty million dollars in fact. Not to mention, that you are the one that killed my only son! This is business and you stepped right into my business without knowing it. I'm the only thing standing between your kids' lives and your death, you motherfucker."

"I know who you are. I know what you do. I have to say that it is you who was in the wrong place at the wrong time, and I'm going to fucking kill you, you motherfucker!" I said.

I leapt towards him with my hands in cuffs behind my back. I nailed him with a headbutt to his nose that caused an instant break. He fell to the ground bleeding. As I stood over him ready for the kill, one of his guards tasered me from behind, and the taser's electric shock took me to the ground. His guard then kicked me in the abdomen several times.

I coughed up my own blood as I lay on the ground staring at El Jefe slowing getting up. His guards sat me down and now cuffed my legs to my chair. They tasered me once again behind my neck, which sent my body into a whirlwind as I was cuffed to the chair by my arms and legs. My joy came from seeing El Jefe's crooked, bleeding nose.

"Look out, Americano. I have no patience, and I have no use for your kids, so I will chop their fucking heads off right now, right in front of you while you sit there in handcuffs, just useless, you bitch. Do not try anything else stupid like that again!" El Jefe said.

He spit his gross, bloody spit onto my face. It dripped down my face, as I couldn't wipe it while being tied to my chair.

"You'll help me, or you and your family will disappear, and your pinche SEAL Team Six will bury your body parts, cabrón."

I decided that I had to get down to business. "Look, just tell me what you need me to do. I'll do what you say, and I'll take my kids away from here, and you'll never hear from me again, OK?"

"That is more like it, Captain Williams. Listen to me very carefully. Don't interrupt me until I say I am finished. What I am about to tell you is something that you will not believe at first. My following words will make you want to hurt me once again, as you will not want to believe them, but you will believe me once you absorb them." El Jefe said.

"Captain Williams, have you ever seen this picture?" El Jefe asked.

He showed me a picture that I had seen many times in the past. It was a picture that I couldn't remember when or where I saw it, but I knew I had seen it before in my lifetime. The picture was in old black and white with fading and folds.

He then showed me a picture of my family that was taken at our home during my birthday celebration. It included my wife, kids, brother, and my mother. Natalie had posted it on Facebook. I became angry as I wondered why the hell he was showing me these pictures, and I was pissed that he got them off of Facebook.

He then showed me a picture of my mom from that same picture that zoomed onto her face and neck.

"Captain Williams, do you recognize that pendant that your mother is wearing? El Jefe asked.

I did. I did recognize it. At that moment, my stomach turned. I threw up in my mouth.

"You know what I am about to tell you don't you, Captain Williams?" El Jefe said.

I churned in my seat. He showed me the old photograph once again. I remembered the photo. The photo was the only photo and only personal possession my mother had when she left Mexico. She always said her father gave her the pendant. The photo was in her pendant that she wore on her necklace ever since I can remember. I didn't know what to think or say, so I sat in silence. I didn't want to believe what I was imagining.

"You see Captain Williams. Your mother is my older sister. She left our family at a young age, but she was old enough to realize what our father did for a living. She left Mexico and never looked back. This was the last picture we took together. She promised me as a young boy that she would come back for me. I have spent my entire life trying to find her without luck. It wasn't until we saw your wife's posts on Facebook that I saw my sister, Elena, and her pendant that my father gave her as a child. My father had that pendant made especially for his one and only daughter, as a reminder to her of his protection of her. The moment I saw it I knew she was my sister.

We have been following your family since you killed my son in San Diego. Even I had no idea that my sister was your mother, as I had lost all contact with her. She also changed her name when she made it into the United States.

I have no doubt that she is my sister, which makes me your uncle." El Jefe recited with confidence of being correct.

Time stood still.

I didn't know what to think or say. I couldn't fully absorb what he was telling me. I tried to think back to my childhood trying to remember any clues my mother may have shared with us. I tried to grasp how she could have left the cartel's family without a trace. Fury raged through my arteries and veins as now the realization became clear that my family had direct ties to the cartels who I despised.

My ability to think clearly became muddy. This information was too overwhelming to process with everything else going on around me. I also knew that my window was getting narrower and narrower. I knew my team was probably close, but they wouldn't make a move until I could give them some type of audio intel. I had to activate the earpiece, but I was in fucking handcuffs. I had to think fast.

"If what you say is true, then what is your real name?" I asked him.

"My name?" El Jefe asked. "Fuck, I barely remember my name aside from my alias/secret name of El Jefe. You see, Captain Williams, my secrecy is my biggest weapon. What is your biggest weapon, Captain Williams?"

"My biggest weapon is always my team and our dedication to each other all the time," I said.

"For you, my nephew, may I call you that now that you know the truth?" El Jefe asked.

"Fuck no! I am not your nephew. My mother is not your sister, and we have no relations to you now or in the past. Even if my mother is your blood sister, she will never admit to it. She will never care about you, and she especially will not care when I kill you!" I said.

"I understand your displeasures in realizing the truth. Even so, if you get lucky and you are able to see your mother again, ask her about her younger brother. If she denies me, then you will know she has no cares or love for her only brother. If she cries, then you will know that her love is still there for her only brother and family. I would do anything to see my sister once again. I know my father would also do anything in his power to see her once again." El Jefe explained.

"I know my mother. Even if she feels anything inside, she will deny you. She left a family that believed in killing people to make money, and she will always deny any relation." I said adamantly.

"Please listen to me for a few more minutes, and I will then let you see your kids. When my father inherited the control of the South American cartel, he was smart enough to know that he had to be involved in Mexico if he wanted to be able to do more business in the United States. In order to do this, he lived in both South America and Mexico. After a couple of years of living in Mexico, he married a young Mexican woman in Mexico City even though he was already married to another woman in Colombia. That woman, Mariana Chavez, was our mother and your grandmother." El Jefe stated.

"Look, I don't want to hear any of this I DO NOT care!" I exclaimed.

"I don't care if you care. You will know the truth, so shut up and listen or I will not let you see your kids. My mother was an angel and a very naïve young girl when she married my father. She was taken in by his wealth without realizing how my father made his money.

When your mother was fourteen, we all found out what my father did as his pictures and background were all over the newspapers one day. We found out he ran the South American cartel and was also working with the Mexican cartels. Our mother vowed to have our father captured, as she did not agree with his doings and she felt betrayed by him for not telling her the truth before they married. When her threats became real and she sent my father's personal information to the chief of police in Mexico City, my father dealt with what he thought was the right thing to do. My father had my mother killed even though it was made to appear as an accident. When Elena, your mother, found out about our father and how he had our mother killed, she was devastated. We talked about it for hours and how we didn't want to be with our father anymore. We had our housekeeper take this picture. She wrote me a note that stated she loved me more than anything and that she would come back for me one day soon. The next day she vanished. We believe she stole money from our father's vault while he was in South America, and she never looked back even though she made a promise to me that she would come back for me. I was only seven years old.

I was demolished, as I had lost my mother and my only sister in the same month. I cried everyday and every night. I hung onto this picture everyday and night, and I prayed that she would come back for me. I hated my father for years, and I tried to run away several times.

Once I knew that he was the leader of the cartel, my father knew he could not let me ever get away from him especially after losing his daughter who he loved very deeply. After losing his only daughter, he was also lost and depressed for several years. I believe his loss of Elena was the main reason he stayed mostly in Mexico, so he could try to find her. He wanted to find her not to punish her, but to love her. Although you think of us as being the devils of the world, we do feel love for our family just like you do for your wife and kids." El Jefe said.

I was again at a loss. I knew I hated the man that sat in front of me for everything he had done and for kidnapping my kids. I became angry with myself for feeling any sympathy for his story, but somehow I couldn't help feeling sorry for the seven-year-old boy that never had a chance. He drew me in, but I knew I had to still hate him and kill him when I would have the chance. I would have to deal with my mother at some later point.

"Ryan, when I started in this business, I knew enough to know that trust does not exist in this line of business. My father later inherited control of both the South American and Mexican cartels. As he advanced in age and his ability to evade capture became too hard, he passed the leadership to me. Many think my father, El General, is dead as his killing and funeral were all fabricated. He is still alive and well-protected. I am the only one that knows his whereabouts in order to protect him. Congratulations once again, as you are the only soul on this earth who knows all this information." El Jefe said.

"Julio or whatever the fuck your name is. I don't care what you say. I do not believe you and I will never believe anything you are telling me." I said.

"No, you listen to me. How would you like it if you never saw your kids or wife again? How would you like it if I make sure the entire world knows that your grandfather is the leader of the South American and Mexican cartels? I want you to think about all of those things for a moment and how your life would change. You see, I know how it feels to lose my mother and sister. It is a pain that no battle or loss of your men will compare to in your lifetime. Trust me," El Jefe said.

32

THE GATHERING

"I admire your Seal Team Six and what they stand for with your ethos. I wish I could have a Seal Team Six, as there are some motherfuckers that I'd like to make disappear. The thing with your government is that you kill people all over the world, and your government calls it legitimate because you label as what needs to be done for democracy or national security. I call it bullshit, you see?" El Jefe said.

"I am curious. Why did you bring my kids and me all the way to South America and not Mexico since Mexico is so much closer?" I pondered.

"Ah, great question. You see in South America I have full military support despite our line of business. We provide the government with millions of dollars, and they protect us from being harmed. It is an arrangement my father perfected and also what helps him stay safe. We used to have that same arrangement in Mexico, but your government has become too involved in Mexican affairs to allow a legitimate level of military protection. I assumed that if we brought them to Mexico that you would be able to mount a successful rescue attempt." El Jefe explained.

"You see this little red button?" El Jefe asked.

"Yes, why?" I asked.

"If I hit this little red button, I have one hundred men run in here heavily armed and ready to shoot to kill, no questions asked. It also notifies the Colombian army that I am under attack. The Colombian army then presents to my house immediately ready for a war. It is quite impressive, as we have actually done drills with them. They have made it here within seven minutes ready to engage with full land and jet air support. So before you think about doing something stupid to me, please realize that you'll never see your kids again if something happens to me, you understand?"

"Yes, I understand."

He uncuffed my hands and ankles. My first instinct was to kill him by breaking his freaking neck, but I knew he did hold the key to my seeing Jaxon and Emma again as I still didn't know where they were.

"Captain Williams, you may go to the restroom and clean yourself up. Then I will take you to your kids. You'll get five minutes with them. Then you'll come with me and learn about your mission. You'll then have four days to complete your mission. Once your mission is completed, I promise you I will send your kids with you home in a car. You have my word as a father that I will not bother you again in the future if you leave me to my business. You live your life with your kids and your wife, and you'll forget this ever happened. If you try to find me or cross me, I will have you and your family killed while you are out to dinner or the movies. I will deliver all of your heads to your mother, you understand?"

I went to the restroom. I knew it was time to activate the earpiece. I turned it on by placing my finger deep into my ear to activate the earpiece.

Not knowing if El Jefe could hear me or not, I prayed. "Lord, thank you for bringing me here today. Thank you for allowing me the chance to see my kids. Please protect us from El Jefe and the cartel, who are in this house. El Jefe is an evil man. Please protect us from this fortress that lies on top of what feels like a pyramid with so many stairs. Please protect us from the forty or fifty heavily armed men, so they don't hurt us. Please, realize that we have only about one or two hours before they hurt us. Please, come with your heart and soul and rescue us. Please, send your two strongest angels with wings that will take us out of here, and may they strike this sinful ground, so it is no longer ever fertile. Be swift."

I prayed with the intention of prayer, but also, to let my team know it was time to strike and strike heavily, as I hoped the earpiece was working, and that my men could now hear all the intel I was conveying in my prayer. Our plan had to work.

I came out of the restroom. I hoped both God and my team heard my prayer. I really had no idea if the earpiece was working, but I had to have faith that it was. I was pretty confident that the pill GPS was working. They both had to be working.

"OK, please let me see my kids." I said.

"Yes, of course," El Jefe said. He walked me toward a separate part of the house. I kept thinking, "What the fuck? This house is huge." I thought about just how many lives were lost to drugs, human trafficking, prostitution, and whatever else the cartel did. I knew how much blood money had to be won to build this house.

We approached a door. For some reason, El Jefe kept me uncuffed. Maybe he thought I wasn't stupid enough to try to do something to him, since he had my kids, and he had that stupid little red button chained to his necklace. I wondered if it was real and if it would work.

I knew I had to remove it from him either way, as it would be the only way I could take my kids away from him as well as the only way to help prevent the Colombian army coming in to kill us all. "Before I do anything for you, I have to see my kids to make sure they're OK. Also, you have to promise me that you won't hurt my kids."

"Patience, Captain Williams, I will promise you that I will protect them if you do your mission for us, but remember, if you try anything stupid, my men have orders to slaughter your kids while you watch, and I haven't forgotten about your beautiful wife either," El Jefe said.

My first thought was to tackle him and kill him, but I knew I had to confirm that my kids were alive. I had to relay to my team that my kids and I were together and ready to be rescued.

"Come with me; I will bring you to your kids," El Jefe said.

I was baffled yet again by his story about my family. I was confused as to how I got in the middle of this crazy story. Seriously? I just wanted to see my kids at this time. We walked up a flight of stairs. My knees felt weak. I'd faced so many things in battle, but I'd always known my family was safe.

This was different than any war or challenge I'd faced in the past. Now my kids' lives were at stake. El Jefe opened the door slowly. I fell to my knees. I looked straight ahead, and my kids were lying down on a bed with their hands tied. Their mouths were gagged, and they were crying while their screams were muffled from their mouth gags.

The sight almost made me grab El Jefe's arm with the intention of bringing him down, so I could kill him. He threatened me by grabbing his red button.

I froze, as I knew if he was telling the truth, my kids and I would be shot to death execution-style. I yelled out to him, "Release my kids now, you motherfucker!"

El Jefe laughed and kicked me in the leg. "You release them!" El Jefe said. "Captain Williams, why don't you untie them yourself?"

I stood up with bouncy knees. I ran to both of them. I took off both of their gags, eye covers, and the ropes that bound them as I quickly as I could. I held them tight as I didn't want to let them go.

"Daddy, Daddy," Emma cried.

"Dad, you made it," Jaxon said in relief.

I hugged them both as tight as I could. I wished we were home. I wished we were anywhere except where I knew we were.

The reality hit me too quickly. I had no idea when the cavalry would come, so I had to figure out a plan.

I kept holding them tightly as tightly as I could, knowing that the next phase of the escape was going to be nearly impossible.

Both Emma and Jaxon had been beaten up badly. Jaxon's right eye was not visible under the bruising. Emma's wrists were red and irritated from trying to escape from her ropes. Seeing them in this state was my worst nightmare come true.

My body felt like it was dead. My brain kept trying to reprocess the reality of it all. My confusion reared its ugly head. I'd seen men tortured in war. I'd seen men tortured for information. But now it was my kids, and I prayed to God that we would make it out alive. We had to make it.

I pictured Natalie at home waiting for us. Seeing my kids alive and home again with our family all together was my only motivation left. We had to survive, and I had to get my kids home.

"Senor Williams, you have very beautiful kids. The only thing more beautiful is your wife's chest," El Jefe said.

"Fuck you, fucker, I am going to kill you!" I said

"No, no, no senor, stop dreaming. Gustavo, put on the video!" El Jefe said.

I went silent.

He put a smart phone in front of my eyes. To my dismay, he was showing a video of my wife at home in the front of the TV. She was on the phone talking and crying. The troubling thing was she had a red laser light on her chest. I knew immediately that El Jefe had someone at my house watching my wife. He was trying to intimidate me even more.

At first, I didn't know what to do. I didn't want my kids to see, as I knew at least Jaxon would realize what was going on with a laser on Natalie's chest. I tried to think about something fast. I then remembered that I had my earpiece on that was hopefully transmitting everything that was being said.

I started talking softly toward El Jefe and saying, "You can go fuck yourself. You might have a red laser dot on my wife's chest while she is in our home, but I guarantee you will never get to her. My next-door neighbor is a Sheriff's deputy and my other neighbor is a former US Army Special Forces sergeant. We always watch out for each other, and if they even recognize something suspicious I guarantee that they will protect my wife as they would their own family."

"Whatever, my men will kill your wife without a trace, and the first time they will know something happened is when they read about it in the newspaper. You see I have my best men watching over your wife to make sure you do what we need you to do for us," El Jefe said.

"I am sure you will not touch her because you need me! If you touch her or my kids I will never do anything, so you might as well kill us now!" I said.

I spoke softly to Emma and Jaxon. "My loves, I'm sorry this ever happened to you. I pray that you forgive me for what has happened. For now, you have to believe me that we are going to survive. We will make it home. You'll see your mother again. I promise you. We're together now on the highest floor of this house. We will stay in this room that is in the northwest corner of the house to stay safe. Whatever happens, know that angels will come and save us. They will come with such wrath and swiftness that you'll be home before you know it. We are ready to be home." I chose my words to calm my children and to alert our team that we were ready to be rescued.

I had to believe that my team could hear everything I was saying, as I had no other way to communicate with them, and I hoped they sent a team to help protect my wife. I had faith they would watch over her for me. For the first time in my life, my life depended on the help of others. It had always been the other way around for me.

33

THE LIGHT

"**S**eñor Williams, you have had enough time with your kids," said El Jefe. "Just remember how it feels to hold them. How it feels to look into their eyes. How it feels to know they are alive. You see, if you do not do what I need you to do, your wife will receive their heads in boxes. If you fuck up here, I will order them to kill her right away."

"Absolutely not! I'm not leaving my kids. Whatever you need me to do, I will do it, but I'm not leaving my kids until it's time for the mission."

"Listen, cabrón, I'm the boss here, not you," El Jefe said. "I will fucking kill you and your kids, you understand!"

"Kill us then, right now. Kill us. I'm with my kids, and I'll die with them in my arms. Go ahead!" I yelled.

"OK, OK, calm down. I will let you stay with your kids for the night. My people will make you a nice dinner, and we will start our business tomorrow morning. You'll have one of my men stay in this room with you to make sure you don't try anything stupid."

"OK, thank you. I'll do what you ask for my wife and our children," I said reluctantly.

"Dad we haven't eaten anything or drank anything for a long time. He is telling the truth that we can have something eat and drink finally," asked Emma.

I brought her close to me and I said, "Yes, my love, we are going to eat something for dinner and then we are going to go to sleep and wait to go home. I promise you.'

34

THE PICKUP

"I will have my private, Mexican chef make you my favorite meal that my Mexican mother used to make for us as kids. Captain Williams, I think you will find it familiar. I wonder if your mother ever made you chicken enchiladas?" El Jefe asked.

"Yes, yes, grandma always makes her chicken enchiladas for us as they are our favorite thing to eat," Emma yelled happily in her ignorant bliss of what El Jefe was really saying.

He had his private cook make us dinner. They brought us a dinner with chicken enchiladas, beans, rice and tortillas. Jaxon and Emma ate their entire plate within two minutes. In fact, they asked for a second plate, and they ate all of their second plate as well. They hadn't eaten in nearly two days.

I also ate some, but I didn't want to eat too much, which might cause me to be bogged down during a rescue. I hated to admit it, but the food was really good. It was the same as my mother's recipe, which I hated to assume but was likely passed onto her from her Mexican mother.

I was just so pleased to see Jaxon and Emma eat. Jaxon joked that he felt like it was our last meal. He was just trying to make light of the situation, but I told them that they would be home eating their mother's lasagna before they knew it.

El Jefe's men left us alone in the bedroom with one of his men in the room with us. I knew this was the opportunity we needed. I just hoped my earpiece was still working and that my team could hear what was happening. Otherwise I knew that a rescue would be more challenging.

Nightfall came. It was about nine o'clock in the evening. We all slept in the same bed as I held my kids tightly. I caressed them so tightly that I wondered if they were able to breathe well.

With the nightfall came an eerie silence. I had no idea what to expect. I didn't know what morning would bring. I just knew that I had to stay close to my kids in case my team was planning a night attack. It could happen at any minute. I knew that.

My kids fell asleep in my arms. They also held me tighter than they ever had in my life. My daughter's wrists were so red from trying to escape, and my son's face was so badly beaten from the assholes that I couldn't wait to kill them all myself.

How could any man hit a child? How could these men do this to my kids? They would all pay for their wrongdoings.

I wished I could have given them a bath like when they were little kids. They were filthy from not bathing, being beaten, and dragged to South America where they had never been.

I couldn't fall asleep, as I knew I couldn't trust the cartel, and I knew that at any moment we might be forced into action. I had to be ready to be saved at any moment.

There was a strange man sitting in our room. He was one of El Jefe's men and the only man watching us for the night. He was armed with a sidearm and an MP-5 automatic weapon. He also had a bulletproof vest on him. Honestly, he looked like a chump that my son could take to the ground even on a bad day with one of his arms tied behind his back.

My kids stayed peacefully asleep. They said they had not slept since they were captured. They had not rested. After they ate dinner, they were pretty much ready to pass out from exhaustion.

I could only imagine the impact their kidnapping had on them. I was used to war. I was used to pain. I was used to death. To them, violence was only what they had watched on TV or in the movies. I was glad that they were able to rest, as I was sure they felt comfort knowing I was next to them.

I started drifting off myself. I tried to fight the urge to fall asleep even though it was so challenging. I had to stay awake and protect my kids. I also didn't want to fall asleep and face my nightmares and further confusion. My body was so tired from the last twenty-four hours of running and trying to find them. I didn't want to lose them again.

I could hear a sound in the sky. It was a quiet sound, but a familiar sound to me. It sounded as the unmanned drone was making rounds to gather intel for my men. I knew they were close. I knew we didn't have the usual Seal Team Six ability to formulate a plan with our best resources, but I had faith in my men and my brother that we would be going home soon.

35

THE KNOCK

There was a knock on the door. My eyes opened wide. I didn't know what to expect. I woke up my kids quietly.

We had always practiced quiet wake-ups in the past when they would wake up and be immediately aware. We practiced waking up before going to sleep. This way their brains could immediately understand what to expect when they woke up. I always tried to train them in some ways for whatever could happen in life.

Jaxon and Emma were now awake. The man in our room asked who it was in Spanish.

"Café, señor?" the strange voice asked. The man opened the door slowly. There was a man holding a tray.

I didn't recognize him at first, but I recognized the boots under his butler-type uniform. I knew this was it.

The tray was put down. El Jefe's man on watch was not too smart. I think he wanted only to go to sleep. I don't think he knew who I was or what could happen. He must have assumed we were just another kidnapping. I couldn't wait to kill him.

El Jefe's man took the carafe of coffee and poured a cup. As the coffee filled the cup, a knife came out of nowhere and slit the man's throat. I had confirmation that my team was here.

"Captain, good to see you, sir," Loco said. "SEAL Team Six and US Rangers are here to take you and your kids home."

I was so happy to see him. My brothers were here to save my family and me.

"Captain, we have two stealth birds on loan, and they are seven clicks away, waiting for my order to blaze this fucking place. I've taken out three men already, and our intel on from the drone shows that this crazy fucker has about forty to fifty men on site. We have eight men, two McMillan Mk 15 .50 cals with glass and special tips and the men that know how to use them, a bunch of explosives, and two stealth birds with enough firepower to fry a few miles of this fucker's ass. Don't ask how, but he does appear to have an Apache helicopter that may or may not have military capacity, as it looks. We have no idea if it works. Anyhow, sir, we will get you home and get home safely."

"Outstanding. Loco, from the first heard bullet, I am certain the cartel's leader will notify the Colombian army, so we have to act quickly. I don't have to explain, but the Colombian army is owned by the South American cartel. I don't know if he was telling the truth, but the cartel leader said he can have the army here within seven minutes with full air and land support," I said.

"Copy that Sir, I will notify our team that we must act quickly to get out a dodge in seven Mikes as I don't think we have enough manpower to take on an army. Same shit, different day, Cap'n," Loco said confidently.

"Cap'n, I brought you your Sig sidearm, two grenades, and now you have this fucker's MP-5," Loco said. "Here's your audio. We are on channel seven. We have to move. Can you believe these fuckers let me walk right up here, pendijos, right?"

"I can," I said.

"We had one sheet on intel that the butlers here wore these fucking cheesy outfits. I back packed right into the yard, dumped my parachute, and walked right into the kitchen. Talk about some crazy stealthy shit, right, sir?

"God blessed me by being Mexican-American, sir, just to be here today to help you; I'm going to walk you guys right into the kitchen. I'll say that I'll be making you something for dinner. Once we get into the kitchen, I'm going to order the raid. We think El Jefe must be staying upstairs, so we'll try to get low with the ability to get out a dodge. We will start our timers at first heard shot, so we can blaze out of here within seven Mikes."

We rushed down the stairs. I kept my sidearm and MP-5 hidden under my jacket. We passed two men in the hallway. They approached us after we passed them. Without hesitation, Loco shot them both. He had a suppressor on his sidearm, which helped conceal the sound.

We kept walking. We approached the stairs. There were four men at the bottom. They looked at Loco. Loco told them that El Jefe ordered him to make us dinner. We kept walking. We made it into the kitchen. There wasn't anybody in the kitchen except us.

I felt a quite calm at this time, as I gained a sense that we were going to make it. My kids seemed scared but immune, at this point, to what was happening. I guess it was my line of work—what they'd seen already during the kidnapping, TV, movies, or all of the above.

Loco spoke into a microphone hidden on his lapel, "Listo por pisto." His words meant we were "ready for drinking alcohol." It seemed fitting for the occasion at hand.

Loco turned to me. "Cap'n, you remember when the stealth birds came in to help us in Iran? We knew they were coming, and we still didn't hear them. Badass stealth shit. I still remember staring at them and saying, what the fuck is that?"

We walked out of the house. It was pitch-dark outside. You could hear the sounds of crickets everywhere, as well as chickens and other animals moving around the compound. Their sounds actually helped us to cover our movements in the night.

Loco put on his night-vision goggles. I wished I had a pair. I couldn't see anything in the darkness except the lights from the house. I was just holding onto the back of Loco's pack, Jaxon had my other hand, and Emma had Jaxon's hand. We made our way through the pitch-black darkness. I prayed that my head would hold straight.

36

THE FIGHT

I heard a hum in the background. I knew what it was. It was our stealth helicopters coming to our rescue!

To the untrained ear, the hum sounded like an electric fan blowing in the still of the night. You couldn't hear an engine sound, just the sound of a fan in the background.

I could hear El Jefe's men talking in the distance. They were asking what the sound was and where it was coming from. One of the men said it must be one of El Jefe's women coming to visit. His men were laughing in the background with complete ignorance of what was about to happen to them. Their ignorance was bliss.

I heard the hiss approaching. As a seal, you always knew the sound of a missile coming. It grew louder and louder, and then it happened. BOOM! Our timers started in unison. We had seven Mikes to get out and survive.

The missile took out most of El Jefe's house. All you could hear was screaming followed by more and more explosions. It was the perfect strike to take out the asshole's compound.

Even though we were only about sixty meters away, we were not injured. The sound was deafening. The impact rocked us to our knees, and I felt the pressure from impact in my bones. Our ears were ringing from the noise, which made it difficult to hear anything aside from the loud ringing. We all tried our best to keep our feet. I felt concussed. I lost my bearings for a few seconds. Please God keep my head straight.

A tremendous firefight started. It lit up the night in such a way to make it appear as day. I could see some of my seal brothers firing their assault rifles in the distance. As always, their shots were calculated and precise.

Loco took us to the rendezvous spot. He kept throwing red smoke screens in order to provide us with a shield of smoke for cover. I had to trust his navigation, as he was the only one with night goggles. He led us through the pitch-black darkness.

We were running for our lives. We kept running away from the destroyed house and where the firefight was happening. I had no idea how many men El Jefe had, but they kept coming from all angles. Four black SUVs approached the house. I didn't know if they were our men or El Jefe's.

I could see at least ten men exiting the SUVs and heading toward the remains of the house. The men ran with assault rifles blazing and green lasers pointing everywhere. Bullets flew with total random abandonment throughout the combine. It was almost as they didn't care if they hit their own men as they shot at anything that moved.

It was El Jefe's men who came out of the SUVs. I assumed they were looking for El Jefe and us—or just El Jefe.

The firefight became more intense, and I knew my brothers were outnumbered at least four to one. My first instinct was to join the fight to help them, but I knew I had to keep my kids safe. We had to make it to the rendez-vous point. If we didn't make it to the rendezvous point, I knew we would not make it home alive. I held Jaxon and Emma's hands so tightly I must have cut off their circulation.

"Cap'n, we need to hunker down here and wait for our ride. They are circling with return fire on El Jefe's men, so we can make a clear run for our ride," Loco said.

"OK, let's take cover and make sure we can see 360 degrees, so we are not attacked blindly," I said.

I could see one of the stealth helicopters landing about thirty meters away from us. My heart was pounding out of my chest. My head pounded. I became confused. I wasn't scared, but I was not myself. My head disease, whatever it was, picked a bad time to present itself once again. I could hear Loco yelling to me. He said the words, "move out, move out!"

I stood up low and started running toward the helicop-ter. I heard Loco once again. His words were clear to me then and now. He shouted, "grab the kids, grab the kids!"

Fuck, fuck, fuck. My confusion made me hesitate and forget to grab my kids. Fuck, I had only ran about 10 yards ahead, so I rapidly ran back to grab Emma and Jaxon.

I picked up Emma to run toward the helicopter.

Emma's face was blank and pale. My baby girl was so scared. We were all scared. She was crying without making a noise. She was terrified, as was Jaxon at this point.

I was used to being in battle, but my poor kids had no concept of what it was really like. They had no idea what odds we faced in trying to escape from this crazy fuckers combine. I was so angry at myself for forgetting them for a split second. How could my mind play tricks on me at the worst time of my life with my kids' lives on the line?

We started on a mad dash toward the helicopter. There was intense firing toward the helicopter from El Jefe's men. The firefight exchange was blinding in the night's black darkness. Loco returned fire as he was running backwards toward our ride.

"Williams, this one is for you and killing my only son!" El Jefe yelled in the distance. In a split second, I caught El Jefe's image in the background as he fired his assault rifle toward us.

I turned to put my back toward the shooting. Before I knew what happened, I felt his bullet pierce me in my right back flank of my abdomen. Emma was in my arms. I couldn't stand, but I couldn't fall, as I was holding my precious cargo, my little princess.

I had to keep running toward the helicopter, even though I felt immense pain in my abdomen. I knew I had been hit. I could feel blood leaving my body while it gushed out onto my clothes and it ran down my legs. Anger enraged my body.

I felt weakness setting into my body, but I controlled it with my mind. I had to get my kids onto the helicopter. Once they were in the helicopter, I knew they would be safe.

We made it to the helicopter. I threw Emma into the stealth bird. Jaxon, Loco, and I then jumped in also. Loco kept firing toward El Jefe's men as we loaded.

We could hear the bullets hitting the sides of the helicopter. We made it inside, but we were still not safe. The helicopter door closed. The stealth bird started rising despite taking on heavy fire. We made it. We made it! So I thought to myself.

I looked down at Jaxon. He was crying uncontrollably. At first, I thought he was crying from the entire fiasco and battle that was going on around us. I didn't blame him for crying in such a chaotic moment of his life.

He was looking at Emma. In a flash of a second, I looked down at my baby girl. She wasn't breathing. She was covered with dark red blood. At first, I thought it was my blood, and that she had passed out from the shock of the event. I felt for her carotid pulse. I didn't feel anything. I put my ear to her chest. I couldn't hear or feel anything moving. I froze in complete fear and loss of hope. I was in a blackened disbelief.

The assault rifle bullet had gone through my abdomen and into my baby girl's left abdomen. I started CPR immediately. I did chest compressions then gave her breaths. I rechecked her pulse. Nothing. I repeated the process. I could feel her little ribs breaking from my chest compressions.

More breaths. No reaction. This couldn't be happening. We were also still in a heavy firefight. My little girl could not die. She just could not die.

I reached for the defibrillator in the helicopters ceiling, as I best could with our helicopter trying to maneuver away from the firefight. The G forces were hard to overcome with the lift. I turned the defibrillator on as we lifted higher into the air. I put the pads and gel on Emma's chest. My tears flooded my hands and her tiny chest. I gave her two more breaths.

The automated defibrillator's voice was surreal and senseless to the gravity of the situation. It said, "Charge… ready…shock!"

I checked her carotid pulse. Nothing.

Two more breaths with the firing from the cartel's men becoming heavier and heavier than it was when we boarded the helicopter.

I had to keep trying to rescue my little girl.

"Charge…ready…shock! the defibrillator shouted.

No carotid pulse.

Two more breaths.

The amount of her blood loss seemed to be equal to the amount of blood from five men. Images flashed in my head of seeing her being born, the first time I held her, the first time I kissed her, the first time she cried, the first time she laughed, the first time she walked, the first time she swam, and the first time she told me she loved me more than anything in the world. I was breathless. Everything went black. I was in the dreaded black zone.

"Charge…ready…shock! the defibrillator shouted.

I prayed. I checked. My little girl had a weak, but viable, carotid pulse. My little angel was gone, but now I had her back and I wouldn't lose her again.

Jaxon and I held her in our arms tightly. I kept checking her pulse and listening for breath sounds. I refused to believe what had just happened to my little girl. Her pulse remained and she was breathing, but I knew we had to get her to a hospital quickly.

All I could do was picture Emma competing with Jaxon in everything. She always acted tougher than her age. I guess most little sisters likely have to be tough when they have an older brother. Emma's biggest strength was her loyalty to her brother and mother. She struggled sometimes warming up to me. I couldn't blame her as I blamed it mostly on the fact that I was gone for more than half her life. Her school counselor mentioned that my absence might cause her to be angry with me, which might cause her to be angry in general. I didn't know what to do aside from loving her when I was away and home.

Now, more than ever, I prayed to God to take care of my baby girl. She didn't deserve this. She deserved to be home in her bed. She deserved to be home with her family. She deserved so much more. I prayed to God that he would take my life in replacement for her precious and innocent life. She was my baby girl, and she hadn't had a chance to live her life. Time stood still in complete blackness while our helicopter kept taking on heavy fire. Her breaths were weak and very labored. I placed the oxygen mask on her in order to provide her with much needed oxygen. I had faith and the will to get us out of there alive.

37

THUNDER DOWN

"**E**leven, Eleven, this is Thunder," said the helicopter pilot of helicopter one into the radio. "We have secured our pickup, and we are heading out. We have one civilian severely injured. We need immediate medical attention upon arrival. We are still in heavy gunfight, Over."

"Thunder, Thunder, you are clear for rapid return," said the voice—somewhere close, I hoped. "We will have medics ready on arrival for civilian care. Over."

"Holy shit, we are taking air fire, air fire," the pilot said. I could hear loud beeping in background. "Shit, someone is on our tail."

"What the fuck is that?" I said loudly.

"Sir, it looks like an Apache helicopter, where the fuck did it come from, who the fuck is this guy? I have to face him, sir. We won't be able to outrun his range if he has missiles. Lightning, Lightning, this is Thunder Taking on air fire from Apache attack helicopter. Need assist ASAP."

Our helicopter made a hard turn. A missile from the Apache helicopter flew right by us. Thunder then went vertical trying to make a getaway. The G forces from the vertical take off trapped us down to our seats. I struggled to hold the oxygen mask on Emma, but I had to be by her side.

We couldn't lose the Apache, as it seemed the pilot had some experience. "Lightning, where are you, we can't shake this fucker, over," the pilot said frantically.

"One Mike until engagement," said the pilot of Lightning.

We made another hard turn and then we were facing the Apache head-on. Before the pilot could evade, I could see a missile coming right at us. We were hit at the top edge of the tail body by one of the missiles, the helicopter destabilized for a moment, but it held together somehow. Black smoke filled the helicopter's cabin.

The missile likely grazed the top edge without having major body damage. I could see smoke and fire coming off the edge of our helicopter.

Time stood still once again in complete darkness. My baby girl's body was still in my arms. For once in my life and career, I didn't know if we were going to make it out of this horrible situation. She was still barely breathing.

We could hear bullets hitting our helicopter. We were still under fire. We could not outrun the firepower of the Apache. If Jaxon were not with me, I would have accepted the inevitable, which was death. I refused to lose my son and daughter on the same day by the same asshole who had corrupted the world. I refused to lose.

"Thunder, Thunder," said the pilot of the second stealth helicopter. "We are twenty seconds away. We will engage. Over."

"Surface to air, surface to air! Fucking shit," said our pilot. "We are hit with a missile strike! Fuck! Mayday, Mayday. We've been hit. We're going down for a hard landing, brace yourselves!"

Our helicopter was crippled this time. I could feel how unstable it was, and I could smell the burning fuel this time. This was it. I could feel us going down to the ground quickly.

Fuck! We were going down hard. I held Emma and Jaxon as tight as I could. I wasn't sure if we would survive the impact. We had only a few seconds before we'd hit. I started talking to Jaxon in my most calm voice. He was shivering from fright, begging God not to let us die, and crying hysterically while I held him. Emma was breathing, but unresponsive.

I started singing in his ear one of our kids' lullabies. What had to be only seconds seemed like our lifetime at this insane moment. I sang as best as I could to help calm them down.

We hit and hit hard. I couldn't move for a few seconds. I thought I was paralyzed. I could hear the sounds of bullets all around us. I woke up out of my daze. I looked over to Jaxon. He had passed out. Our stealth helicopter separated into several pieces, and we were exposed to the elements including El Jefe's men who were now getting closer to us.

"Jaxon, Jaxon, wake up, wake up!" I kept yelling at him. I started to get up, as I realized that we went down right in the middle of El Jefe's compound yard. I knew we had only a few seconds. "Jaxon! Get up! Get up, son!" I kept yelling. He finally responded.

"Eleven, Eleven. Helicopter down. Thunder down, Thunder down," Lightning's helicopter pilot said.

Jaxon awakened. He was alert, thank God. I gave Emma to Jaxon to hold. Our pilot did not survive the impact. The copilot was just coming out of being knocked out. Loco was still passed out, but he was alive.

I grabbed the pilot's helmet, so I could use his radio. "Eleven, this is Captain Williams in downed Thunder. We are OK. One pilot did not survive. We will scatter for pickup. Over."

"Roger that Sir, Lightning coming in hot for ground sweep, flare when at 100 meters out, over," said the pilot of Lightning.

I couldn't wake up Loco. "Loco, bro, we have to go. Wake up, wake up now!" I kept yelling.

"Loco, you are a fucking frogman, get the fuck up!" Fuck! I knew I would have to carry him out as he was knocked out unconscious. He was still breathing, and I could feel a strong pulse. I could not leave my brother behind after he had saved my life.

"Jaxon, you'll have to carry Emma out while I carry Loco, OK? I'm not going to leave my baby here!" I exclaimed.

I could hear men approaching while they were firing their assault rifles at us. Luckily, they were still out of range, but they were closing in fast. I grabbed the MP5, so we could make a run for it.

I started firing a few shots as cover fire as we started to make our way out of the helicopter zone. El Jefe's men were now close enough to us, so I started taking motherfuckers out left and right. My clip ran out, and I reloaded, knowing that I would have to preserve ammo to make a run for it. It bought us a little time until Lightning came to make it rain.

I picked up Loco. He was heavy, like a gorilla on steroids. Jaxon held Emma. We had to abandon the oxygen that helped fill her lungs with life. She was pale and barely alive. We got out with the pilot and made a run for it. Lightning kept sending ground fire around us to keep men from coming in on us.

We made it out about 100 meters from the crashed helicopter, and I pulled the flare to let Lightning know we were clear from their upcoming light show. It lit up the sky then Lightning lit up what was left of El Jefe's compound and men. The boom of their firepower and the smoke from the fires were both overwhelming. The blast force knocked us to the ground.

Emma flew from Jaxon's arms. She was lifeless lying next to a rock. I ran to pick her up again. She wasn't breathing. She wasn't responding. She had no color to her skin. I lost it. This was a disaster, and I couldn't do anything to make it better at the moment.

A few seconds later, Lightning came toward us with a hard landing for themselves to help ensure we could get out of there in a hurry, as the Apache was still a threat. It had disappeared for a couple of minutes after we went down, but I could hear it coming toward us from a distance.

The Apache must have retreated to reload its weaponry or something, as I was not sure why it left for a few minutes. I didn't care as its temporary disappearance allowed us to stay alive. Emma's pulse was barely present.

I knew we were fighting for all of our lives. I looked at my timer. Five minutes had passed. It seemed like an eternity. I knew we only had another minute or two to try to evade the possible attack of the Colombian army if what El Jefe said was true.

38

HEAD TO HEAD

We quickly loaded into Lightning. When I threw Loco into the helicopter, he woke up frantically. "What the fuck? Where are we? What the fuck?" he yelled.

"Loco, you're OK. Our helicopter went down, but we made it out and now we're on Lightning.

"Buckle up, men," said our new pilot. "We have to get the fuck out of here before that Apache gets on us, or we will never make it out of here. Captain Williams we are showing five jets on radar that are approaching from our north and two jets approaching from our west. Both sets of jets are about three minutes away from us, Sir, we have to move and move fast, as we don't want to establish contact!"

We took off, and almost immediately we took on heavy fire from the Apache. Our pilot tried to outrun the Apache, as we were now down to one attack helicopter.

"Fuck, I can't outrun that son of a bitch! Captain, I'm afraid we'll have to fight our way out of here, sir! We have a Blackhawk nearby, but we didn't have time to load it up with its weapons. It's only for picking up the terrorist when we've cleared the area. They tried to come in with only assault rifle support, but they were no match for the surface-to-air missiles. We took all of the surface-to-air out, but this crazy son of bitch has a fucking Apache helicopter."

I had to agree with the pilot, even though I just wanted to get my kids to safety. I knew I couldn't leave our men, including my brother, behind, as they would not survive a second-wave attack from El Jefe's men or from the Colombian army. It appeared as El Jefe was telling the truth about the Colombian military, as we were sure they were in transport from outside the compound including their air support from the jets approaching.

"Roger that, I said. "Go head-to-head. I trust you, and I know you can take out that piece of shit!" I yelled. The pilot made a hard turn and began his transition toward the Apache helicopter. We were in another dogfight. I just prayed that we would win this one.

We were heading straight toward the Apache. El Jefe's Apache engaged with heavy gunfire. We fought back with heavy artillery.

Our guns went dead. I thought we ran out of ammo or our guns jammed. Before I knew what happened, we were hit with the Apache's gunfire to our weapons system. "Fuck, fuck," said the pilot. "Our missiles and guns are dead. We can't return fire. The Apache's gunfire must have taken out our main firing systems. We'll have to retreat!"

Fuck, I had a feeling of impending doom in my heart that felt as my heart was going to explode. I had to decide between my kids' lives and the lives of my brother and our men. Emma appeared dead in Jaxon's arms. Jaxon was crying uncontrollably. Emma's bleeding stopped, as she had no more blood to bleed. I looked to heaven to ask for God's help. I wanted to give up my own life for my kids, my brother, and our men. We had no backup. We had no other way. I prayed for an answer.

"Bullshit, we are not leaving our men behind!" I yelled. "Roll back around! We have to take the Apache out, or they won't survive."

"Sir, we have no weapons. We have nothing we can do. If we go back for them now, we will be shot down for sure and then we will all be killed. I have to get you out of here. We will do our best to come back for them after we drop you off," said the pilot.

"Fuck that! If we leave them now, they will all be killed. There is no time to head out and come back. They are sitting ducks with limited ammo and no retreat zone," I said.

I kept thinking to myself. I kept praying.

I knew we were fucked if we didn't try to take the Apache out. I knew it was our only option of surviving and making sure we all survived, including my brother and our men who had fought hard on the ground. They had placed their lives on the line for my family and me. I knew Jaxon would understand. I knew the Colombian's Air Force jets were now about one minute away and then we would be really fucked!

"Eleven, Eleven," said the pilot. "Lightning's weaponry is down. We are taking on heavy air fire. We need QRF (Quick Reaction Force) developed and activated. Repeat we need QRF!"

I knew there was no QRF. Even if we were lucky, a QRF team would take several hours to be activated and several hours to reach us. I knew we were all about to die.

"Ask the general to activate the Air Force's drone. It should be able to provide some gunfire support for our men. Hurry, get that fucking drone here right away!" I exclaimed.

"Gator, Gator, Activate the bat (drone)! Activate the bat! We need gun support for hot spot!" the pilot shouted.

"Lightning, Bat in route, repeat, Bat in route, 15 mikes," said Gator (forward base).

"Fuck that, this will be over in two mikes! Get that fucking drone moving!" I said.

The cartel's gunfire was picking up in the background. I could see the gunfight fire exchange. Our men were trying to get away as the cartel's men outnumbered them. I felt my abdominal pain tearing my insides out. I couldn't let pain weaken me now at our last minute of hope. My bleeding intensified. I felt faint as I kept losing more and more blood.

I turned to my Senior Chief Special Warfare Operator. We both looked hopeless. Jaxon was crying feverishly. Emma lost her pulse and her chest was no longer moving up and down. We had no more time or way out.

"Loco, hand me the McMillan! When we get on angle with them, I'll have to take the Apache out with the McMillan .50-cal as we have no other fucking options," I said.

"Gator, we have to utilize our onboard assault rifle to try to take out what looks like an Apache helicopter," the pilot said.

"Lightning, the men on the ground are OK," Gator said on the radio. "Take out that cartel motherfucker and light up their fucking place. Lightning, men on ground will flare you where they are so you can make a roundabout, over."

"Captain," said the pilot. "I'm going to swing a hard right with an angle to their backside. Fire as many shots at their rear as you can. It should take out their rotatory or fuel tanks."

I gave Emma to Jaxon. Her body was peaceful, as if she was sound asleep in her bed at home. I asked Loco to start CPR on Emma, as he couldn't support the long-range assault rifle. I found that in the last 24 hours I had to make the hardest decisions in my life. Now I had to decide between giving my little girl breaths of life or trying to save all of our lives by taking out the Apache helicopter with the rifle. God help us, as I had to try to save all of our lives. If I gave CPR to Emma now, the Apache would shoot us down for certain. Then we would all be dead. Fuck, I had to take out the Apache.

I opened the helicopter's window hatch. We made the attack angle. I took aim. We loaded special exploding tips to the McMillan .50-cal to act as armor piercing ammunition that could take out the Apache's important workings.

I could see El Jefe in front seat of the helicopter with a pilot. He was close enough that I could see his face. He was actually blowing me a kiss. He was no longer firing back. He must have been preparing to lock on us with a missile. Time stood still. My heart stopped. I was about to pass out from lack of circulatory blood.

I wasn't going down to my knees although this was misery and torture for me. I had to kill him. My thoughts were tangled in some fucked up way, as I knew he was my mother's brother. Even if he was my mother's brother and my uncle, I didn't care as his blood brought us there and my little girl was dying or dead because of him. This fucking asshole was going down.

"Here comes hell in a special package from the men and women of the United States of America, you asshole! All the way from Phoenix, Arizona!" I yelled loud and proud.

I prayed to God. I knew if this was my last day on earth, and if He was calling me up to heaven that I'd rather die in a pile of my own empty brass. It was our only chance of survival.

I rolled the bolt on my first load, and I fired. It hit the Apache and the specialized, exploding tips detonated on impact. I reloaded and rolled the fucking bolt two more times for a total of three fired shots with the McMillan. The special tips all detonated on impact with the Apache. A fireblast followed the last bullet's impact.

"Missile lock, missile lock, prepare for hit, prepare for hit!" our pilot yelled.

I could see the Apache's missile trail lighting up the pitch-dark sky. I jumped on Jaxon and Emma in some effort to protect them from the missile's deadly strike. Images of Natalie shined in my mind as I prayed. She was smiling.

I spoke out loud.

"Natalie I love you. Jaxon I love you. Emma I love you," our end of time was here.

"Hard right, hard right!" our pilot yelled as he maneuvered our helicopter.

"Sir, the missile missed us. It fucking missed!" he yelled again.

I could see the missile's trail flare right by us. I couldn't breathe. My chest tightened. I held Jaxon and Emma close.

I looked out the helicopter's window. I didn't know what to expect. The three hits had a delayed reaction, but they finally caused the Apache to explode. The explosion was like the sun bursting in dark, mid air. It started smoking and spinning. It spiraled down violently to the ground.

"Tell Elena I love her. I'm sorry, I'm sorry," El Jefe said as his Apache went down.

Somehow El Jefe jumped on our frequency to say his last words. I didn't care.

"Go to hell, you motherfucker!" I said. We swung around and confirmed the Apache went down and exploded. El Jefe was killed. The leader of the South American and Mexican cartels was dead. I felt an immense desire to jump out of the helicopter to confirm his death and chop his fucking head off as he threatened to me.

I looked back at the Apache crash site again. A wild fire broke out on the ground where it crashed. I didn't see any signs of El Jefe getting out of the Apache. He had to be dead. His evil reign had to be over.

I could barely breathe. My chest kept tightening and my arm started to go numb. I knew I was in bad shape from the gunshot wound.

A green flare lit up the sky. It was my men. It was a view I had seen many times in battle, and this time it meant more to me than ever.

They were about two clicks away from the house. Our pilot prepared our pass. We had one bomb left on our bird. It was for groundbreaking and groundbreaking only. They called it the Big Boy, as it would pound the ground and kill anything within a five hundred meter radius. I hoped that it would work, so we could send an even bigger message. A message to say the cartels' days were over. It was what we should have done years ago with Operation Sol.

We flew toward the green flare. As we approached the flare, I could see my men and my brother. The Blackhawk helicopter was also landing to help carry all the men back to safety.

My brother survived. We hit the ground hard yet again. I opened the door. "Bro, you made it. I love you, brother," I said.

"Ryan, you came back for us, you crazy fucker," he said. "Next time get yourself safe, brother, we can take care of ourselves" Then he saw that Emma was pale and hanging on to her life by a thread. "Oh my God, Ryan, I'm so sorry."

We held each other tightly. I couldn't help but wonder what the hell we were doing there. How did this happen? I held Emma and Jaxon tightly. I was never going to let them go. Tears flowed down my face.

"Here you go, fuckers, eat some good old-fashioned American metal blast," our pilot said.

The Big Boy bomb dropped onto the remains of the cartel's compound. There was an enormous explosion. We were at a safe distance with all of my brothers loaded in our stealth bird and a Blackhawk. I just hoped the bomb took out all the cartel's men.

As we climbed and began our escape, our helicopter's alarm started sounding, "Beepppppp!"

"Fuck, we are being engaged by their military's jets! They have us in a missile lock," our helicopter pilot shouted.

"Este es el comandante Pérez del Fuerza Aerea Colombiano. Te ordeno que aterrice de inmediato o que te destruiré. Me encerré en usted para el fuego de misiles inmediata." the Colombian pilot said in Spanish. *Translation: This is Commander Perez from the Colombian Air Force. I order you to land immediately or we will destroy you. I am locked onto you for immediate missile fire.*

"Fuck, we are locked on Captain Williams. We must land or be killed!" our pilot exclaimed.

We were trapped. We were already dead either way. We hovered. I looked at Jaxon. He was in a dead fright. I looked at Emma. She needed whatever little life I had left to breathe back air into her dead lungs.

The Colombian pilot repeated his statement with urgency.

I looked at Emma once again. I started CPR. Ten chest compressions. Two breathes. Nothing.

Ten chest compressions, two breathes. Nothing. Repeat again. Nothing.

Our helicopter's alarm kept sounding.

"Repito, repito! Este es el comandante Pérez del Fuerza Aerea Colombiano. Te ordeno que aterrice de inmediato o que te destruiré. Me encerré en usted para el fuego de misiles inmediata. Tienes cinco segundos para cumplir!" the

Colombian pilot said in Spanish. *Translation: Repeat. Repeat. This is Commander Perez from the Colombian Air Force. I order you to land immediately or we will destroy you. I am locked onto you for immediate missile fire. You have five seconds to comply.*

Time stood still. I closed my eyes for the first time.

"Uno, dos, tres, cuatro…" Commander Perez started his death countdown. He voice had complete resolve.

I kept giving Emma CPR. She wasn't responding. I would give her CPR until my own last breath. I knew we were about to be shot down by the Colombian jet. We had no way out. There was not QRF this time. We reached the end yet again in just a few minutes. I accepted it. I could hold my two kids and my brothers until the end.

"Cinco…misil viniendo su manera," Commander Perez gave his last warning that his jet's missile was about to be fired.

I felt my soul falling into an abysses blackness void of space and time. My CPR wasn't working on Emma.

"Commander Perez, this is Lieutenant Colonel, Nathan Jones, of the United States Air Force, Florida Fighter Wing. I am leading five, United States F-22 Raptors, and we are also engaged on your two outdated jets. It seems that you do not have your government's authority to be engaged with our men at this time and that you are breaking your country's laws and international law by engaging with our men. We have your president's authority as well as our commander in chief's authority to engage. Do you wish to engage Commander Perez? We'd be happy to let you go, so you can assume your training exercise for the day," Lieutenant Colonel Jones stated factually.

"Colonel Jones, I don't see you on my radar. Nice try asshole. We are locked for missile strike!" Commander Perez stated.

"Commander Perez, I am right on your six. Your outdated radar can't pick up our Raptor nor can anyone else's radar. If you continue to engage our men, you and your men will be killed. I guarantee it. This is your last warning, sir!" Lieutenant Colonel Jones stated sternly.

"Colonel Jones, you do not have authority or jurisdiction here in Colombia. I repeat to you to abandon your unauthorized mission before we engage. I have your men on missile lock. They are about to be killed if you do not disengage! This is your last warning!" Commander Perez stated.

"Senior Perez, do you see that red flashing light at your twelve?" Lieutenant Colonel Jones asked.

"Yes, that is my missile lock on your men!" Commander Perez shouted.

"Do you see it now? Lieutenant Colonel Jones asked.

"What the fuck, it disappeared?" Commander Perez asked.

"Commander Perez, our Raptor has locked your jet's weapon systems. You are at my twelve with five seconds to disengage or I will have you and your men killed. I can guaran-fucking-tee it! Uno, dos, tres, cuatro…" Lieutenant Colonel Jones counted in Spanish.

"Fuck you Americano. We are out!" Commander Perez said desperately as the Colombian Air Force jets flew away.

"Hoorah!" Loco shouted as he heard the communication.

I gave Emma another breath. I looked at her. She opened her eyes. Tears formed against her dry eyeballs.

Her chest expanded as she coughed out blood. She was alive! Barely alive. I kissed her forehead without letting go of my little girl.

The pilot passed me his headset, so I could communicate with Lieutenant Colonel Jones.

"Captain Williams, you hold your family tight, Sir, we will be escorting you to our nearest military base. Sir, we have two options at this time. First, we land at our military base outside Bogota. We have you and your men board a C-130J-30 that has medical care capacity and a long range. We then fly you directly to Houston, Texas where Emma can be transported to the Texas Children's hospital for immediate care. Or second, we land at our military base outside Bogota, and we have Emma transported to their children's hospital in Bogota. Sir, I will tell you that we prefer option one even with Emma being unstable, as we can't guarantee your safety in a Colombian hospital especially after word gets out that you killed El Jefe," Lieutenant Colonel Jones stated.

I looked at Emma. She was still smiling at me as blood trickled out of her mouth and abdominal wound. It was if she had no doubt that we would make it out of there. Her pale body needed blood. I knew what was at stake. I knew I also was on my last few breaths.

"Sir, will the C-130 have ability to provide my daughter with fluids and blood. She needs blood now more than anything, and she may need surgery immediately," I said.

"Yes sir, the C-130 is equipped with a full service operating room. There is a flight surgeon on board from the United States Air Force reserve that is trauma surgeon who is already aware of the critical condition that Emma is in at the moment," Lieutenant Colonel Jones stated.

"Ok, we will plan to board the C-130 and head to Texas immediately," I said.

"Roger that, we will also provide air escort for your ride to Texas. We are able to refuel in the air," Lieutenant Colonel Jones said.

We flew back to an American military base outside of Bogota, Colombia. The helicopter ride was silent as we pierced the dark night sky with just the wisp of our silent bird in the air. The F-22s stayed by our side. They were such a welcome sight. I wondered how the Raptor jets got there. The president must have had them sent to our aid. For once in my life, I was at a complete loss for words. My emotions were so depressed by what had happened to my little girl. I couldn't stop the feeling that I had to cry. I felt weak. My body wanted to pass out. My mind had had enough. I had to remain strong for my family and men. Although at my weakest physical state, I finally had hope that we were going to get my kids home safely.

We all boarded the C-130J-30 airlifter plane with urgency. The medical team immediately started working on Emma. Her blood pressure was 65/40 and her pulse rate was 120; both were very abnormal. Her oxygen saturation was 87%; also abnormal. All of her vital signs displayed that she was in shock and dying. I looked at my little girl in prayer and desperation, as bright red blood dripped out of her mouth and abdomen. She had to live even though she had died already. We had to get back on American soil. Our quickest route was to fly to Houston, Texas.

39

THE REPORT

"In what appears to be a team effort with the South American government, the elite SEAL Team Six and US Army Rangers captured and killed El Jefe, the infamous leader of the South American and Mexican cartels. His remains have identified him as Julio Chavez, who was long believed to be the second in command to El General, but in fact, Mr. Chavez was confirmed to be the actual leader of both the South American and Mexican cartels. El General, the former leader of the South American cartel, was killed by a rival cartel in the past. It was El Jefe who helped the terrorists enter the United States for their failed assassination on the president of the United States two years ago. SEAL Team Six led a secret mission after intelligence confirmed that El Jefe was hired by four Middle Eastern men believed to be from the Taliban, ISIS or another terrorist group based in Afghanistan. US intelligence confirms that the terrorist group had concrete plans to make another assassination attempt on the president of the United States when he visited the governor of Arizona in two days.

"The president of the United States, the governor of Arizona, the Colombian and Mexican presidents were scheduled to meet to finalize plans to start operations to fight the cartel in their own backyard. With El Jefe being killed, rumors are starting to fly as who would be his successor or if the days of the South American and Mexican cartels are over. The president will still speak at his scheduled meeting with the governor, and the Colombian and Mexican presidents. It is rumored that they will enter an official agreement to allow US military to begin strict drug and legal enforcement within South America and Mexico with the goal of ending any cartels or crime families within South America and Mexico. This agreement will be the first of its kind, and it will represent the only time that US troops will actively engage in war against the cartels especially in Mexico and South America. The president is expected to comment on the importance of ending the cartel's desires to make deals with any terrorist groups attempting to cause havoc in the United States. If last night's battle against the cartel represents the planned actions of the United States, Colombia and Mexico and what the United States is ready to do, then it appears that the war on the cartels is for real. This is Richard Martinez reporting from NBC news here in Phoenix, Arizona."

40

TEXAS

We landed at the Houston International airport. The flight medics and air evac were ready. I could see they had more blood already hanging and ready to transfuse as soon as she exited the C-130J-30. My brother, Loco and I all helped get Emma and Jaxon secured. My men stayed by my side and prayed the entire flight. Even though they had food and water available to them, I didn't see anyone take a sip of water or a bite of food. They kept their heads down and prayed for my Emma the entire six-hour flight.

It was the third helicopter ride for us in less than 8 hours. With every turbulent draw from our current flight, I felt myself thinking about our recently doomed helicopter flights. I had flashbacks of our helicopter crashing at El Jefe's compound. The crash's immediate memory over-powered my will. The flashback kept me feeling that we were still stranded dead to rights of El Jefe's missile strike. He had us dead to rights.

To make things worse, I kept flashing back to hearing Commander Perez's Spanish, death countdown. Why did

I have to keep remembering these awful near death experiences? What kept us alive? I kept asking what kept us alive? The horrendous flashbacks had to stop. I had to focus back on my family.

I had to remain strong to get my little girl to the hospital. I could rest when she smiled back at me once again.

The helicopter flight kept getting more and more choppy as it had started raining heavily. The powerful wind gusts plowed us side to side. Jaxon started crying again as he was just so traumatized at this point. How could an eight year old congeal his mind to survive anymore after such nightmarish realities? I told him it was ok to cry. I was crying, as I had no other emotional expression left in me at this point.

We landed atop the hospital. Despite the rain, the surgical team was on the roof again with more blood and a team of eight personnel including the surgical and nursing team.

The flight surgeon had accompanied us from Bogota was also on our air flight from the Houston airport. He started telling the surgical team the following,

"Five year old girl with acute abdomen, likely intestinal and splenic injuries. She received eight units of packed red blood cells, four units of fresh frozen plasma, and 10 packs of platelets. She had one episode of cardiac arrest with response after epinephrine and three defibrillator shocks. She was intubated about 2 hours prior to secure her airway. Her father administered three separate defibrillator shocks while in Bogota with return of threaded vital signs. She was hypotensive for last hour of flight into Houston with systolics in 50s while on two vasopressors. Father also suffered high powered rifle shot to abdomen and will need assessment when she is in surgery."

They placed Emma into a stretcher atop the hospital's top floor. They ran her from the helicopter into the elevator. I ran with them despite my weakness and pounding abdomen.

We were in the elevator. Calm music played that seemed out of touch.

"Sir, I am Dr. Merrill. I am the Chief of Pediatric Surgery here. I will be taking Emma directly to the operating room to perform an exploratory surgery to find out the extent of her injuries while also gaining control of her internal bleeding. I realize that this is a terrible time to ask you, Sir, but do I have your consent to perform surgery on your daughter?"

"Yes, please save my daughter's life. I have faith in you doctor," I cried.

"Sir, I promise you that I will do all in my best to save your little girl. I advise that you let our medical team wheel you over to our adult trauma center, so they can take a look at you," Dr. Merrill said.

"No, I need to stay with my daughter. I'm ok. I can wait."

"Sir, it looks like you have a severe abdominal wound in your right flank that needs medical attention, and I'd be surprised if you were not in shock yourself."

"Ok, but only after I know Emma is in the operating room."

The elevator arrived at the level of the operating room. I shook the surgeon's hand. They wheeled Emma into

OR room 7. Seven was her favorite number. I knew she needed more than luck, and that her life depended on a miracle. My little medical experience kept reminding me that her chances of survival were remote. How could a five year old survive being dead several times? Fuck I hated that I couldn't be ignorant to the dire fact.

They wheeled me over an inside bridge to the adult trauma center. They wheeled me into the emergency room trauma bay. The flight surgeon again informed the team.

"Forty-two year old healthy male that suffered a high powered assault rifle shot to the right flank approximately 8 hours prior. Patient reports only mild complaints of abdominal discomfort, but has visual signs of acute abdomen and shock," the flight surgeon said.

They placed a blood pressure cuff and pulse monitor on me. My blood pressure was 82/54 and pulse raced in the 140s.

"Sir, I'm Dr. Feinstein. I'm the trauma surgeon that is going to get you back to your daughter and family. Your vital signs are very unstable. I'm going to do an exam and get an ultrasound and possible cat scan of your abdomen to see what injuries you have suffered. Ok sir?"

"Please just patch me up and get me back to my daughter, please!" I pleaded.

They examined me. I had an isolated gun shot wound to my right flank as advertised. The trauma surgeon squirted some cold lube onto my abdomen and did a fast ultrasound. He pressed hard on my painful abdomen. I could now feel more pain than I had felt since being shot.

"Sir, you have an extensive amount of blood in your abdomen. I need to take you to surgery immediately," Dr. Feinstein said.

"No, no way. No fucking way. I have to be awake when my daughter comes out of the operating room!"

"Mr. Williams, you might not make it if you keep bleeding internally. Your body is in shock. I will get a cat scan to give us a little more time to see if we hear anything about your daughter, but I do need to get you to an operating room as soon as possible."

"Ok, I will agree to that if you get me an update," I requested.

They put me through the cat scan. Jaxon waited outside the cat scan machine. It was the first time we had separated since I was reunited with him in Colombia. It hurt me to let his hand go for the first time. It only took a few minutes, but it seemed like days.

I felt my body dying. Images of Natalie filled my brain. I remembered when we first met in the coffee line at the hospital. I remembered when she gave birth to Jaxon and Emma. I remembered my promise to Natalie to keep Emma alive. I had to fight for my own life now. My chest became heavy. I felt an elephant sitting on me. I couldn't breathe. My pulse raced.

Beep, beep, beeeeppp…it was the last thing I could remember.

"Fuck, get him the fuck out of there. We just lost his blood pressure. Go, go, go. Straight to the OR!" Dr. Feinstein exclaimed.

I felt myself going in and out of consciousness. I knew what was happening. I could see the surgeon staring at me as he pushed my hospital stretcher frantically toward the operating room. My gunshot wound bled more now than ever. The warm blood soothed my icy skin.

"Mr. Williams, you have a major injury to your liver. I need to bring you to surgery now in order to stop the bleeding. I communicated with the surgical team taking care of your daughter. She is still critical and they are still operating on her. They had to remove her spleen, which was likely the source of her major bleeding. Dr. Merrill is the best surgeon I have ever met, Sir, and I know he will save her life," Dr. Feinstein stated confidently.

I struggled following his words. I barely had enough energy to mutter the following words, "Let's roll. I want to be awake to see my little girl. Jaxon, you hold tight, buddy. Your momma will be here soon. I will be ok. I promise you buddy."

"Sir, we just got word that your wife is here now and is on her way to see you. She wants to see you before you go into surgery. Is that ok?" one of the nurses stated.

"Yes, please. I want to see my wife."

"No, we need to get him open right away or he is not going to make it. Sorry, Sir, but I need to stop your bleeding."

I stayed still on my stretcher. My abdominal pain intensified. I no longer had enough in me to say anything. I had to see Natalie. I fought for strength.

"Fuck that, please let me see my wife," I requested.

The nurse opened the door right before entering the operating room. My wife and mother stood right in front of the operating room door entrance. Jaxon jumped into his mother's arms. Natalie cried. Her tears soaked Jaxon's clothes. My mother grabbed my hand. My eyes closed. I was taken to my childhood when I fell out of tree and broke my wrist. For a brief moment, my mother made my pain go away. She still had her motherly touch, as I felt at peace for the first time in a long time.

Natalie kissed me. Her lips caressed my dry, chapped lips. I felt peace, sorrow, and anger all at the same time. I couldn't tell her now, but I blamed myself for Emma's injuries as I hesitated when bringing my kids to the helicopter. How could have I forgotten them even for that split second? Why did my mind have to play tricks on me at such a terrible time?

"I love you honey. I know Emma will be ok and back at soccer practice before we know it," Natalie said.

Her words tried to soothe the potential reality of losing Emma. I kissed Natalie, Jaxon and my mother goodbye as they wheeled me into the operating room. It was my time. I passed out before they transferred me on the operating room table. I had no more life left in me. I prayed that my life was being taken in replacement to save Emma's life.

41

CRITICAL

I was dreaming or was I still alive? I could see my body on the operating room table. I could see myself looking up at the bright and blinding lights. The room's arctic freeze pierced my soul. I felt my body shaking. I could see everyone working on me to try to save my life. Was this the end? Was this what everyone talked about as far as an out of body experience?

"Sir, I am the anesthesiologist. I thank you from the bottom of my heart for your service, Sir," the anesthesiologist said.

I could see him placing the oxygen mask on my face. I could smell the awkward smell of moist plastic. I had no nightmares to have as my nightmare was still living.

Lights disappeared around me. I could no longer see my body lying there on the operating room table. What happened? Was I dead?

Dark silence was all I could see or hear.

I must have been waking up now as I could hear a voice around me. A familiar voice spoke to me. My mother was at my bedside. She was praying for Emma and me.

I looked up at my mother. Her eyes were burnt red from hours of crying. I hadn't seen her cry since my father died. I had to say something. I felt too weak to speak, and I didn't know if I was alive or if I was just seeing my soul escaping my dead body.

I had to speak. I had to know.

"How is Emma doing?" I asked in a quiet voice.

"Ryan, she is in critical condition. You rest honey. You just had surgery yourself. Natalie and Jaxon are at her bedside in the intensive care unit (ICU)," my mother stated.

"I need to see her right away. Have the doctor come talk to me, please."

"Ryan, you have to rest. The surgeon said they had to put you on a massive transfusion protocol to save your life. He said they had to pretty much replace all of your blood, as you went into shock before surgery."

"Mom, please get me the doctor. Please," I begged.

"Ryan, I will go find him and ask"

I waited patiently. I had no other choice.

"Sir, I spoke with Dr. Merrill. He said he had to remove Emma's spleen and repair part of her small intestine. He believes he has stopped all of her bleeding. She is in critical condition. When you are more recovered, he states that he will speak to you directly," Dr. Feinstein stated.

"Bullshit, I need to see my daughter now. We had a deal man. I don't care if I have to tear out all my IVs and I bleed to death while walking over to her bedside. I need to see my daughter now. Please have someone take me to her bedside," I requested without compromise.

"Sir, I can only imagine what you and your family have gone through and how much you want to see her. I will wheel you over to her bedside myself. Let me get your nurse to help us over there. I am sure the children's hospital staff will understand," said Dr. Feinstein.

I was so inpatient now. I just wanted to see Emma and hold her hand. I knew I was in the best of hands.

Dr. Feinstein did exactly what he said. He wheeled me in a wheelchair through the trauma center, over the connecting indoor bridge, and directly into Emma's ICU room. There was my little girl. She had lines going and coming from everywhere including her nose, arms, abdomen, and bladder. The illuminated ICU lights made her pale skin appear as fresh snow in the bright sunlight. She had lifeless blood being pumped into her tiny veins.

Natalie and Jaxon crawled into bed with my little Emma. I wanted to do the same, but I barely had the strength to sit up. Natalie barely looked at me. She wanted every second with Emma. I knew the situation was grave.

I thanked Dr. Feinstein, and I asked him for one last request as to have Emma's surgeon come speak to me.

He shook my hand and gave me a hug. Tears scurried down his face. He couldn't speak, but he said "of course" with tight lips.

I held Emma's hand. I grabbed her little feet and rubbed them. Natalie always gave her foot massages after soccer practice, which she loved. I looked at all of her vital signs. Her blood pressure was still low. Her heart was still racing. She was fighting for her life.

Dr. Merrill walked into her room. He didn't look me in the eyes at first, but rather, looked down at the ground. I had to face the news. I had to accept whatever he said.

"Mr. Williams, I shared the news with your wife already, and I apologize for having to share the news with you. Sir, I am afraid, Emma, suffered some complicated injuries to her abdomen from the rifle shot. She was not stable in transport and suffered from hypoxia, or lack of oxygen, for several hours. Even if she survives, her internal injuries, I just don't know if the lack of oxygen to her brain for several hours will allow her to have any cognitive function. It is too early to say for sure. I just want to be honest with you when I say I am sorry, but I am not sure she will survive through the night. She is still unstable, and we can't keep her vitals stable. She is on multiple medications to try to keep her heart working and her blood circulating. She has receiving blood transfusions to match about three times the amount of blood she had before the injury. She is in kidney failure. She might go into multiple organ failure at any moment, which at her age is not survivable. Sir, I'm truly sorry. We will do all we can, so you can spend time with her. I'm sorry," Dr. Merrill stated.

I couldn't take the news. It was my fault that she was in this position. All those times in battle; all those times I helped save my men. Now when I needed it most, my brain failed me and I failed my little girl. I didn't want to live. I fucked up.

I was still in disbelief about what happened. I kept wishing the bullet had hit me in the chest, so maybe my bones or spine would have stopped it. I would rather have been paralyzed from the bullet than losing my little girl.

I kept wishing we were never there. I kept closing my eyes while trying to imagine that night had never happened. I'd tried to imagine that we just decided to stay home that night. We could have had dinner at home followed by a family movie.

It wasn't fair for my kids to be put in that position and have to suffer through the horrible experience. Emma had to live. I prayed to God. I prayed for a miracle.

42

MY FAMILY SECRET

Seconds, minutes, and hours passed. Emma's monitors would alarm and nurses and doctors would run to her bedside. They would do assessments and adjustments. The alarms would stop temporarily. Emma kept fighting. The staff's smiling faces turned to regrettable frowns.

We barely moved from her side. Twenty-four hours passed. Emma was not making progress, and she seemed to be withering away with more frequent alarms. More frequent doctor visits. More frequent talks. More despair in her room.

Thirty-six hours passed. Dr. Merrill had another sit down talk with Natalie and me. His speech was clear and grave. He talked about letting Emma pass peacefully. He talked about her pain and suffering. I couldn't bare the thought. Natalie began to accept that Emma might not make it, and that we would have to make the upsetting decision of withdrawing her care.

Forty-eight hours passed. My mother took Jaxon away from the hospital. They visited the zoo. They went to the park. Each time Jaxon would come back, he returned with a big smile while running into her room hoping Emma was improving. I hated to see his smile turn into tears when he realized she was worsening.

After two days had passed, Natalie finally asked me what happened. I had to speak with her truthfully. Usually I told her a safe story just to calm her fears, but I knew this time that I had to be truthful. My father used to tell me that it was ok to sometimes tell a lie to help calm a person.

I took her through all of the events with the exception of telling her that my mother may have been the daughter of the cartel leader and that my possible grandfather was the notorious leader of both the South American and Mexican cartels.

Most importantly, I had to tell her about my self-diagnosed dementia and PTSD and how both keep worsening. She knew about the nightmares already, but she had no clue that my head was not straight. This truthful admission was hard enough, but I knew I had to tell her what happened.

As I told her more about my dementia and PTSD, I flashbacked to the helicopter run. I could hear the whistling sounds of bullets flying around us. I reverted to being in that awful place. I saw myself running toward the helicopter. I saw myself realizing I forgot to grab Jaxon and Emma. I cost us several seconds by forgetting them. I saw myself running back to get Jaxon and Emma. Their faces were pale in disbelief that I forgot to bring them onto the helicopter.

I will never forget that appalling moment at which time I realized that I forgot them. My fuckup was costing

Emma's life right now. My forgetfulness caused enough hesitation and passing of time that the cartel's men were able to get off an in range shot that pierced my abdomen and tore up Emma's innocent little body.

I started shaking as I cried in abandonment. My words of explanation to Natalie of the event were no longer comprehendible. As I tried to explain to her how I fucked up with agreeing to leaving our kids at Momma's place, how I let them get kidnapped, and how I left our kids behind on the run to the rescue helicopter, she put her finger on my lips. She said the following words that I will never forget.

"Ryan, you brought my babies home. You did nothing wrong my love. I will never let you blame yourself for Emma and Jaxon's kidnappings. I will never blame you for Emma's injuries and loss. You brought my babies home. I've been able to hold them again and tell them that I love them again. For that my love, I will never blame you. We will get you help. You will be strong again. You are a frogman. You are my man, and I will always love you more than life itself," Natalie said with Niagara tears.

I promised my wife that I was done with the Navy at that point. I'd learned that my place was home with my family. I shook in her arms as she held me tight.

I couldn't think about ever spending another day away from them. I felt guilty for being gone for so long prior to the event, that now, especially, I felt that I had to be with my family more than ever.

I missed my kids growing up, and now I was facing the death of my baby girl. The pain from her loss would be too overwhelming for all of us. I had no idea what to do, but I had to have faith in God more than ever.

I felt like a zombie at that point, as I had not slept in several days, or weeks, for that matter. From being on an active mission to traveling home to going through the kidnapping, rescue, surgery, and now watching Emma die, I just couldn't rest.

I had to be strong, as Natalie was worse off than I was. She couldn't get out of Emmas's bed at all, as she cried day and night. She held on to Emma as long as she could.

43

SILENT DAWN

Four days now passed since we were admitted to the hospital. Dr. Merrill's talks deepened in his sympathies. His tone became more negative. I could see the angels trying to take my little girl to heaven. I wouldn't let them take her.

Dr. Feinstein checked in with us each morning and night before he left for his home. He changed my dressings. He said he hadn't had to round on a patient in the children's hospital since he was a resident.

Natalie's parents flew in the day prior. Natalie had told them that Emma wasn't going to make it, and if they wanted to say their last goodbyes.

Dr. Merrill sat us down once again. I knew what he was going to say. He appealed to us to let Emma be in peace, as she was no longer responding to treatments. How is a parent of a five-year-old girl supposed to be able to make that decision? She was playing soccer a few days ago. She was shouting out in Ninjutsu classes a few days ago. Now we had to let her go?

Natalie agreed. We argued. I made a promise to my little girl, and I was not going to break it now after everything she had gone through in a span of a few days. I disagreed. I asked Dr. Merrill for one more day. Emma's birthday was tomorrow. She was going to be six years old. I begged him to just let her celebrate her sixth birthday.

Natalie agreed with me with flowing tears in her eyes. I had to hold on to her hand just one last time. One last birthday. One more red velvet cake. I prayed for a miracle. The memory of kissing her good-bye that last night seemed so real. It seemed as though I was just in a bad dream and that Emma was going to run up to me and jump into my arms. I kept feeling that she was going to school the next day and that I would drop her off and pick her up as I'd been doing for the last several days before the event.

Natalie and I slept next to Emma through the night. They withdrew her vasopressor medications that were keeping her heart going and her blood pressure up. A silent dawn arrived. Emma's blood pressure dropped. I grabbed her hand as tightly as I could. I didn't want her to suffer anymore. I prayed for her peace. I cried my last tears.

The sun pierced through the closed blinds. It covered Emma's pale face. I moved over to cover the sun from her resting eyes. I didn't want her to be blinded by the bright light even though I knew she was no longer aware. I wanted to scoop her up and hold her for her last breaths. I had no strength left in me, but I didn't want to regret not holding my little girl for her last moments.

I reached my arms around her back and legs. I felt my abdominal incision stretching as the ends sliced open.

Blood oozed from my body as the force of lifting her was too much for the injured surgical site. I didn't care about my own pain anymore. I didn't care if I bled to death. I had to hold her one last time.

I felt something. I felt my heart stop. I felt Emma grab my neck. I thought it was just a spasm or something. I held her tight in my arms as I bled onto her frail body. I felt it again. She grabbed my neck again.

I didn't know if it was real or my dream. Suddenly, she opened her beautiful brown eyes to the blinding dawn's light. She smiled at me through her breathing tube. My baby girl was alive and coming back to life. My body weakened from shock and disbelief.

I woke up Natalie, as I couldn't trust what I was seeing. Natalie stared at our baby girl's smile and started yelling and crying. Emma's nurse and pediatrician ran into the room. They saw Emma's eyes open. They saw Emma move her head towards them as she tracked their movements. I looked at her blood pressure and heart rate. For the first time in a long time, they both looked normal and all of the alarms stopped buzzing. Gently, I placed her back down on her hospital bed. She was now soaked in my own blood.

Emma was alive and she was now breathing on her own. They called in Dr. Merrill. He ran into the room. He was in disbelief. He started looking at the breathing machine, her vitals, and her urine output. He realized the blood on Emma was mine. He directed his concerns toward Emma.

His amazement cried out to all of us. He spoke to Emma. He asked her to move her hands and feet. She followed his commands. He gave her a pad and pen, so she could communicate. He asked her if she could write something down on the paper. She took the pad and paper out of his hand as quickly as she could. She wrote down the following words in her best writing as her hands were shaking.

Yes, please get this thing out of my mouth. It does not let me talk.

Dr. Merrill looked pale himself. He double-checked everything. He couldn't believe his eyes. He mumbled a bunch of medical jargon with the pediatrician. They stepped out of the room. They came back in immediately and said they were going to remove the breathing tube out of her mouth. He told the nurses to call Dr. Feinstein to assess my bleeding.

We sat patiently. I held pressure on my wound as the staple line opened up from the pressure exertion of lifting Emma. Jaxon and my mother came into the room in complete disbelief. Jaxon cried. He crawled in bed next to Emma. We all held some portion of her tiny, weak body.

The doctors removed the breathing tube with slow hesitation. We all watched not knowing how she would respond. The sunlight shined on my little girl almost as she was on stage with bright lights.

Emma spoke her first words with her lips moving and barely any sound, "I'm hungry. Where am I?"

We all hugged her. We laughed with tears running. The silent dawn brought our little girl back. It was a miracle. I wasn't going to give up on my little girl. She lived to celebrate her sixth birthday.

Natalie and I laughed and cried. We looked at each other without say a word. We both then said, "Red velvet cake."

Natalie would have to scramble to find her favorite cake, red velvet cake. A pleasurable task at such a time of near gloom.

Dr. Feinstein came into the room. He was short of breath likely from running from the trauma center. He looked at Emma and tears formed in his sharp surgeon eyes. He glanced at me and realized I was bleeding.

"Mr. Williams, your wound opened up. I need to get you to the operating room to make sure you are not bleeding internally," Dr. Feinstein demanded.

"Doc, I'm fine. I'm not leaving my little girl. You know that," I said.

"Mr. Williams, I understand, but you could go into shock again if you are actively bleeding inside," Dr. Feinstein stated.

"Doc, please. Please just staple me back, and I promise you if I start feeling bad again I will head on back to the trauma center," I said.

"Sir, that is a bad idea. If your body goes into shock again, you could be causing some permanent damage," Dr. Feinstein said.

"Doc, I promise. You will be the first to know. Please just don't take me out of Emma's room," I requested.

"You win, sir, let me get some supplies and I will patch you back up," he inclined.

He stepped out of the room for a few minutes. We all continued to hold onto Emma. I wasn't going to leave her side. He came back in with a bunch of medical supplies.

"Mr. Williams, I'm going to give you some local to numb up the wound edges once again, so I can staple it back up. You ok with that?" Dr. Feinstein asked.

"Hell no, Doc, just staple the fucker shut. I'm cool without the local medication," I said, as I just wanted to get it over with and be with Emma.

He approached the wound with sterile gloves and a stapler with steady hand. Click…click…click about fourteen times. He stapled the wound back together. It felt like several bee stings tagging me at the same time. It was nothing compared to everything else that my body had gone through in the last twenty-four hours. He was quick and that was all I wanted at this point, so I could hold Emma close to me.

44

OUR RECOVERY

My body and mind begged for a rest. I was crushed physically, mentally, and psychologically. My flashbacks of the last few days tormented my spirit. I had to get help. I knew that things would have to change after what happened. Emma and I had a long recovery ahead of us. I knew mental recovery would take longer than the physical.

Emma and I spent another five days in the hospital. Miraculously, Emma appeared to be making a full recovery as her kidneys recovered, her blood counts normalized, and she was getting out of bed with physical therapy.

We started to make arrangements to fly home. I couldn't believe it.

Part of me also realized that I could have lost Natalie that fatal night, as the Cartel's men were watching over her. I still have nightmares of the video El Jefe made me watch with the red laser on Natalie's chest with her crying. Helplessness can't describe what I felt at that moment. I was so far way from her that there was literally nothing I could do.

When she was crying on the phone in the video, she was on the phone with our neighbor who is a Sheriff's deputy. He knew something was wrong, and as I had prayed, he came to her rescue. He had his men arrest the cartel's men when he saw them snooping around our home. The cartel's men were then later deported back to Mexico. Luckily, Natalie ended up staying the night with our neighbor and his family. I knew he saved her life, and I would always be indebted to him.

There were too many variables involved with the last few days. We could have all ended up dead including my wife, my kids, my brother, and my men. I couldn't sleep. I couldn't find peace from my inner demons. What was I going to do I kept asking myself?

The Navy was in my blood. I'd dedicated my life to the Navy, my men, and the people of the world, not just the United States. But I think most would understand that I had to make a change in my life now for my family after what happened to all of us. We were finally heading home.

45

MENTAL STATE

Despite having safe travels home, the flight home was painful for Emma and me. She cried and screamed the entire way home from stabbing abdominal pains caused by changes in the air pressure during the flight. I just wanted to get her home into her own bed, so we could continue to comfort her and help her recover.

I think my exhaustion didn't allow me to feel any more physical pain. I refused to take any pain medications although I could have downed several at once; as I worried I would spiral in my addictions. I couldn't handle any more problems at this point.

Soon after Emma's miraculous recovery, I reflected back upon the events, and what may have been best for my family. I couldn't leave my family again. I had to make a change in my life. My physical and mental states were now too exhausted to even fathom making a come back to the SEALS.

Emma continued to improve, but she was still broken just as I was. She cried day and night for several days even after arriving home. Sometimes she cried from the physical pain and other times she cried from her mental inner demons that haunted her each night.

All of us saw psychologists in order to help sort out the situation for our family. According to the psychologists, we all suffered from some sort of mental post-traumatic stress disorder (PTSD) from the events that occurred. I knew I had suffered from PTSD for a long while, but now it felt substantially worse as the recalled events included my own family. It was hard to believe, but somehow the event enhanced Natalie's understanding of my PTSD and why I struggled so much. She now knew firsthand why the inner demon of PTSD was so hard to control and manage.

Nights at our home were fucking crazy. It almost resembled a psychiatric ward as one minute Emma was screaming mad from her nightmares, Jaxon was crying out loud from his memories, Natalie was yelling at someone or something, and I was hitting my bed in recourse to whomever I was flashing back to in my thoughts. I just wanted it to end.

We all attended sessions with a psychologist at least twice weekly. At first, I thought there was no hope for us. I figured I had dealt with it so long, and I tried to suppress it for so long that I just needed to figure out how to do it again. However, this time was different, as we all had to get through it. We were only human. We all had suffered in so many ways. We had to trust the guidance of a complete stranger that may or may not have truly known what we were suffering through at this time.

In regards to my other mental issue, a little dementia is what they called it. I finally saw a neurologist who ordered and did a battery of tests to see why my memory and action recall was fading. Fuck, I had had enough.

From one doctor to another, I no longer knew what I was supposed to think, do, or say. We soon discovered what I suspected. The neurologist did an MRI that showed certain changes in my brain. He explained it to us that my many concussions as a teenager and in adulthood led to scarring of my brain that caused the condition I had self-diagnosed myself with over the last two years. It was called dementia pugilista. The neurologist said it was treatable with medications, but that I should not remain in active duty especially in combat missions. Easy to say, but not easy to do.

I didn't disagree with their assessments, as I knew my hesitation in Colombia was from this process. I agreed to begin treatments. Medications, therapy and a bunch of other bullshit I thought. I just wanted the quick fix. Give me a pill and tell me when I need to swallow it. I could fake a smile and play a part. I had done it for so long that I thought I could just return to playing my part once again. This time however I knew I couldn't bullshit anyone.

I finally realized that I had to retire from the Navy. The neurologist and psychologist explained to me that the PTSD might decrease, but that it could often worsen without warning. They were right; as I would often wake up in the middle of the night in a cold sweat while thinking we were still in Colombia trying to get away from the cartel. My body debated with my bed as it recalled both of our hard landings in the helicopter. My mind kept thinking it was a nightmare and that Emma was asleep in her room.

I found it so difficult to try to motivate to do anything aside from staying home with Natalie, Jaxon, and Emma. All of these feelings overwhelmed us. To make matters worse, Natalie couldn't sleep and she was always sick in the bathroom. I tried everything I could do to help her. We tried to do things together as a family, but everything we did reminded us about the kidnapping and the near loss of Emma.

I knew the Navy would be calling soon even though they had agreed to give me a temporary leave with pay. I just didn't know how I could continue to leave my family in the future, and how my mental issues could hurt my service. With all of this in mind, I decided to resign from the Navy SEALs and the Navy altogether. My mental state reached the end of the line. I finally realized I was human.

There were no questions when I turned in my resignation. At the time, I'd reportedly been the most active Navy SEAL ever. In other words, I'd served more missions than any other Navy SEAL in history. I was told that I was also the longest serving Captain of the Navy SEALs.

I think everyone understood that I had to stay home with my family. I'd given my life to my country and the world. Now it was time for giving my life to my family, which I had not done in a long time. I had so many regrets from putting my family second for so long that I had to make better by Natalie and our kids.

Prior to my resignation, the Navy had offered me an administration position or a teaching and coaching job at the Naval Academy. I did consider it for a few minutes, but I knew that now I had to be with my family. My head was still underwater, and I had to resurface on my own so I could breathe again.

I did consider the teaching job at the Naval Academy. Natalie did say she would support us moving to Annapolis, MD if I wanted to take the job. I did like living in Annapolis when I went to the Naval Academy. Part of me wanted to take the job just to leave Arizona in order to avoid being reminded of the events every time we went for a drive.

The teaching job was combined with being a swimming coach for the Naval Academy. I always spoke to Natalie about how my dream was to become a swimming coach at the Naval Academy when I retired from the Navy SEALS. In fact, I pretty much always told my co-SEALS that when I retired they would find me teaching swimming somewhere. I really didn't care where.

Even after talking about the job seriously with Natalie, I knew that even a teaching job combined with being a swimming coach would take me away from my family. I was always the Type A personality who had to do everything at 110 percent, with only perfection accepted as an outcome. Therefore, I knew that the only thing for me to do for now was to stay with my family. I still needed more time to recover, and I knew my presence was vital to the recovery of my own family.

I told the Naval Academy and my commanders that it was my time to retire from the SEALs and the Navy altogether. I knew I would somehow have to figure out how to be a civilian again. I am not sure what being a civilian quite meant, as I grew up into a Navy family and civilian life almost sounded as a foreign concept.

We had saved enough money to keep us comfortable for at least a certain period of time, until we figured out the next chapter in our lives. Natalie took a temporary leave from her work to help her cope with all that had happened. She acquired a lot of paid time off (PTO) as well, so she was using her PTO to help us manage our finances. We had always led a modest life, so we really didn't miss anything despite our cutbacks in our finances.

When I did complete my letter of resignation, I read it over and over for several days before I submitted it to the Navy. I edited it a few times, but my message was clear. I often reflected on my father's words, before he died, when trying to figure out what my true mission in life was supposed to be and how I might not always recognize it. My letter of resignation contained my father's words and thoughts.

Time kept passing. To me, time was not always a measureable state. They say time heals all wounds, but what I didn't know was just how much time would be required to heal our wounds from what had happened and the possible loss of Emma.

I enjoyed staying home with my family. At first, I didn't know what to do. Natalie's parents moved to Phoenix to help us. My in-laws were very helpful throughout the entire situation. Jaxon and Emma liked having their grandparents around, as it helped him learn so much about them. I think they helped all of us cope with such a challenging situation. My mother also spent a lot of time with us at our home.

I often wished I could go back to that night, and we could start all over without any badness entering our much-needed night together. I wished we had it back. I wished we just decided to stay home that night.

My wife woke up crying and went to sleep crying. Jaxon and Emma rarely smiled. I also cried every day, when others weren't looking. It was hard for all of us to hold back tears from our eyes with the thoughts of what happened.

That night, I cried even more in the shower. I locked the bathroom door, as I couldn't let Natalie or the kids continue to see me breakdown. The difference now was that my tears and breakdown were finally tears and reactions of joy. I finally began to realize that my family was slowly returning to some sort of normalcy. I prayed day and night that we would survive the mental battle that had overwhelmed all of us.

I had stayed away from Jack somehow in my biggest time of need with my heaviest of cravings for alcohol. Jack was an affordable and tasty whiskey. Each time we went to the grocery store, I felt myself walking toward the beer or alcohol aisles. In my past, these would have been times that I would have had a Jack sandwich to put me out of my misery. A Jack sandwich is what we called a six-pack of beer, followed by a bottle of Jack, followed by another six-pack of beer. It was enough alcohol to kill two or three people, but for some of us alcoholics especially those with PTSD, it was just enough for us to forget and become comfortably numb.

In the past, I had broken too many promises to Natalie and my kids that I was going to give up alcohol. I'd make a promise to quit and then the very next day I would be on the back porch drinking a beer or a slug of Jack. After I almost lost my kids, I truly promised to them that I would not start drinking again.

I felt the spirit that my prayers were being answered to keep me away from the bottle. I had to fight the urge to drink each night. I returned to deep meditation as I had learned from Ninjutsu. Meditating helped me focus and channel my energies toward a deeper relaxation state than I could have achieved in the past. I think with the psychologist's help, meditating, and staying home with my family that I finally had a chance to beat my inner demons.

That night, I slept a peaceful sleep. I think we all finally slept a peaceful sleep. We were helping each other heal.

Jack no longer existed in my world although he owned my thoughts. I refused to lapse back to Jack's grasp. I had fucked up too many times and things were finally looking right for us. It had taken me too long to shake the disease.

If it wasn't for Jaxon and Emma, I think Natalie and I would have been isolated in our house for months. I couldn't find the energy to motivate myself. I tried so hard to be the strong one in the family who could pick everyone up. Generally, my PTSD isolated itself to horrible flashbacks and scary nightmares. Now, my PTSD took a hard hit on me with a very deep depressive phase.

Jaxon and Emma were still not themselves. How could they ever be normal again? Fortunately, Emma had a full recovery of her physical injuries. She had lost a lot of weight from her internal injuries, as I had as well. We both tried to regain muscle strength and endurance. Jaxon, Emma and I started working out together by doing pushups, sit-ups, and light jogging and cycling. We enjoyed the cycling the best as it got us outside. Natalie would join us every now and then.

I think our physical recovery progressed more efficiently than our mental recoveries. Many nights Natalie and I could hear them crying in their bedrooms, sometimes at two or three in the morning. We couldn't blame them. It was hard enough for an adult to try to forget the event, but we witnessed first hand that our two children were struggling even more.

Even though Jaxon was eight years old, he would still crawl into our bed at night. He said it was the only way he could fall asleep. Emma slept in our bed for the first few weeks before we could even get her back into her room. They both pretty much ended up in our bed at some point in the middle of the night.

They both suffered from nightmares about the kidnappers and the night we escaped. Natalie and I didn't mind having them sleeping in our bed. We understood how distraught their emotions must have been. I think having them sleep with us was also comforting for us.

Even though we all attending sessions with the psychologist, Jaxon would still not engage with the psychologist very much. He just kept telling her that he was OK. We knew that he kept bottling up his emotions, and that it would make it worse for him. Emma found speaking with the psychologist helped her try to get over the situation. She was now making it through her sessions without crying the entire time. The psychologist said she was taking steps forward, but of all of us, the psychologist she would possibly need the longest time to recover.

We held them every night that they came into our bedroom. I wished I could take their memories of the entire event away, since it seemed impossible for a child to understand, accept, and try to move forward.

It was hard enough for Natalie and I to cope and move forward, so I understood that an eight-year-old boy and six year old girl would struggle for a very long time just as we would. As more time passed, we all recovered more physical and mental strength. I wasn't sure we would ever quite recover.

46

MY MOTHER

I knew enough time had passed. As my mother visited us almost everyday, a feeling inside of me kept pressing me to speak with my mother. I no longer knew if I should share the news with her or not. I felt I had to confront my mother and find out if what El Jefe said was true. One day, I invited her over for lunch with the full intention of speaking with her about El Jefe. Jaxon and Emma were finally back at school, and Natalie was back at work. Overall, things were starting to return to normal or at least as physically normal as possible. Mentally, we were all still pretty beat up without a light showing us the end of the madness.

My mother entered our home. I felt awkward having to confront my mother on something that she likely still felt was isolated from her. I was angry as to what she was thinking especially after the event occurred. She had to have known that El Jefe was her brother by seeing his photograph all over the news, as well as her father's photograph. Was she also waiting to tell me when we were alone? I had to give her the benefit of the doubt.

As her son, I couldn't just bring it up. We ate our lunch. I asked her if she had anything to share with me that I would understand. She laughed at first and asked me what I meant. She knew I was clear with my question. She looked me in my eyes and started crying, as she knew I knew.

"Ryan, I'm so sorry, mijo. I never thought this would happen. I left my family when I was fourteen, and I never looked back. I never in my wildest dreams thought this would happen. I never even thought of ever returning to Mexico. You have to believe me. When all this happened with the kidnappings and with Emma and you being shot, I promised myself that I would not bring up my past as I thought it would only hurt you more. I'm so sorry my son," my mother said while crying.

I held her tight. I had no hatred or blame. I knew she was telling the truth. My tears soaked her blouse. I hadn't cried in front of my mom probably since I was five years old. My father swore against us boys crying in front of anyone, so my falling tears in front of my mother made her cry even more than me.

I saved the photo and other photos that El Jefe had shoved into my shirt pocket. He pinned my shirt pocket closed, as to prevent me from taking them out or losing them. At this point, it was as if he knew I would survive to show his sister, my mother, the photos of them when they were innocent, little kids.

I guess I obliged as I knew my mother did have a dear love for her little brother since she left him when he was only seven and Godly innocent. She stared at the photos that she had not seen in over fifty years. My mother was now sixty-four years old. She cried like I'd never heard her cry in my lifetime. She knew that I killed her brother, El Jefe, or Julio as she knew him.

I couldn't blame her. I had to love her at that moment. She was sincere in her apology to me even though she didn't have to apologize. She thought she had left the cartel family a long time ago.

We talked about it for a long while. She told me stories about Mexico. She told me stories about her little brother and how he was so smart and athletic for his age. I saw a smile on her mouth and twinkle in her eyes that I had never seen. I knew she missed the innocence of her childhood, and that the memories of once being a little girl with her little brother brought a unique calmness to her in such a fucked up time.

She cried some more. In some ungodly way, she almost wanted to believe her brother was still alive and that she could see him in another way outside of his cartel life. We held each other for a long time. The only thing that separated us was my phone alarm that reminded me to pick up the kids from school. We swore to each other that we would put the past event behind us, and that we would bury our family secret. At least for now, I thought it could be buried. My mother must have covered up her past well, as all of the Navy's security checks of my family did not recognize that my mother was the daughter of the notorious cartel leader, El General, and the sister of the most wanted and dangerous man on earth, El Jefe.

47

GETTING WELL

To my amazement, Emma wanted to play soccer again. She finished her physical therapy treatments and was cleared to run again. She convinced the psychologist that she was ready to tackle the physical game. The psychologist said that both Jaxon and Emma would benefit from playing a sport to rechannel their energies from suffering to having fun once again. It made sense to me.

We contacted Emma's soccer coach the day we found out she was cleared to practice again. He was just as excited as we were as he missed our little fireball. When I saw Emma walk out of her room with her soccer practice gear, I couldn't help but remember the first time I saw her at practice when I first returned from my last mission. It seemed as such an unbelievable surprise. I knew it was a miracle. My little girl that laid dead in my arms more than once was now standing back in front of me with a smile, her cute little pig tails, and her infamous shirt that said, "Girls kick balls hard." I loved it.

Although Jaxon was not physically injured during the event, he hadn't returned to doing anything that resembled playing a sport or activity. He used to like video games, but he hadn't touched a video controller or even considered it. When he saw Emma practicing at her first soccer practice since the event, it was as if a flame lit Jaxon to return to himself or at least try. After her soccer practice, we came home and Jaxon begged me to throw the football with him. I hadn't touched a football in months, but I didn't hesitate to fulfill his request. Tears filled my marble eyes as I began to realize that we were slowly inching our back to a normal life.

The next morning shined a special light. Emma woke up running up and down the hallway. Jaxon asked if we could throw the football again after school. I thought we were finally departing from the evils of yesterday.

48

PROTECT HERO
FOREVER

For the last two years, I rarely answered my phone or emails. There were too many calls trying to pull me back into the Navy somehow. I was honored by the offers, but I had not been in any place near being able to function in a stressful situation. I was much better now, but I still was not the same person after the event.

I had been offered work as a consultant for a few security companies locally and nationally that were organized by former military or police officers. I was offered a lot of money to help lead security companies in Mexico, Iran, South Korea, Afghanistan, and basically, all over the world. I turned them all down because I didn't want to be put into another situation that might jeopardize my family. My medical treatments also had me functioning at a higher level without any major lapses in my memory or judgment, but I still questioned if I was well enough to perform in tactical situations. I hadn't been in a stressful situation to test my mental status, but I felt confident that I was improving.

We were on our way to church one Sunday We were running late and without thinking about it, I drove by the "place." We all stared at the place without any real reactions. We figured enough time had passed or we had gotten better at suppressing the memories and holding back the tears. Natalie and I avoided passing the place for several months, so we wouldn't cause any bad memory recall.

It was too painful to call it by its real name. After the kidnappings, all of the Momma's Place businesses were closed by the state because they had several violations of state codes regarding childcare. We found out later that not only did they have expired licenses from the state, but also, their security system was not working, because they had missed several payments. The security company had shut their system off two months to the kidnappings. We really didn't know if it would have made a difference in stopping them, but I am sure the cartel knew that their security systems were not working.

The corporation that ran Momma's Place filed for bankruptcy. There was a class-action lawsuit against them for their failures in preventing the kidnappings. We knew that we would never see any financial compensation, since they had filed bankruptcy. I didn't pursue any legal actions as I knew it wouldn't make a difference. I knew that even with a working security system that the cartels would have still taken the kids without question.

The CEO of the corporation that owned Momma's Place had killed herself after "the event." It was said that her guilt was too overwhelming for her to live anymore. She had three kids of her own, and one of them was also kidnapped that dreadful night. I did feel bad for her kids, as they also suffered from losing their mother.

As we drove past the place, I had the same empty feeling in my heart. Aside from my mother and me, nobody else knew the truth about the cartel and my family's blood relation. I didn't want anyone else to know for many reasons mostly because I just couldn't stand the harsh reality myself.

I struggled so much with the memory of learning that our kids were kidnapped. We were so helpless at first. I thank God we prevailed.

When I looked over at the door of the place, I remembered Emma's face looking out the door. I remembered the night of the event when she was smiling at me and saying good-bye on that night they were kidnapped.

All of a sudden, Emma said the following to me while we drove past the sight, "Daddy, protect others like you protected us. Don't ever let this happen to anyone else."

It was at that moment that a warm feeling overcame me. Her words were so clear and special. They provided me with an epiphany and a God given spirit that I hadn't felt before in my lifetime.

It was that day that I decided that I would start a full security company focused on providing protection to families and especially kids. I called it Protect Hero. The name fit, as it was the name we gave to the idea originally, before we actually had to utilize it to rescue Emma, Jaxon, and the other kids from the cartel that unpleasant night.

I developed the company with the help of two of my SEAL team members who had also retired recently. My brother was still enlisted in the army, but he also helped with advice and consultation. He connected me with two of his former US Army Ranger brothers. Both of them lived locally, and they were now police officers in Phoenix. They worked security details for extra money on their days off, so they had a vast amount of experience in many different things.

When we announced the start of Protect Hero, I didn't know what to expect. To me, the company made sense, but I had no idea that it would take off so quickly or what to expect.

Protect Hero grew from a small local security company in Phoenix, Arizona that consisted of three retired Navy SEALs and two retired US Army Rangers to a national security organization. The public's need for safety seemed to be underserved before our company opened its doors.

Our world had changed since I was a kid, and it seemed that dangerous acts were all around us at all times from lone gunmen killing people at a movie theater or mall to terrorists acts on an airplane or bus. We provided top-level security for anyone from senators to presidents of corporations to families having private events. But most importantly, we provided families with protection of their kids.

It was the protection of kids at schools, field trips, and games that provided me with the most satisfaction. Although those jobs paid the least or we sometimes did them for charity, it provided all of us with the highest satisfaction, as we all had kids, and we all knew that they were safe when we were on duty. We protected all.

In the span of two years, Protect Hero became the largest private security company in the country that provided security services designed for everyone. We had streamlined the process so well that every major corporation asked for our services. In just two years, Protect Hero had over 80 employees. We had multiple security service contract requests in any given day. Our major struggle was finding enough highly qualified men and women to work for us. I made it a point to hire every single person and our job qualifications demanded only top-notch individuals.

I'd received multiple buyout offers from other private security companies because the growth in our business revenues was actually becoming a big deal. I had no idea that we could run such a successful business protecting people in a dangerous world.

I served as a consultant for the military, corporations, other ally countries, and for my favorite category, schools. I'd seen too much violence occur with kidnappings and shootings at schools. It had been out of control prior to Protect Hero, but we now were having an impact at more and more schools daily. I felt our presence and influence on protecting kids directly decreased the violence against them. For all the things I'd done in my life, I felt peace in knowing that Protect Hero was keeping kids safe and happy at home.

49

REMEMBERING WHY

Although I had retired from teaching, as Protect Hero's growth required my full attention, I still made the time to take and pick up Jaxon and Emma from school. Emma could barely contain her excitement when I picked her up from school, as it was now her tenth birthday. Natalie made her famous lasagna that night. We all sang "Happy Birthday" to Emma at home.

It was four years since the event. We celebrated Emma's birthday every year since the event without any mention of what had happened. We almost lost her that day. I will always remember that silent dawn and how the sun's rays opened my Emma's eyes.

Natalie made Emma's favorite cake: red velvet. We ate red velvet cake or cupcakes only on Emma's birthday. Each time I bit into the red velvet cake, I remembered that day in the hospital when we celebrated Emma's sixth birth day. I remembered her words that day, "Daddy, I love red velvet cake. It's my favorite. I could eat red velvet cake all day. Yummy, yummy, yummy for my tummy! I want more please."

I cherished those memories so much. I could still picture her face covered with red velvet cake crumbs. Even at age ten, she would always get so hyper after she ate red velvet cake. She would always say it was her jet fuel, and that when she ate it, she could take off like a jet.

Bella looked up to Emma since she was her big sister. I couldn't imagine not having Emma around to show Bella the ropes. We were blessed. Bella would always fight with Jaxon and Emma to be the first one in our bed in the morning, especially on the weekends. It was all these little things that I cherished the most.

I made it my number one priority to always protect my family. Even with four years passed since the event, I still had nightmares of the cartel retaliating against my family. My contacts in the government and Navy SEALS kept tabs on any cartel activity. Since we had taken out El Jefe and the cartel, there was four years of silence on the cartel's end. We assumed our destructions enabled an end to the cartel or at least we thought.

50

THE CALLS

As we sat and ate Emma's cake, I was lost in memories of the past both good and bad. I appeared to be in the white zone.

"Ryan, your cell phone is ringing," Natalie said.

I didn't hear my phone ring or feel its vibration. Maybe I was just subconsciously ignoring it.

It was a familiar number—a number that I hadn't seen on my phone in over four years. I had to answer it, even though it was Emma's moment, as I knew who was on the other line.

"Hello," I said.

"Mr. Williams, please," the voice said.

"This is he," I said.

"Ryan, this is President Johnson. I'm sorry to bother you today of all days. I know it is Emma's birthday. I just want to let you know that my prayers have always been and will always be with your family. I hope you have been able to move on since that awful event."

"Sir, thank you. Your words and what you did for my family four years ago mean the world to me. You helped me save my family. My son, Jaxon, my daughter Emma, and my wife are right next to me because of you, sir. I am and will always be indebted to you," I said, with tears developing in my eyes.

"Ryan, I need your help now," the president said while his voice was cracking.

"Yes, sir. Anything. You name it, sir."

"Ryan, my children have been kidnapped while they were at school four hours ago. My wife and I are devastated. The Secret Service, FBI, and CIA are all involved, but I need you, Ryan."

"Yes, sir, I will do anything you ask. Do you have any more details at the moment?" I asked.

"Ryan, the CIA and NSA think it might be the former leader of the South American and Mexican cartels, El General. He was presumed dead after his murder and funeral were demonstrated for all to see. It appears as if he faked his own death, so he could live in peace despite his murderous and criminal past.

When we were tracking you during the rescue attempt, we intercepted a text sent by El Jefe to his father, El General. Ryan, what I am about to tell you is only known to a handful in the NSA and myself. Ryan, El Jefe texted his father a message stating that El General's long lost daughter, Elena, was your mother. He also texted a photo of you and your family with your mother in the photo. His text pointed out to his father that she was wearing a pendant, El General gave her when she was a child. He described it as a custom, one of kind pendant that proved that she was his daughter. His text also said that you killed El Jefe's son, as he was one of the terrorists that tried to assassinate me.

Ryan, I hadn't done anything with this information, as I didn't think I had to until now. Ryan, they also think that the cartel combined with a newly formed terrorist organization from the Middle East. Ryan, I need you to find my kids. I need you to bring them home to us. I need your help, Ryan. I need Protect Hero. Can you help me, please? We will provide protection for your family," the president stated.

My heart sank, but at the same time an overwhelming warmness came over me—a calm sensation I'd never felt in my lifetime.

I felt the presence of my father. It was this moment that I remembered why.

I looked up to Heaven. I gave thanks to my father and said, silently, "Father, I know my mission. Thank you for always watching my six, father. I love you very much. I miss you. Help me keep my head straight and my family safe."

The phone was still in my hand. I hadn't said anything for a few seconds. The reality of the situation sank into my soul. I had only one option, which I would take gladly, but with reserve. Here are the words I said that day, on Emma's day, her tenth birthday: "Mr. President, I'm on my way."

Fuck I needed a drink.

My phone rang again while still in my hand. Who the fuck was calling me now?

"Hello," I said.

"Mi sobrino querido como estas?"

"Who the fuck is this?" I asked.

"Ryan, how quickly you forget. You really thought you killed me? Surprise motherfucker! Come find me. I took the president's kids, so you would be forced to try to rescue them. Come get it!" El Jefe stated.

"Fuck you! I'm going to fucking to kill you just like I killed your son!"

"I love to hate you my own flesh and blood. I'm waiting, bring some help. You will need it!"

"I'm going to fucking kill you just like I killed your son! I will then burn you, and piss on your ashes!"

"I'm looking forward to it!" El Jefe said.